Fiona Leitch is a  chequered past. She
motoring magazines, childbirth videos and mail order
catalogues; DJ'ed at illegal raves in London, been told off
by a children's TV presenter during a studio debate; and
was the Australasian face of a series of TV commercials
for a cleaning product. All of which has given her a
thorough grounding in the ridiculous, and helped her to
write funny stuff.

twitter.com/fkleitch
facebook.com/fionakleitch

Also by Fiona Leitch

The Nosey Parker Cozy Mysteries

The Cornish Wedding Murder

The Cornish Village Murder

The Perfect Cornish Murder

A Cornish Christmas Murder

A Cornish Recipe for Murder

A CORNISH SEASIDE MURDER

A Nosey Parker Cozy Mystery

FIONA LEITCH

One More Chapter
a division of HarperCollins*Publishers* Ltd
1 London Bridge Street
London SE1 9GF
www.harpercollins.co.uk
HarperCollins*Publishers*
Macken House, 39/40 Mayor Street Upper,
Dublin 1, Ireland, D01 C9W8

This paperback edition 2023
1
First published in Great Britain in ebook format
by HarperCollins*Publishers* 2023
Copyright © Fiona Leitch 2023
Fiona Leitch asserts the moral right to be identified
as the author of this work
A catalogue record of this book is available from the British Library

ISBN: 978-0-00-852539-2

This novel is entirely a work of fiction. The names, characters and
incidents portrayed in it are the work of the author's imagination.
Any resemblance to actual persons, living or dead, events or localities
is entirely coincidental.

Printed and bound in the UK using 100% Renewable Electricity
by CPI Group (UK) Ltd
All rights reserved. No part of this publication may be reproduced,
stored in a retrieval system, or transmitted, in any form or by any
means, electronic, mechanical, photocopying, recording or otherwise,
without the prior permission of the publishers.

Prologue

M y dad was always fond of a good chat. My mum used to say that he was worse than her when it came to gossip, but that really wasn't true. Whereas Mum was (and still is) fond of the opportunity to pass village news around without being too fussed whether or not it was true, my dad mostly just listened. He liked to keep his ear to the ground, in a professional capacity. Being in charge of the police in a small, close-knit community like Penstowan, it was (and again, still is) very useful to know the ins and outs of the inhabitants' lives.

Being dead, of course, meant that my dad, Chief Inspector Eddie Parker, formerly of the Devon and Cornwall Constabulary and now of St Botolph's churchyard, was rather out of the loop. I tried to keep him informed but my life had become so busy lately that I didn't get the chance to visit his grave very often. Ironically, I'd moved back to Penstowan after quitting the Metropolitan Police Force (and a bad marriage), searching for a quieter, safer life for me and my teenage daughter Daisy than the one we'd had in London; but the Cornish coast had proved to be much less sleepy than I remembered from my own teenage years.

'Hello, Dad,' I said, feeling a bit daft. I sat down on the grass next to his headstone, and scraped away the thin layer of green moss that had started to cling to it. The summers in Cornwall are beautiful, long hot sunny days that stay light later in the evening than up country; but the weather can turn without warning, sea mists quickly rolling in to envelop the land and then staying there for what sometimes feels like weeks on end. Mould and damp are constant problems when you live near the ocean, even for the dead.

I shuffled my bottom on the damp ground and sat and thought about my dad. Now that I was here – I hadn't actually made a special effort to come, I'd just been passing on my way home from picking up some supplies for a catering job – I realised why I didn't visit his grave more often. He wasn't there. My dad – his spirit, anyway – was in Penstowan, watching out for troublemakers in the King's Arms; and on the bench at the top of Fore Street, where he'd kept an eye on me and my friends playing on the beach when we were kids, and on Daisy when I'd brought her down for a visit when she was little. And most of all it was in the police station, where DCI Nathan Withers, current holder of the (unofficial) title of Cornwall's Sexiest Copper and possessor of my heart (along with various other parts of my anatomy), carried on my dad's good work, albeit with more technology and a touch less local knowledge. Luckily he had me for that.

'So,' I said, clearing away the weeds that had sprouted up around the headstone. 'Things are still going well with me and Nathan. I wish you could've met him, Dad, you'd really like him. He's a good copper and a lovely bloke. He's so good with Daisy, and Mum – you wouldn't believe it, but he's got her eating out of his hand. She keeps trying to iron his shirts for him and stuff like that.' I smiled. 'I think – I think he's The One, Dad—'

'Ahem…' I looked up at the sound of someone clearing their throat. Tony stood behind me, smiling but looking a bit awkward. 'Thought it was you. Come to see your dad?'

'Yeah.' I jumped up and brushed the earth from my jeans. 'Just filling him in on current events. What you doing here?'

'Believe it or not, I'm here to see the vicar.'

I raised my eyebrows. 'Don't tell me you've found religion? Weren't you the little boy at St Buttholes primary who made the RE teacher hand her notice in after you asked her what day God invented the dinosaurs?'

He laughed. 'I still think that was a reasonable question. Dunno why she got so upset about it...' We turned and headed up the hillside, through the graves, towards the church; my new catering van was parked in the neighbouring car park, and Tony's assignation with the vicar was presumably in the church itself. Although I'd been sad to replace my old van, the Gimpmobile (so called because I'd bought it cheap from a sex shop that was closing down, and there was a surprisingly graphic decal of a cartoon man in full BDSM gear, holding a whip, on the side), I was also slightly relieved, because it wouldn't have felt entirely appropriate parking it next to the church. I hadn't had a choice, anyway, as it had resolutely refused to start, despite the close attentions of Rob Trevarrow, the town mechanic.

'How's the new van working out?' asked Tony, gesturing towards the car park. 'It looks good, although I did have a soft spot for the old one.'

'Yeah, me too. But I have to admit Gwyneth's more reliable.'

'Gwyneth?'

'Yeah. After Gwyneth Paltrow.' I grinned at Tony's confused expression. 'It used to belong to the fishmonger on Fore Street – he's gone electric now. When we first went to look at it, it absolutely stunk of fish. Debbie said it reminded her of that candle Gwyneth Paltrow's company brought out, the one that supposedly smelt like her va—'

'Oh my God!' spluttered Tony, laughing. 'That sounds like Debbie, all right. I'm sure there's something in the bible about not talking about Hollywood actresses' unmentionables on hallowed ground...'

'Talking of which, why are you meeting the vicar?'

'My mum comes here, and she was talking to her last Sunday—'

'Her? We got a female vicar? I didn't know that.'

'No, nor did I. For some reason they got talking about Merrymaid, and Mum volunteered me to help.'

Penstowan's Merrymaid Week was one of those uniquely Cornish festivals that supposedly harked back to the olden days and celebrated the area's historic fishing industry, but nowadays was an excuse for fun and games for locals and tourists alike, culminating in a carnival, a costume contest, and a huge booze-up with fireworks at the end. It was based on the legend of the Penstowan Siren, a fearsome mermaid who had once been the scourge of the local fishing fleet. The name

Merrymaid *Week* was a bit of a misnomer, as it only ran for five days, Monday to Friday, but that was because changeover day at the nearby holiday camps tended to be on a Saturday. Like I said, it was completely traditional and in no way seen as an opportunity to liberate the holidaymakers who flocked to Cornwall in the summer from their spending money.

'Do they want you to dress up as the mermaid?' I asked, sniggering.

'Let's face it, I've got the legs for it,' said Tony, giving me a saucy pose.

'Mr Penhaligon?' A female voice stopped us in our tracks. We turned around to see a very attractive woman in her late 30s, early 40s, straightening up from behind a grave. She had long blonde hair, tied back in a ponytail, and was holding a pair of gardening shears. Tony leapt out of his daft pose and straightened up. I suspected he was holding his stomach in. 'Sorry, didn't mean to sneak up on you, I was just trimming the grass around Agatha and Jim.' She waved towards an ancient-looking headstone, which I assumed was the last resting place of the aforesaid couple. 'Between you and me, Jago Thomas is meant to keep the grass tidy, but he's getting on a bit. You must be Tony, and you are…?'

'Jodie, Jodie Parker.' I held my hand out to shake, then nudged Tony when he didn't move. I glanced at him and thought, *uh oh*... His mouth was open and he looked absolutely transfixed by the vicar.

'Uh, yeah, I'm Tony...' he said, finally. She gave him a big, friendly smile, completely without judgement, which I thought was very kind of her seeing as he was acting like a moron. She shook both our hands.

'I'm Carmen Sommersby. The vicar.' She laughed. 'Obviously. Why else would I be lurking in a graveyard?'

'I was,' I said, smiling. 'But I was visiting someone.'

Her expression changed to one of sympathy. 'Ah, I hope they're not one of our more recent residents?'

'Nine years ago,' I said. 'My dad. I don't come to his grave very often, but I was just passing.'

'We're not together,' blurted Tony, and I had to restrain myself from groaning out loud.

'No, Tony just spotted me and came to say hello,' I said. 'Well, I'll leave you to it...'

'You're welcome to stay,' said Carmen. 'I was rather hoping we'd have a few more recruits by now, but so far it's just you and me, Mr Penhaligon.'

'Tony,' croaked Tony. He really was hopeless. I decided I should stay and make sure he didn't make a complete muppet of himself.

'Well, I'm not sure how much help I can be, but count me in,' I said, and they both looked at me gratefully.

Chapter One

'How did I get into this again?' I asked, looking at my reflection in the mirror. This was not the sort of thing I usually wore on a Monday morning. My mum, who had sat on the bed watching me squeeze into the costume with an amused look on her face, snorted.

'With difficulty.' Next to her, Daisy laughed and reached over to high five her. My family can be so disloyal.

Studying my tight costume carefully, though, I had to admit she was right; it had been touch and go whether I would get into it. The long, curly blonde wig suggested Dolly Parton to me, but the skin-coloured mesh top with built-in seashell bra cups definitely had more of a mermaid feel. A slightly slutty mermaid feel, unfortunately. Thank God the mesh was tightly woven and opaque enough to protect my modesty.

The tail/skirt was just plain ridiculous, particularly as it had been specially modified for Merrymaid Week. It was long at the back, but very short at the front (so short I had to wear Lycra cycling shorts underneath it, to prevent passersby getting a glimpse of what I only allowed myself, my gynaecologist and Nathan access to). The back was shaped like a fish tail, covered in a shiny, scaly-patterned material in shades of blue, green and silver. Tony had had the good grace to look slightly embarrassed when I'd taken the costume out of its packaging, but as he pointed out, if they'd left the skirt as it was – long, back and front, all the way down to my feet – I would hardly have been able to move; I'd have found it hard to muster up even a waddle. So now it just stuck out behind me, like a weird padded dinosaur tail. My most comfortable (but shabby) trainers completed the look. I was, after all, going to be running through the town, chased by a pack of feral children, so I needed to be nimble on my feet. Across my cheeks, pale, silvery face paint gave me an ethereal, unearthly glow, while my eyes were rimmed with red eye-liner to make me look evil, or like I was suffering from the worst bout of hay fever ever.

I sighed and made my way to the top of the stairs,

stopping for a moment to get my misbehaving tail under control, as it seemed determined to trip me up. Downstairs in the kitchen, I could hear Nathan getting ready to go out. He had to go into work that day, but he'd promised to come and watch at least some of the chase if the inhabitants of Penstowan behaved themselves, or at least didn't get caught. *Oh good*, I thought sardonically.

'I'm off in a minute, babe,' he called out, as I carefully descended. 'Good luck with the chase in case I don't see – Jesus Christ Almighty!' – this, as he turned and caught sight of me. He recovered his wits, clearing his throat and quickly replacing the shocked expression on his face with one of calm. 'Is that what you're wearing?'

'No, I still need to get changed,' I said sarcastically. He grinned.

'Sorry, stupid question. It's a … you look very…' He gave up. 'Bloody hell.'

'That about sums it up,' I agreed.

'Can you run in it?'

'Let's hope so, or the little angels will catch me well before I reach the church.'

Nathan looked surprised. 'You have to run all the way to the church? I wouldn't have thought you'd make it that far even *without* the costume.' I swatted him with my tail. 'No, seriously, why do you have to go to the church? I thought you'd just lead them around the town and end up on the green by the car park.'

'Because then the vicar will subdue the evil mermaid and lead us all back down to the harbour, where she'll bless what's left of the Penstowan fishing fleet,' I said. 'Part of the legend, innit.'

The Siren (so the legend went) was a beautiful creature. She would sing to the fishermen of Penstowan when they were lost in the sea mists that had a habit of suddenly appearing from nowhere, guiding them back to the harbour. In return the fishermen would avoid her part of the bay, around a rocky promontory near the harbour; all the fish in that part of the sea were hers, so no nets were cast there, and no crab or lobster pots put out. But one day a fisherman called John Hawken, who had no time for anyone or anything other than money, noticed that the biggest lobsters lived in the Siren's fishing waters. He secretly cast his pots there, and sure enough, his catch was the biggest he'd ever had. He sold the lobsters for top price, and after drinking away half of his profits in the local pub, he mouthed off to the other fishermen about his new secret fishing spot. The next day, one of the other fishermen sent a boy to spy on Hawken and find out where he was fishing. Soon all the fishermen were setting out their crab and lobster pots there.

The Siren was furious. And now, instead of guiding the fishermen back to shore, she began to lead them astray, hypnotising them with her beautiful song until they were claimed by the huge waves that broke far out in the ocean. Many fishermen were lost, and no one understood why their luck had changed. Apart from one boy; the same boy who had followed Hawken. He alone knew that it was the Siren luring men to their death, and he knew why. But the fishermen had got used to making more money and were unwilling to go back to their old ways. There was only one thing to be done.

The boy built the biggest lobster pot anyone had ever seen, and early one morning, as the sun rose, he went to the Siren's fishing grounds and cast the pot out on a line. The other fishermen laughed at him, but they were beginning to think that he was right; too many of their number had drowned. That night the whole fleet – those that hadn't met watery graves, anyway – went out to help the boy haul in the lobster pot. Sure enough, as they pulled at the rope they could hear the song of the Siren; but instead of being beautiful, it was heartbreakingly sad. They carried on pulling and finally the pot broke the surface of the waves. Curled up inside, sobbing, was the most beautiful creature they had ever seen; a mermaid with flowing hair and big blue eyes, her long eyelashes heavy with tears. She pleaded with them to let her out. The boy had planned to release her after showing the fishermen who they had been upsetting, hoping that they would apologise and that things would get back to normal; but the fishermen refused. They jeered at the Siren; not so powerful now, was she? At that the mermaid changed, her eyes turning red, her pearly white teeth becoming evil fangs, and her fingers clawing at the rope. The fishermen dragged the pot to shore with her inside, then hauled it all the way through town and up the hill to the church. The Siren howled with fury and pain, and as they entered the church she gave a bloodcurdling scream and turned to stone. The stone Siren was placed on a ledge inside the entrance to the church to stop her returning to the sea, halting her campaign of terror among the fishermen. John Hawken used his ill-gotten gains to buy a whole fleet of fishing boats, and he became extremely rich and powerful, but he never went out to sea himself again. As for the boy, he became the vicar of St Botolph's so that he could watch over the Siren and pay his respects to her every time he entered the church.

'Poor Siren,' said Nathan, and I had to agree.

'It's just another misogynistic myth, created by a patriarchal society,' said Daisy firmly. Mum looked at me with a *here we go again* look on her face. Daisy had just discovered feminism, and I was simultaneously extremely proud and a little bit over it; I'd spent near on twenty years in the Met, and I knew what it was like to stand up for myself against a room full of men, but Daisy seemed to think I'd never even heard the words 'toxic masculinity', let alone been subjected to it. She was at that age where she knew *everything*... 'Every time something bad happened back in those days, it was the fault of a woman. The fishermen couldn't just have been drowning because they were stupid and went out when it was too rough. No, they had to blame it on some mystical female monster. Medusa, Scylla and Charybdis, the Harpies – all women. Crops failed? Probably a witch. Find a stroppy woman who doesn't know her place, then burn her. Men have always been scared of intelligent women.'

Nathan looked taken aback. 'I *wasn't* scared but I think I am now...'

We let Nathan go to work, while I had a last cup of tea. I hoped I wouldn't regret it. I'd had serious issues getting into that skirt (and the cycling shorts underneath), so the fewer toilet breaks I needed, the better.

The Mermaid Chase was due to start in an hour and a half, although families would already be gathering on the beach and enjoying breakfast from a selection of food stalls in the car park. I wished I'd been a bit quicker on the uptake and not allowed myself to be talked into playing the mermaid, because I could've had my own catering stall out there now. It was the beginning of the holiday season, and according to a text from my friend Debbie (who was also helping out with the festival, registering teams of mermaid hunters) the stalls were swarming with tourists as well as locals, tucking into bacon rolls, waffles and all manner of breakfast goodies. I might actually have made myself some money, rather than risking a hernia from that stupid tail. I had still ended up doing some baking – there was a charity cake stall at the church, where the hunters could celebrate the mermaid's capture and replenish their sugar levels, all for the sake of the stained-glass window restoration fund – but that just meant any money would be going into the church's coffers, rather than my pocket. Oh well. I'd get my reward in heaven, if it existed. I'd driven my contribution to the cake stall over the night before, in Gwyneth, who still smelt somewhat of her previous vocation, despite repeated scrubbings. I hoped my coffee, choc chip and nut cookies would not have a faint suggestion of haddock about them.

I somehow managed to get behind the wheel of the car and drove myself, Mum and Daisy (and Germaine, our dog) to the town car park, where Tony was lurking not far from a large group of families, both local and holidaymakers, who had just signed up for the hunt. He smiled as he spotted the car and rushed over, carrying a large blanket.

'Here,' he said, chucking the blanket over my head as I climbed out of the car. I threw it back.

'Bloody hell, Tone, let me get myself straight first! What are you doing?'

'We can't have the kids seeing the ug – scary mermaid yet,' he said, looking me up and down properly. 'Good Lord, that skirt's tight…'

'Oi you, eyes up here!' I snapped, more because I knew that I looked a right state, not because I suspected Tony of perving over my figure in that costume. 'Can I at least take a breath before you go smothering me with a blanket?' I looked down as I felt a tug on my tail. Germaine was growling at it, then pouncing on it, giving it a shake and letting go, only to start the game again. 'Get off, Germaine! Where's the other mermaid? The beautiful one, not the *ugly* one.'

Tony grinned. 'Sorry. We should probably call you the

"Before" and "After" mermaids – before and after the Siren gets caught and transforms into an evil harpy. The festival budget didn't cover Hollywood-style special effects for the transformation, hence your dodgy costume… The lifeguard's parked his truck on the beach and our "Before" mermaid is hiding in there until we get started.' He squinted up at the sky. 'Glad the sun's out and it's nice and warm, her costume's a bit less…' He waved his hands vaguely at my dreadful outfit. '…just *less*. A *lot* less.' I was suddenly pleased to be the ugly – or rather the *'Before'* – mermaid, after all.

'Say cheese!'

I whirled around to see my friend Nina standing there with her phone raised. 'Oh my God!' she giggled, as she snapped a picture. 'That's a *fantastic* photo … Tony said your costume was bad, but…'

'Oh, thanks a lot,' I said, grumpily. 'You know I could have you arrested for breach of privacy or paparazzi-ing or something?'

'You *could*, but it's my turn to do lunch next week and you wouldn't want to miss that, would you?'

One of the things I'd simultaneously looked forward to *and* dreaded about moving back to Penstowan was catching up with old friends, some of whom I'd lost touch with on purpose. But Nina wasn't one of them, and after a slightly awkward start – I'd run into her at the council, where she worked, and hadn't even recognised her at first – we'd put together a 'ladies who lunch' club, consisting of the two of us, Debbie, Lily Swann (who now lived over near Bodmin in a flipping massive 13th-century abbey hotel), and Louise Gifford, who worked part time at an engineering works in Launceston. We'd meet every couple of weeks, taking it in turns to host and each of us bringing a plate. We'd sit and cackle and gossip and OH MY GOD it had just occurred to me that we were basically my mum's Wednesday morning coffee club, only with alcohol.

'At least let me do a better pose,' I said, giving her a snarl and arching my fingers into claws. 'What's this for, anyway?'

'For the council website,' said Nina. 'It'll be on the local events page, so everyone can see you. You could go viral.'

'She definitely looks contagious,' said Tony, and I elbowed him.

'Daisy!' My daughter's best friend Jade, who lived just down the street from us, appeared. Germaine barked and leapt up at her, but she was a Pomeranian (the dog, not Jade), so she only came up to Jade's knees. 'Hello Germaine, who's a good girl then?' said Jade, turning to look at me with a smile. 'Hi, Mrs Par – bloody h—' She stopped abruptly, her eyes wide.

Daisy sighed. 'Only my mum could have that effect on my mates,' she said. 'Come on, let's get out of here.' They toddled off across the car park, Germaine following dutifully at Daisy's heels.

'Keep her on the lead!' I called. Daisy raised a hand in reply, not stopping or even turning around, and I got the feeling she was pretending to not know the mad woman in the terrible wig and bizarre scaly costume. I turned to Mum. 'You coming with us?'

'What, you think I'm going to follow a bunch of screaming kiddies around town, with my bunions?' She grimaced. 'Bugger that. I'm off for a cuppa.'

We watched her toddle off to meet some of her more rebellious friends from the coffee club – they were going rogue, meeting on a Monday, and at Rowe's bakery rather than the church hall – and said goodbye to Nina, who was on her way to work. Then we headed down to the beach. Tony did his best to shield me from prying eyes but only succeeded in making me stand out even more. The tide was out, the sun shining on the wet sand, glinting off the rock pools and making the waves out to sea sparkle. I took a deep breath, savouring the tang of salt in the air. *This* was why I'd moved back; not just because I missed being near family and friends who I'd known long enough to feel like they were family too, but because of the sea. I never wanted to live anywhere I couldn't see or at least smell the ocean. London had had its moments – it had been fun when I'd first moved there – but the fun soon wore off. The effect the sea had on me never did.

We reached the long finger of rocks and boulders that protruded out onto the sand, extending from the face of the cliffs. Over those cliffs, just around the bay, was Penstowan Harbour, the tiny but still (just about) working heart of what was left of the local fishing industry. It was picturesque enough, but most visitors ignored it or were even unaware of its existence, preferring to stay on this gorgeous sandy beach, swimming in the icy cold water, or fishing for tiny crabs in the rock pools.

The lifeguard's four-wheel drive was parked on the sand, near Mermaid's Rock, the enormous (and predictably named) boulder that sat on its own a few feet away from the rock pools. It had probably been part of that small promontory once, but the sea had carved a channel between it and the other rocks, a river forming between them when the tide began to come in. The boulder was permanently circled by a tiny natural moat of sea water, making it the perfect mermaid throne. Which was just as well, as the perfect mermaid was sitting in the passenger seat of the truck, waiting to make her entrance. Kira Tiddy, daughter of Maggie, who ran one of the local B&Bs, was back from university upcountry somewhere, and I had to admit that with her pale skin and wide blue eyes, she had the undersea ingenue look down to a T.

Tony nodded to the lifeguard, Billy Trevarrow (son of Rob – everyone in Penstowan seemed to be the son or daughter or second cousin of someone I'd been to school with), as he got out of the driver's seat.

'All right, Billy?'

'Aye, all right, Tony? All right, Jo—' Billy turned to look at me and stopped abruptly. I sighed. I was getting used to this reaction.

'Yes, I'm fine. Are we ready to get started?'

Billy nodded, taking out his walkie talkie. 'I'll see if the hunt marshals are ready,' he said.They *were* ready, having finally collected all the entrance fees (which were going to the RNLI), and shepherded the multitude of hyped-up kids and their parents into some semblance of order. Tony went to join them, then, at his signal, Billy opened the other door of the truck and lifted Kira out of the passenger seat; she couldn't really move much herself, as she had a proper tail. Other than that, as Tony had said, her costume was very much *less* than mine: she wore the same seashell bra top, but where mine had mesh around it to keep my bits under control, she just had the bra. Luckily her bust was also rather *less* than mine, so it wasn't threatening to overwhelm the seashells in a tsunami of female flesh like it would've done on me. She had a glittery blue piercing in her belly button (*you can tell SHE hasn't had kids*, I thought slightly bitterly, as I noted the lack of stretch marks on her smooth stomach), and naturally long blonde hair, and I had to admit that she looked gorgeous. Which just made me look all the more terrible. Oh well. Good job I wasn't trying to impress anyone with my svelte figure.

She giggled and fluttered her eyelashes at Billy as he gallantly lifted her onto Mermaid's Rock. Billy, bless his cotton socks, blushed, but seemed to be enjoying himself immensely. He set off a large bubble machine, and soon the beautiful Siren was surrounded by iridescent bubbles. He signalled for me to hide behind the rock, as the crowd of juvenile mermaid hunters made their way down the beach, led by the infamous fisherman, John Hawken (or Tony, in what looked like a medieval peasant's costume).

The children *oohed* and *aahed* at the pretty lady sitting on the rock, until Tony stepped forward and did his bit, telling them how the Mermaid had been very naughty and had sunk some of the fishermen's boats (the committee had decided to gloss over her sending the fishermen themselves to watery graves, in case it scared the kiddies). At that point Billy set off a massive smoke bomb that made all of us jump (as Tony had said, no Hollywood-style special effects here…) and Kira almost fall backwards off her rock; but he was there to catch her. He unceremoniously elbowed me out from behind the boulder and towards the shrieking children.

I stalked towards them through the smoke, scowling and flexing my plastic claws, channelling my inner Harpy, but my motivation was slightly ruined by one of the mums standing nearby, who guffawed loudly and drawled, 'Oh my God…' I turned towards her and snarled loudly, causing the kids to shriek even louder, and one very small, very cute little girl burst into tears. I don't usually have that effect on children. Not very often, anyway.

Tony led the screaming, giggling children up the beach and into town. We went in and out of a couple of shops (Tony's family's department store, Penhaligon's, of course, plus a couple of others by arrangement – we made sure to avoid the chemist shop, as the owner was an infamously cantankerous Cornish curmudgeon). I followed behind, sometimes getting close enough to grab at the slower kids loitering near the back of the group. I did actually make the mistake of catching one, but his two brothers and some of the more excitable kids turned back and started hitting me with plastic swords until I let go. I made a mental note to tell Tony and the other hunt marshals off for allowing some of the little darlings to have weapons.

After an exhausting (and noisy) ten minutes, Tony led them into the library, where they would be 'safe'. There was paint and glitter and seaside themed craft to get stuck into for a while, so the poor knackered mermaid could have a sit down and a bottle of water. I was boiling hot and out of breath. I was in the best shape I'd been in for about two years; I'd let myself go a little when I'd left the police force, but since I'd been recruited for Devon and Cornwall CID I'd made an effort to do a bit of training and get fit again. Not that I'd had much opportunity to use it. After sitting my National Investigators Exam and attending training courses to get me back up to speed on police procedure – all of which had taken several months – I'd been made a kind of probationary 'floating' detective sergeant. The probation was scheduled to last for a year; I was about nine months in, and so far the only work I'd been given was on a murder case in Penzance (really straightforward, two well-known drug dealers had been involved in a turf war and one had run the other over), where all I'd done was catalogue witness statements, and a week spent helping Nathan cover Penstowan and the surrounding areas when his full-time DS, Matt Turner, had broken his arm and one of the other officers had holiday booked. It appeared that all the criminals had gone on holiday that week too, as it had been *dead*. The whole town had been disappointingly well behaved. Still, it had been nice to spend time with Nathan. I wasn't sure it proved that CID actually needed me, though.

I got my breath back, and then headed up the hill towards the church. Tony and I had worked out that if I waited in the field between the back of the pub and the churchyard, amongst the old standing stones of Morvoren's Circle, the children would be able to spot me there when they came out of the library. Tony would encourage them to 'sneak' up on me, during which time I would hide behind one of the stones and then leap out at them. They would chase me the rest of the way up the hill and to the church, where Carmen the vicar (who Tony clearly still had the hots for but could now at least form a coherent sentence in front of) would be waiting.

I reached the stone circle not a moment too early. I turned round to look back at the town and the kids were already out of the library, Tony and a couple of the other marshals trying discreetly to get them to look up in my direction. I grinned to myself; he might look like a poor man's Pied Piper in that get-up, but Tony would make a great dad. I hoped it wasn't too late for him. Carmen looked like she was still young enough to have children.

I shook my head; I was starting to sound like my

mum. I heard shouts and knew I'd been spotted, so I made my way to the other side of the stone circle. Tourists assumed they'd been put there by the druids for some mysterious purpose – probably human sacrifice, or something exciting like that – but in reality they'd been put up in 1867 by the bloke who owned the land as part of the Victorian craze for garden follies and fake ruins. There was a footpath across the field up to the church, so ramblers would occasionally pass through the stone circle, but the most frequent visitors were the sheep that grazed there.

There was a water trough at the other side of the circle; I could duck down behind it and hide, whilst still being able to see the hunters coming. But as I approached it looked like someone else had had the same idea. A man was hunched in front of it, arms and head over the side. Was he trying to get a drink of water? Yuck!

'I wouldn't drink out of there, mate,' I called, but he didn't look up. He didn't move. He didn't even start at the sound of my voice. *Uh oh*, I thought. I rushed over and looked down. His face was submerged in the brackish water of the trough, and his arms were hanging limply. I grabbed the hair at the back of his neck and pulled him up, but I was obviously too late. He was dead...

Chapter Two

I sat on a boulder and watched as the police did their work. I'd abandoned the stupid padded mermaid tail, and Debbie had brought me a Merrymaid week marshal's T-shirt to put on over the awful mesh top so I felt less exposed, before hurrying off to rejoin the hunt once the police had arrived.

After discovering the body, I'd called Tony (you don't want to know where I'd been keeping my mobile phone in that get-up, but it was on vibrate) and told him to lead the children to the church via the road, and maybe get Kira to meet them there so they would still find a mermaid. I hadn't gone into detail, but he knew me well enough to realise that there would be a good reason for the change of plan. Then I'd hung up and immediately called Nathan.

Everyone had swung into action. Debbie, who had been waiting at the church and who had received a garbled text from Tony, had reached me within three minutes, and the police had got to me within five – I could see the roof of the station from where I'd been standing, so there'd have been no excuse for them to take much longer. Now, half an hour later, the Scene of Crime team from Barnstaple were here, too, in their white hazmat suits. They were scouring the area for clues; footprints in the grass, fibres from clothing that might have been caught on the rough edges of the metal water tank... I didn't hold out much hope though, as the sheep hadn't been grazing around the stones recently, and the only evidence I could see was some trampled-down long grass by the trough, which had probably been caused by me, finding the body.

'You okay, babe?' I looked up as Nathan stood in front of me, a look of concern on his face. 'Room on there for one more?'

I shuffled over so he could sit next to me on the boulder. 'That wasn't a pretty sight,' I said, shuddering as I remembered the bruised and bloated face. 'Do you know what cause of death was yet?'

'It looks like he drowned.'

I nodded. 'I thought that. Someone held his head under the water.'

'We won't know that until the ME looks at him. Maybe he was drunk and needed a drink of water, but then passed out or hit his head as he bent over—'

'Nah, to even consider drinking that filthy water you'd have to be too drunk to make it up the hill,' I said. 'And if he was coming from the pub, where was he going? There's nothing but the church up here. Look at his hands. Look at the side of the tank. He was grabbing on to the side, trying to push himself away. There'll be scratches on the tank, or metal under his fingernails or something.'

Nathan looked at me shrewdly. 'I think you're probably right, to be honest, but with the town full of tourists we don't want word to get out until we know for certain that it was murder.'

I laughed softly. 'Spoken like a true local. We don't want to put the tourists off and let them go home before they've spent all their money.'

'I was more thinking that I don't want a load of them traipsing up here to have a look and getting in my way…' Nathan stood up and I followed suit, as DS Matt Turner approached us. 'Matt, any luck getting an ID?'

'Yes, Guv.' Matt swallowed hard. 'I recognised him. Although he looks a bit different to the last time I saw him. Mick Tyler. We hired him last summer to take us out fishing on me dad's sixtieth. Nice bloke.'

'And you're sure it's him?'

'Yeah. Davey Trelawney found this.' Matt held out a plastic evidence bag. Inside was a leather wallet. 'It's got his driver's licence in it.'

'Where did he find it?' I asked. 'On the body?' Matt shook his head and pointed to the other side of the stone circle.

'No, in the long grass over there. There's a faint trail of flattened grass leading from there to the water trough, so I reckon they dragged him across the circle and stuck his head in the water.'

'And his wallet fell out of his pocket as they dragged him,' said Nathan. 'That's a reasonable theory. Although he could just have been really pissed. He could have fallen over and then crawled over to get a drink of water.' Matt and I looked at him. He grinned. 'Yeah, I can see from your faces how likely you think that is. But we can't rule anything out just yet.'

My phone, which was still clasped in my hand, rang. I glanced down at it, expecting it to be Tony wondering what was going on, but it was Daisy. I moved away from the two men and answered.

'Everything all right, sweetheart?' I asked.

'No, the vicar's going potty up here,' said Daisy. 'Where are you? Tony said you were at the stones.'

'Yeah, there's been an accident.' It didn't look like an

accident to me, but as Nathan had just said, we couldn't rule it out. Yet. 'You're at the church?'

'Yeah, me and Jade and Nana. We thought we'd come up and see the end of the hunt and have some cake.' There was a pause, during which I thought I could hear her chewing. She swallowed loudly. 'Is that Nathan and all his lot down there with you? I can see people in hazmat suits. It's not like a chemical spill or something, is it?'

'No, that's just the forensics team. It's quite safe.' My brain caught up with something she'd said earlier. 'Why's the vicar going potty? Isn't the mermaid there? I told Tony to get Kira up there—'

'Oh, *she's* here. It's the other one that's missing…'

I left Nathan and carried on up the hill to the churchyard, where the juvenile mermaid hunters were celebrating by stuffing their faces with cupcakes and running wildly in and out of the graves, chased by a small, fluffy white dog who was barking loudly and excitedly. I was relieved to see it wasn't Germaine… As Daisy had told me on the phone, Kira had made it there, her costume hastily put back on, and she was now sitting awkwardly on a small, raised dais under the grand old oak tree that shaded the graves, smiling and waving in what I assumed was meant to be a serene, otherworldly expression but was starting to look a lot like boredom and needing a wee. It was chaos. *Not my circus, not my monkeys*, I thought, and left them to it. I waved to Daisy, who looked relieved that I'd lost most of my mermaid costume now, and glanced around to see if I could spot the vicar. But she found me instead.

'Jodie!' I turned to see Carmen's concerned face behind me. 'I was about to call the police, but Tony told me to wait for you.' She shook her head. 'And in light of what's happening down at the stones, I'm not sure it's that important.'

'Well, I *am* the police today, so let me be the judge of that. What's happened?'

Carmen looked around, then took me by the arm and led me over to the church. The heavy wooden door was wide open, welcoming visitors, and inside it was cool; a relief, after the march up the hill I'd just undertaken, and it was a hot day anyway. She stopped next to the first pew, and turned to me.

'What's happened?' I asked her again. She reached out and took me by the shoulders, then spun me around to face the door. I was confused. 'What?'

'Up there.' She pointed to the stone shelf above the door.

'What? There's nothing there.'

'Exactly. She's gone.'

I looked at her, sudden understanding coming to me.

'The stone mermaid? You mean someone's nicked her?' I was incredulous. Who would steal from a church? And if you *were* degenerate enough to steal from a church, why take a worthless stone ornament and ignore the massive bejewelled brass cross that stood on the altar? Or the brass candlesticks? They'd actually be worth something.

'Aye, they have, and no good will come of it, neither!' We both turned at the sound of the old man's voice. Jago Thomas, who looked old enough to have been here while the church was being built (but could actually only be about eighty), had been sitting, unseen, in one of the pews. He approached us, waving his hands about in a warning manner, his voice a portent of doom. 'There's a man dead at the stones, is there? Drowned, was he?'

Carmen looked at me, confused, then back at Jago. I crossed my arms – it just feels like a 'police' thing to do sometimes, a personal barrier that means I'm not taking any crap or giving anything away to anyone – and stared at him.

'You listening to gossip, Mr Thomas?' I asked. He grinned toothlessly at me (honestly, he was *so* portentous I wouldn't have been surprised if his next words had been 'don't go on the moors', or 'don't feed them after midnight' or something like that).

'I keep me ear to the ground,' he said. He was a wizened little man, so both his ears were pretty close to the floor already. I nodded.

'You mean you've been on your phone to your grandson.' Darren Thomas was a young PC who had recently finished police training college, and had only been stationed at Penstowan for a couple of months. He was currently down at the stones, stopping anyone going near them. *Note to self: have a word with young Darren and tell him he's not allowed to blab to his family about an ongoing investigation,* I thought, but then Nathan had blabbed to me plenty of times before I'd been made official by the superintendent of the Devon and Cornwall constabulary, so maybe I wouldn't say anything. 'What has the accident –' Jago scoffed, but I ignored him '– at the stones got to do with the mermaid going missing?'

'It's the legend, innit? Don't tell me you don't know it. That statue was the only thing stopping her coming back.' Now Carmen and I both scoffed, Carmen's escaping her before she could stop it.

'Honestly, Jago, I don't think—' she started, but he interrupted her.

'That stone statue was put there to stop her reign of terror, and it worked, didn't it? It kept our fishermen safe. And now it's gone, and one of our boys is out there, drowneded.'

Carmen turned to me, her eyes wide. 'This – accident. Is Jago right? Did someone…?'

I sighed, and nodded. 'Yes. Mick Tyler. A fishermen. Drowned in the water trough by the circle.'

'See? See?' Jago was so excited he was practically jumping up and down on the spot. I held up my hands.

'Mr Thomas, you're a grown man. Don't tell me you seriously believe this mermaid malarkey?'

'Course I do. These stories may sound fantastical, but they come from *somewhere*, don't they?'

'Okay.' I fixed him with a steely look. 'So how did she get down off that ledge?'

'I dunno, she—'

'Why did she wait all these hundreds of years to come back to life? *How* did she come back to life? And a water trough, when the sea is just down there? Surely she'd head back to open water, wouldn't she?'

'I don't know! You're not taking this seriously—'

'I *am* taking it seriously, Jago. Very seriously. Which means I'm not going to go back down there and tell DCI Withers that we're looking for some scaly bint with fishy breath and a tail. We're looking for a human person, someone who had a motive to target Mick Tyler, not a mythical creature who just wanted to knock off the first random fisherman they came across.'

Jago looked at me for a moment, then slowly shook his head. 'You'll see. When the next body turns up, you'll see I'm right.' He pointed a long bony finger at me. 'It's the Siren!' Standing there in the church, a sudden shaft of light through a stained-glass window falling upon him, it *did* look very dramatic and portentous and omen-like, but the effect was somewhat spoilt when his mobile phone rang, the ringtone a cheery chorus of 'Don't Worry, Be Happy'. It wasn't the right ringtone at all for a portent of doom, and he knew it. He took it out of his pocket and mumbled, 'Sorry, I have to take this,' and walked out of the church, leaving me and the vicar to share a bemused but troubled glance.

Chapter Three

'So what you're telling me,' said Nathan, 'is that our chief suspect has gills, and until recently identified as a stone statue.'

'Killer's a mermaid,' I said, holding up my hand for Matt to high five. Nathan shrugged.

'She should be easy enough to find, then,' he said. 'Not many of them around…'

Nathan and Matt had joined me at the church, leaving the forensics team to hunt for evidence back at the stone circle. We stood at the back of the churchyard as the vicar plastered on a smile and got back to the celebrations, joining Kira on the dais and giving a short speech thanking everyone for taking part in the hunt. As ever, the entry fees were going to a good cause – the RNLI – and Carmen praised the brave men and women who put their own lives at risk to save those in peril on the high seas.

I nodded over to the vicar. 'I asked her about the theft of the statue, but she couldn't tell me much. She *thinks* it was there yesterday during the Sunday services, but she couldn't say for absolute certain. It's a church, so it's open all day, and she only locks up late at night before she goes to bed. And everyone in town knows about the statue. Half the holidaymakers probably do, as well. It's a local legend.'

'You think the theft and the murder are linked?' asked Matt.

'I don't know,' I admitted. 'But if you wanted to throw suspicion off yourself, or even just muddy the waters for a while to cover your trail, it wouldn't be a bad idea to get the locals convinced the murderer's some supernatural being, would it?'

'Surely no one's seriously going to believe this mermaid nonsense—' started Nathan, but one look at me and Matt stopped him. 'You're kidding me.'

'Nope. Fishermen are a superstitious lot. If you're out fishing at night, no whistling because it's bad luck. And traditionally the fishermen only count their catches using an old Cornish chant.'

'Except not many of them know it these days,' said Matt.

'But a mermaid? Come on…' Nathan shook his head. 'When did the vicar realise the statue had gone?'

'Around the same time I discovered Tyler's body,' I said. 'But she reckons it could've been taken long before that. It's high up on a ledge over the door, so it's not exactly the first thing you notice when you enter the church.'

'How high up? Could someone reach up and get it?'

I shook my head. 'No. I reckon they would've had to stand on something.'

'Like what? Is there anything in the church they could've used?'

'I had a look round. The only thing is the organist's chair. They could've dragged it over to the door, then put it back after they took the statue, but who knows?'

'Before or after they'd murdered Mick Tyler?' said Nathan. 'I know he was a fisherman, but… I think it's a stretch that the murderer would bother to steal the statue and try to implicate the mermaid.'

'Unless that's not why they took it,' said Matt.

'What do you mean?'

'Maybe they weren't trying to blame it on the Siren. Maybe it was a warning.'

'A warning that there are more deaths to come?' I looked at Nathan. 'In the legend, she kills the fishermen for fishing in her spot. Maybe someone's been fishing – or whatever – in someone else's spot…'

'A turf war? In *Penstowan*?'

I bristled indignantly, which was stupid because I really didn't want my town to be in the middle of a turf war, and I probably would've been just as incredulous had someone else suggested it. 'Well, why not? It could be anything. Drugs, maybe? A lot of these coastal towns have big problems with heroin. Look at Penzance. Further upcountry, too, places like Hastings. Poor seaside towns are a breeding ground for smack addicts. Let's face it, the killer's not made any attempt to hide the body, just dumped it somewhere it was likely to be found. And leaving him draped over the water trough like that – it's nasty, and not exactly discreet, is it? So maybe it *is* a warning that anyone else thinking of crossing them will go the same way.'

'Hmm…' Nathan looked thoughtful. 'Does Mick Tyler have any previous, not just for drugs, but for anything?'

'Dunno off the top of me head,' said Matt.

'Then we need to find out. What was he involved in, and who did he piss off?'

. . .

I left Nathan and Matt talking to the vicar and her band of helpers. They'd been there since early on that morning, and although it seemed to me most likely that Tyler's murder (or 'accident' – yeah, I wasn't buying that) had taken place overnight, there was still a chance they might have seen someone lurking around the stones, or even running away from them.

I gazed down towards the stones, where a tent had been erected. The forensics team often did that to protect outdoor crime scenes, to stop any evidence being contaminated or degraded by the weather or the environment, but in this case I thought it was probably more to shield the body from view; it – *he* – had been left in a hunched-over position, and with rigor mortis well set in by now, it would be impossible to lie him down and get him into a body bag without forcing and damaging the already broken body. It was like the body was clenched, trying desperately to hold on to life; but give it a few hours and it would start to relax, admitting defeat and beginning to soften into death and decay. I shuddered; it didn't do to start getting all fanciful when it came to murder, and God knew Mick Tyler's wasn't the first (or worst) corpse I'd seen.

I went to round up my mum, my dog and my daughter before I headed home to change into something more sensible. This would be the first investigation with

Nathan that I would legitimately be part of, and I was nervous but excited. Which probably made me a bad person (someone *had* died, after all), but I couldn't help it. I loved running my catering business, and I'd actually started to turn a profit now, but… I couldn't deny the tingle that ran through me whenever I got involved in police work. I'd had good reason to leave the Metropolitan Police; London was becoming more dangerous, and after I'd been caught up in a terrorist attack, Daisy had cried and begged me to quit, because she was terrified that one day I wouldn't come home. I'd resigned immediately, because I remembered how I used to feel when my dad, Chief Inspector Eddie Parker, went off to work, and he'd only been based in Penstowan and the surrounding villages, which at the time were very sleepy and quiet. I'd signed up for catering college, because I'd always enjoyed cooking, with barely a pang of regret for my old job. Barely. But I had ended up missing it more than I'd expected to. Helping Nathan made me feel like I was keeping my hand in, and not turning my back on all the skills I'd learnt in the force.

I found Mum sitting on a bench, feeding Germaine bits of cake.

'I hope that's not one of my mocha choc chip cookies you're feeding her,' I said, sitting next to her. 'Dogs and chocolate don't mix.'

'I know. This is one of Anthea's vanilla cupcakes.' She pulled a face. 'I'm not saying they're dry and tasteless, but they're like eating sand with coloured sprinkles on it.'

Daisy joined us. 'Come on then, spill the tea.'

Mum looked hopeful. 'Is there tea? I could do with some after Anthea's cake.'

'Are hers the vanilla ones?' Daisy screwed up her face. Anthea's baking really wasn't going down well. Germaine gave a little cough and spat out the bit Mum had given her.

'Everyone's a critic,' I said. 'There's no tea—'

'Shame,' said Mum. Daisy rolled her eyes.

'Tea means gossip, Nana, and there's *loads* of that. Is it true that some bloke got his head shoved in the water trough and drowned?' She looked at me eagerly. The apple hadn't fallen far from the tree.

'Who have you been listening to? Bloody Jago Thomas…'

'Who's Jago Thomas? Luke Trevally told me and Jade—'

'Yeah, and I heard it from Martha Dooley,' said Mum. 'You know her, she's the one with the hair.'

'Oh, *her*. And where did she hear it from?' I shook my head. 'This place is a nightmare for gossip.'

'Yeah, good innit? So it's true then?' asked Daisy, her

and Mum looking at me keenly. Germaine stopped sniffing the rejected bit of cake on the floor and trotted over to me, putting her front paws on my knees and looking up at me beseechingly. I sighed.

'Yeah, it's true. But it could've been an accident, and I don't know if his family's been told yet, so don't you go spreading it around. Any more than it already has been,' I added in an undertone. Mum scoffed.

'Accident? Not likely. It's the Siren, innit?'

Daisy and I looked at her sceptically. 'Now that *definitely* came from Jago,' I said. 'Don't be daft, Mother. There's no such thing as mermaids, particularly not homicidal ones, or stone ones.'

Mum sucked in a breath. 'You don't want to go around saying stuff like that,' she said. 'She might hear you.' Daisy and I looked at each other and laughed, but Mum shook her head and attempted to look wise. 'I'm telling you, these stories get round for a reason. There're more things in heaven and earth, Mercutio.'

'Horatio,' said Daisy.

'What?'

'It's Horatio, not Mercutio,' I said. 'You're getting your Shakespearean references mixed up.'

'I weren't quoting Shakespeare, I were quoting Bob.' Mum nodded over to the elderly hardware store owner, Bob, who was standing next to the cake stall. He caught her eye and gave her a nod. Mum giggled coquettishly and raised her fingers to give him a little wave. 'He proper fancies me, he does.'

'Eww, Nana!' cried Daisy.

'What? I'm considered a bit of a catch amongst the single gentlemen of the Wednesday morning coffee club,' said Mum, offended. She gave a small sigh. 'Although I'm not sure Bob would remember what to do if he caught me.'

'That does it, I'm off to find Jade…' Daisy leapt up.

'Erm, kiss goodbye first, please, young lady!' I said. She didn't really mind kissing me – she even still enjoyed a cuddle in front of the TV occasionally – but she was at that age where it wasn't cool to do it in public. She gave me a quick peck after checking no one was watching, then bounced off to find her friend, promising to be home for dinner. I turned to Mum. 'Right, I need to go home and change out of this before I go down to the station. Are you coming or staying here?'

'Me and Germaine'll come with you,' she said. 'I've had enough now. After all that gossip I could do with some *proper* tea.'

I changed out of the remains of my mermaid costume and left Mum in front of the telly, watching *Bargain Hunt*. Nathan had texted me to say he would swing by and pick me up, and sure enough by the time I'd wriggled out of my cycling shorts and into a smart pair of trousers he was there, waiting at the kerb.

'All right, babe?' I said, as I got into the passenger seat. He smiled.

'That's 'Guv' while we're on duty,' he said. I snorted.

'Yeah, right... Where're we going?'

'To see the victim's wife. Vivienne Tyler.' He nodded to the glove compartment. 'I got you a sandwich on the way here. I know you can't think straight on an empty stomach.'

'Cheek!' I said, but I couldn't really deny it. It was lunchtime by now, after all, and my stomach was rumbling.

'Do you know the Tylers?' asked Nathan. I shook my head, my mouth already full of prawn cocktail and lettuce on wholemeal (he knew me so well).

'Not really. I know *of* them, but Mick was younger than me so we weren't in the same year at school.' I swallowed. 'Plus I don't think he bothered with it much, coming from a long line of fishermen.'

'What do you mean?'

'Most of the fishing fleet in Penstowan – what's left of

it – have been around for generations. If you already know what you're going to do when you leave school, and that it doesn't require GCSEs, well, a lot of kids just won't bother, will they? Specially if they're not particularly academically minded.' I looked out of the window as we drove through the town, round the one-way system that branched off to lead you towards the police station, or up and over the cliffs to the harbour on the other side. 'Although even in Tyler Snr's day they must've seen that the industry was in decline, and not a guaranteed way to make a living anymore.'

'I wondered about that.' Nathan turned the steering wheel and we began to make our way up to the cliffs. 'How *do* any of them make a living? Matt said Tyler had taken them out fishing for his dad's birthday. If Tyler was having to rely on tourism and day trips rather than actually catching and selling fish, he'd be fine during the summer, but out of season…'

'Out of season, he'd have been stuffed,' I said. 'The traditional industries the locals worked in are dead or dying out. People are leaving. Those that stay behind have to find other ways to support their families, and maybe they're not always strictly legal.'

'Hence your theory about a turf war,' said Nathan. I shrugged.

'It could be that. Or it could just be that he borrowed

money off someone and then couldn't pay it back. I'd be surprised if there wasn't a loan shark or two swimming around Penstowan and the local area. Is there anyone on your radar?'

Nathan shook his head. 'No, not the sort of person who'd do anything like this.' We reached the top of the cliffs, and Nathan pulled the car into the car park that marked the start of the North Cornwall and Devon Coastal Path. The vicar would perform her blessing of the fishing fleet from here, later that afternoon. In the past the clergy had made it all the way down to the quayside; but as tourist numbers grew, so did problems with parking, the narrow streets near the harbour not conducive to a sudden influx of visitors' cars. Nathan got out and looked down at the boats laid out beneath us. I followed, hastily finishing my sandwich.

'I didn't even know there *was* a harbour, for the first couple of months I lived here,' said Nathan.

'No. The tourists don't bother with it much. It's not exactly picturesque. I like it, though. It's kind of … honest.'

'Honest?' Nathan looked at me quizzically.

'Yeah. Like, this is the *real* Cornwall, this is what it's like to live here. It's not all pasties and cream teas and beautiful beaches, although of course it is that as well.'

'The dark and seedy underbelly of Penstowan...' said Nathan.

'Ha! Yeah, something like that.'

Some Cornish harbours, like tiny Mousehole or famous, arty St Ives, are popular with tourists because of their natural beauty and the quaint stone cottages that nestle around them. Others, like Padstow, are bustling and prosperous, still full of tourists come the summer season, but proper, working harbours with proper, working fishing fleets. Penstowan, I had to admit, was neither. It had a kind of rundown charm to it, in my eyes at least, but it wasn't pretty; its recent past as a small but busy industrial fishing port still clung to the scenery, like the smell of fish clinging to my new van.

The tide was out, revealing seaweed-strewn mud and sand. What remained of the fishing fleet lay beached, stranded like manmade whales waiting for the sea to come back and cover all the dirt and rust and rotting wood, freeing them from the salty, slippery green and brown sand and setting them afloat again. Some of these boats did still go out to catch fish – some were probably out there now, bobbing around on the water, serenaded by hopeful seagulls waiting to share the catch. Others had been scrubbed, painted and tarted up to chase the tourist pound, offering trips out to Seal Island or to see the dolphins that occasionally visited the waters nearby. Others still had given up completely and been left to rot, undisturbed by time or tide, slowly sinking into the mud. It hurt to see how many of them there were. The stone-built jetties were scarred and crumbling, rusty metal mooring posts and rings and other unidentifiable bits of industrial iron pockmarking the concrete ramps down into the mud. The sun was bright, but its cheery rays failed to glint off the old tin boat sheds and ramshackle buildings that dotted the quay. The fish market, which had once been a major part of the port, was all but derelict. I remembered my dad taking me there once when I was little, early in the morning as the boats came in, laden with their overnight catches. The sights and smells – the fish laid out in trays of ice, eyes wide, most of them still but some of them fighting, gasping for breath in the inhospitable air, gills fluttering – had stuck with me for a long time, although I hadn't at that point quite made the connection between them and the cod in batter we got from the fish and chip shop for our dinner on a Friday.

Nathan sighed. 'Let's get this over with,' he said. 'I love talking to the newly bereaved.'

Chapter Four

We got back into the car and drove down to the harbour, the narrow streets leading us through winding rows of grey stone cottages and two-up, two-down terraces that had been there for at least a hundred years and would probably be there for at least a hundred more.

'Does she know?' I asked, crossing my fingers. One of the things I hated about my time in uniform was having to break bad news – the *worst* news – to victims' families.

'Yeah, one of the PCs knows her, so they volunteered to go and break it to her,' said Nathan. 'They're with her now.'

The Tyler house was well kept, with a couple of kids' bikes in the front garden. Nathan and I exchanged glances as we got out of the car; these things were always worse when there were children involved.

Nathan knocked, and the door was quickly opened by a young black female PC I knew by sight, but hadn't spoken to before. In my dad's day, every single copper in Penstowan had been white, male, and born within a five-mile radius of the station. As the population of the town had grown and diversified it was nice to see the local police finally starting to catch up.

'Hi, Chrissie. How is she?' asked Nathan in a low voice.

'About as good as you'd expect.' The PC had an accent that was pure South London, and I felt a brief – very brief – pang of homesickness for my own days in uniform at Stockwell. She stood aside to let us in, then led us into the front room. 'Viv, the detectives from CID are here to talk to you. I'll go and put the kettle on while you have a chat.' She turned to us. 'Tea?'

'Yes, please,' said Nathan, and I nodded. I was learning to let him do most of the talking – he *was* the 'Guv' while we were at work, as he'd jokingly said earlier – but I didn't always manage it.

The PC left us standing awkwardly in the doorway of the front room, and we got our first look at the grieving widow.

Viv Tyler sat bolt upright on the sofa, a cardigan

wrapped tightly around her despite the warmth of the day. It looked to me like she was literally trying to hold herself together, physically as well as emotionally; as if, were she to relax even a little, she would completely fall apart and never get herself back in one piece. She glanced over at us, then went back to staring out of the window, into the street beyond.

'Mrs Tyler—'

'Viv,' she interrupted, in a monotone. Nathan hesitated, then carried on.

'Viv, I'm DCI Withers and this is DS Parker.' He sat in the armchair opposite her. There was a small dining table and four chairs in one corner of the room, so I pulled out a dining chair. 'We need to ask you a few questions about your husband.'

'Okay.' She fiddled with a loose thread on the sleeve of her cardigan, absentmindedly pulling at it and making it worse.

'You have children, Viv?' I asked gently, leaning forward. She nodded. 'Where are they?'

'Next door, with the neighbours. They don't know—' Her voice choked off into a sob, which she quickly swallowed down. She drew herself up again. 'They won't disturb us.'

'When was the last time you saw Mick?' asked

Nathan, gesturing discreetly to me to make notes. I took out my pad and pen.

'Last night,' said Viv Tyler. 'We had dinner, and I was just getting the kids ready for their bath when he left, so yeah, it would've been about eight o'clock.'

'Did he say where he was going?'

'Yes. He said he was going out fishing.'

'I see,' said Nathan. 'Did he often go out at night? In the boat, I mean.'

'He used to when we first got together, but then he stopped, said it wasn't worth missing the kids' bedtimes for the size of the catch and the money he was getting.' Her voice wavered, but she carried on. 'And then about four, five months ago he started again.'

Why would he do that? I wondered. I glanced at Nathan, but he kept his eyes on the grieving woman. 'How often would he go?' I asked. I didn't know why, but it just felt – *odd* that he'd suddenly started to fish at night again. It wasn't like the price of fish had gone up or something.

'Not very often. Once a month? Although he did go out a couple of nights ago, so I was a bit surprised when he said he was going out again. And he never normally went on a Sunday.' She looked at me. 'Why?'

'No reason. I was just wondering what prompted him

to start again. I thought there was more money in doing tourist charters and that?'

'Yeah. It got too hard to make a living fishing, and the tourist things pay better so that's mostly what he did. But we were still struggling, until he started going out and doing the odd night trip.'

'Ah, right,' I said, noncommittally, although alarm bells were ringing in my head. I was willing to bet my right arm that Mick Tyler had not been fishing on his nights out.

Nathan glanced at me, and I could see he was thinking the same thing, but he let it go. 'Did he go out on his own?'

Mrs Tyler looked shocked. 'No, of course not, that would be dangerous. If you fell overboard in the dark, on your own...' Her voice trailed off for a moment, and I knew she was imagining her husband's body, face down in the water trough. His precautions hadn't prevented his death. She cleared her throat. 'It's a crew of three, him and the Barraclough brothers. Terry and Ewan. He would never go out on the boat on his own.'

We thanked her for her time and gave her our condolences, then stood up to leave. She reached out and grabbed my arm.

'You will catch whoever did this, won't you?' she said, looking into my eyes beseechingly. 'Promise me.'

'We will do everything we possibly can.'

'That's not a promise.'

Outside, I paused for a moment to take a deep breath before I got back into Nathan's car. He looked at me, concerned.

'You okay?'

'Yeah... I'd just forgotten what it was like, talking to victims' families. The other cases I helped you on, before I was "official" again, they kind of felt like a game. I mean, I knew someone had died and everything, but...'

Nathan reached out and put his hand on mine. 'I know. But you did well in there.'

I smiled at him, then pulled myself together. 'Come on, let's go and talk to the Barracloughs.'

Terry Barraclough, the elder of the two brothers, lived a couple of streets away, closer to the quay. We pulled up outside and went to knock on his front door.

'You looking for Terry?' There was an elderly man in the tiny front garden of the house next door, pruning some shrubs and looking at us with deep interest. A large golden Labrador sat in the shade of a small cherry tree, panting in the heat. I got the feeling the man was out there waiting for someone to talk to, rather than for real gardening purposes. There were a lot of old folk living on their own, from what Mum told me, and they must get lonely. Nathan took out his warrant card and showed him.

'Yeah, do you know where he is?'

'This time of day he'll be down the Admiral.'

'That's the Admiral Benbow pub, down by the quay,' I told Nathan. It was a spit-and-sawdust place, a bit rough, or at least it had been the last time I'd been in there, which had been about twelve years ago. Not the sort of establishment any of the tourists set foot in.

The old man sensed this was an opportunity for a bit of a gossip and seized it enthusiastically. 'Never home, that one. Not got anything to come home *for*.'

'No?' I asked, politely. The old man shook his head.

'Nope. Never married. Not even a girlfriend. Had a mate living with him for a couple of years, but he moved out a while back.'

'Okay... Thanks for your help.' Nathan and I turned away, but he hadn't finished.

'Is it true, then? What they're saying about Mick Tyler's boy?'

Nathan looked at me, confused. 'Mick Tyler's boy?'

'I think he means Mick Tyler *Senior*'s boy, not Mick Junior.' I turned back to the neighbour. 'Why, what have you heard?'

'The Siren came back and did him in.' The old man's eyes gleamed. This was probably the most exciting gossip he'd heard in a long time. Nathan groaned.

'This town! How on earth do you know about this down here, all ready? We only found him a few hours ago.'

'Old fishermen's network, innit?'

'You mean Jago Thomas rang you,' I said.

'It's true, then? I knew it, I knew she'd come back one day if they carried on taking the mick!'

'How are they taking the mick?' asked Nathan. The old man waved his hand towards the harbour.

'Going out all hours, fishing where they shouldn't be fishing... They all do it, mind, not just the Tyler lad.'

'I see,' said Nathan. 'Well, I'll be sure to ask Mr Barraclough about that when we find him.'

We left the old man to his pruning and drove to the pub, although by the time we'd navigated the narrow road and found somewhere to park, it probably would've been quicker to walk. As we approached the pub, I was surprised to hear loud voices and laughter. The last time I'd been there it had been full of salty old sea dogs muttering sullenly into their pints. Things must've changed.

'I thought you said it was the Admiral *Benbow*?' said Nathan, pointing to the pub sign. The name had been changed – only slightly – to the Admiral Rainbow, and the aristocratic 18th-century seafarer himself was now wearing his tricorn hat at a jaunty angle, the waistcoat beneath his military coat coloured in rainbow stripes. Suddenly the old man's earlier words made a lot of sense.

'Terry Barraclough's never been married,' I said, apropos of nothing. 'Not even a girlfriend…' Nathan laughed.

'This town never fails to surprise me,' he said.

'That's what you get with a fabulous gay mayor in charge,' I said, grinning. 'We have *got* to come here for an evening out…'

The changes continued inside. The last time I'd been there it had still been divided into two: the public bar and the saloon. Now it was one big, light, open-plan space, with the bar stretching across most of one end. In the old days, back when many of the pubs in the UK had been built, the publicans would set aside one space – the saloon bar – for the ladies and more genteel folk to sit in, sipping sherry in comfortable surroundings, while the other – the public bar – was for the ruffians, the working-class men who were there to sink a few pints, have a game of bar billiards, and maybe end the night with a punch up. Most pubs these days had done away with that, opening up into one large room, or, if they had gastropub pretensions, using the saloon as a dining room.

There'd also been a dark red or burgundy carpet running throughout on my last visit, laid sometime in the late 70s, early 80s by the looks of it, probably to give the place a more luxurious air of respectability. It hadn't worked. It had felt sticky underfoot, the beer-soaked carpet fibres sucking at the soles of your shoes as you squelched over to the bar. That had been ripped up (thank God), and the original flagstone floor left exposed. It looked lovely, but it was quite uneven and I wasn't sure how anyone would fare on it after a few drinks.

There were comfortable banquette seats and intimate booths along one side of the room, and a pool table and dartboard tucked away in one corner, but most of the bar area was more or less empty of furniture, giving punters plenty of space to stand and chat, to mingle, or (going by the tiny and currently unoccupied DJ booth in another corner) to dance. In the old days the clientele had been mostly male, and they still were now, but they were rather younger, better dressed, and for the most part didn't smell of fish.

We approached the bar, looking around at the punters as we did so; it was surprisingly busy for a Monday afternoon, although I was betting it was even livelier on a Saturday night. I had known Terry Barraclough by sight a while back, but I hadn't seen him for at least twenty years and I was assuming that, like the pub, he'd changed a fair bit in that time.

'All right? What can I get you?' Behind the bar, a young man of about twenty-five smiled at us in a friendly manner. His eyes gave Nathan a discreet (but not discreet enough for me not to notice it) going over, before turning back to both of us.

'We're looking for Terry Barraclough, is he in here?'

The barman looked at us both appraisingly. Everything about us screamed 'coppers', so he was probably trying to decide whether to tell us or not. I smiled at him reassuringly.

'He's not in any trouble,' I said. 'We just need to talk to him.'

Of course, coppers *always* say stuff like that, even when they're trying to find someone who has eighteen outstanding warrants against them, a car full of knock-off gear in the pub car park, and is probably facing a three-to five-year stretch depending on what mood the judge is in, but it worked because the barman relaxed and nodded towards a group of men chatting in the corner. 'That's him, the one with the blond crop and the striped T-shirt. And the muscles...' I followed the barman's gaze; he wasn't lying about the muscles. 'Let me know if you need anything else. Always happy to help our boys and girls in blue.' His eyes dropped to Nathan's suit. 'Or grey, for that matter.'

As we approached the table, one of the group said something and they all laughed loudly.

'Terry hasn't heard, then,' I muttered. Nathan nodded.

'Or there was no love lost between them.'

'I dunno, does this place look like it's part of the old fishermen's network to you?'

'Good point.'

The men looked up at us as we reached them. Terry Barraclough looked at me as if he was trying to place me while the others turned their attention to Nathan. Honestly, a woman could feel invisible in a place like this. It was something of a relief, and one of the reasons why my female friends and I in London had been known to frequent the odd gay club on a night out.

'You need something?' asked one of the other men, slightly belligerently. Nathan smiled at him and turned to Terry, holding out his warrant card.

'Mr Barraclough? Can we have a word?'

Terry looked bewildered. 'With me? What about?'

'Mick Tyler.'

The atmosphere in the group changed immediately. Everyone relaxed, as if Tyler being in trouble wasn't entirely unexpected. Terry sighed and shook his head.

'What's he done?'

'Things have probably caught up with him, at last,' muttered the man sitting next to Terry.

'What things?' I asked. Terry glared at his friend, then looked up at me.

'Do I know you?'

'Jodie Parker. I was a couple of years above you and Mick at school.'

'Oh, yeah… Give us a minute, will you?' His other drinking companions were already halfway out of their seats, but the guy next to him put his hand on his arm.

'You sure you don't need me?'

'Nah, it's fine. Bloody Mick…' Nathan and I exchanged glances; he really *hadn't* heard. We sat down in the newly vacated seats and drew closer to Terry. 'Okay then, what's he done?'

'I'm sorry to tell you that Mr Tyler was found dead this morning, up at Morvoren's Stones.' Nathan watched Terry's face closely as he broke the news.

Terry laughed, in that disbelieving way people laugh after hearing bad news, like you're winding them up. 'What? Nah, you're having me on…' He looked at me, and the expression on my face was enough to tell him we were serious. His own face crumpled in shock. 'No, that's… What happened? Was it an accident?'

'Do you have reason to believe it wouldn't be?' I

asked. 'These "things" that could've caught up with him...?'

Terry shook his head. 'No, I can't believe – I mean—' He stopped. 'Does Viv know? And the kids? Oh God...'

'Were you with Mr Tyler last night?' asked Nathan.

'No, I was in here until closing time, and then I went home,' said Terry, vaguely, his thoughts elsewhere. He looked up. 'Does this mean he *was* murdered? If you're asking for my alibi?'

'We spoke to Viv just now, and she said that Mick had told her he was going out on the boat last night,' I said. 'She said he never went on his own, he always went with you and your brother.'

'I see...' said Terry. He shook his head. 'Bloody Mick. I knew he was up to something.' He reached out a shaky hand for his drink and took a sip before pulling himself together. 'A few months back, Mick asked me and Ewan to cover for him. He said if we saw Viv and she asked, we'd been out fishing the night before and not got back until the early hours of the morning. But we didn't. We ain't been out at night for ages.'

'Why did you stop?'

'We can't compete with the bigger boats. We don't really do any fishing now, it's all tourist charters in the summer and then signing on in the winter.' He sighed. 'I keep saying I'm going to move upcountry where there's more work. Without Mick and his boat to at least see me through the summer I'll have to now.'

'So what was Mick doing, if he wasn't with you?'

'No idea. He was proper cagey about it. I thought maybe he was up to his old tricks—'

'What old tricks?' asked Nathan.

'He was a bit of a ladies man in his younger days, before he met Viv. At one point he had three of 'em on the go at the same time. They found out about each other eventually, of course, and really gave him what for. You can't keep anything secret round here.' He rolled his eyes. 'Believe me, I've tried.'

I grinned at him. 'Oh I dunno, your neighbour seems to think it's strange you've never married…'

'Old Walter? Yeah, he keeps telling me I just haven't found the right girl yet. I reckon I could dress up like the Village People and perform "YMCA" in his front garden, and he *still* wouldn't believe there were gays in Penstowan.'

'Has he seen the mayor?'

Terry laughed softly. 'I know… When I came out, I thought Mick might have a problem with it but nah, he was good as gold. Didn't bat an eyelid…' He blinked, tears forming in his eyes. 'Bloody idiot. What was he thinking?'

'So you think he was cheating on his wife? Seeing

another woman, and then what? Her husband could've done him in?'

'I dunno. Maybe. He definitely wasn't out on the boat with me and Ewan. My brother and his family are away for a few days, they left Thursday and ain't back for another couple of days. And the boat's not going anywhere at the moment, because there was a problem with the starter motor and we're waiting for a part to come.'

'What about a couple of nights before that? Were you with him then?'

'No, I told you, we ain't been out night fishing for ages.' Terry looked from me to Nathan, then back again. 'I'm telling you, whatever got him killed it weren't anything to do with fish. More likely a woman.'

Chapter Five

'So, what do you think? Are we looking for a jealous husband or a homicidal mermaid?'

Nathan and I stood at the quayside, looking out across the muddy sand towards the sea. Past the entrance to the harbour the waves sparkled in the sunlight. A few tourist boats bobbed gently in the swell as they gathered beneath the cliffs where we could see the tiny figure of the vicar, surrounded by a surprisingly large crowd, blessing the fleet from above. Boat trips were popular in the summer season, especially so during the Merrymaid Festival, and even more so today, the day of the hunt, children (and a few adults) eagerly scouring the waves to spot the flick of a mermaid's tail just under the surface. If they were lucky they might spot a dolphin, or the trip might include a brief visit to the seal colony nearby.

I leant against a rusty metal railing and shook my head. 'Neither.'

'No? You don't think there might be something in Barraclough's theory, that Tyler could've been cheating?'

'It's possible, of course, but like Terry said himself – you try keeping something like that quiet in a town like this. You saw how quickly the news about the murder spread. What are the chances Tyler could've been doing the horizontal rumba with someone he shouldn't, without someone knowing about it?'

'But obviously someone *did* know about it – the cheating woman's husband.' Nathan absentmindedly picked at the flaking paint on the railing. 'Maybe she's not from round here. They could have had their secret assignations somewhere else, miles away. How many hotels must there be, within a ten-mile radius? Or further?'

'They could have been indulging in shenanigans at the Aphrodite Motel in Barnstaple,' I said. 'Breakfast included.' Nathan laughed.

'Now *that* sounds like a hotbed of lust,' he said. 'One for date night, maybe?'

'It's more of a honeymoon destination, I reckon.'

'Who needs the Maldives, am I right?'

'Ooh, is that where you're going to take me?' I said. It

was meant to be a cheeky aside, but I felt mortified as the words left my mouth. I wasn't pushing for us to get married; been there, done that, got the divorce. I cleared my throat hastily, as if I could swallow the words down and pretend I hadn't said them. 'But anyway, I *still* think it's unlikely. I can ask around, see if there's any gossip about it. Or rather, I'll get Mum and Tony to ask around. Between the two of them they know everyone in Penstowan, and even if they haven't heard any gossip themselves, they'll know who to ask.'

'I don't doubt it. As long as they're discreet about it,' he said. I raised an eyebrow. 'Yeah, I know your mum so I don't even know why I bothered saying that. But you don't think Tyler was fishing, either?'

'No. He packed it in because it wasn't profitable, and he stopped going out at night because it wasn't worth missing the kids' bedtimes. So why did he suddenly start up again?'

Nathan shrugged, reaching out to start picking at the paint again and then stopping himself. 'Price of fish gone up?'

'I don't think so. And if it has, why limit his fishing to once or twice a month, at night? Why not do it on the days when he didn't have any tourists booked in? Boat trips are popular, but there's a fair bit of competition for tourists and he can't have been booked solid every single day. Plus he *couldn't* have been out fishing last night, because his boat's out of action.'

'True.' Nathan turned to look at me. 'What was it Viv Tyler said about money? That even with the tourist charters they'd been struggling—'

'Until he started going out at night.' I nodded. 'So unless his fancy woman was generous enough to pay him for his time—' I stopped. 'Ooh, maybe he was a gigolo! Maybe he had a secret life, pleasuring the unsatisfied wives of rich businessmen while they were out of town—'

'Yeah, I don't know if you've noticed this, but everything round here smells of fish,' said Nathan, 'including most of the people. I had a mate once who worked on the fish counter at Tesco's. He still smelt of haddock even after a bath and half a can of Lynx. He never had any luck when we used to go out on the pull.'

I guffawed loudly, scaring a nearby seagull. 'Oh my God, I can just imagine you and your mates going out on a Saturday night, all cheap aftershave and fake sports gear from the market.' I put on my best/worst Liverpudlian accent. 'Come 'ed, ladies, fancy a bevvy?'

'Oi!' said Nathan, trying to look offended, but he was laughing too. 'I was *much* classier than that. I had Fila trainers and a bucket hat and everything. I looked boss.'

'Oh, don't!' I gasped. I was laughing so hard now I

was almost doubled up. Nathan snorted, trying to rein in his own laughter.

'DS Parker, you are *so* unprofessional,' he said.

'Wait til you meet the SIO, he's a right scally...'

We managed to calm down. I took a deep breath.

'Okay, so maybe a gigolo from Cornwall who smells of fish –' Nathan snorted again, and I felt my own laughter bubbling up once more, but I squashed it down and carried on '– maybe that's a bit niche. So we can only assume, then, that this extra money that was coming in wasn't from any mysterious bit-on-the-side, and it probably wasn't from fishing, either.'

'Maybe your theory about it being a turf war over drugs wasn't as wide of the mark as I first thought,' said Nathan. 'We need to find out exactly where he went last night before he ended up at the stones.'

We got in the car and headed back to the station. Matt was there, and he'd already put in a request to trace Tyler's phone on the night of his death, so all we could do was wait.

Nathan sat down and started to go through the witness statements Matt and the uniforms had taken, but they all boiled down to the same thing: no one who had been at the church the night before or early that morning, getting the finish line party ready, had seen or heard anything. Carmen had been vicar-ing and seeing off the last of the volunteers until almost ten o'clock that night, by which time it would've been dark. Presumably the murderer or Tyler himself would have needed a torch to find their way to the circle, and the vicar probably would've seen the beam from it dancing amongst the stones. Plus, the surrounding area was quiet, and any noise, like arguing or fighting (or murder), would've carried up the hill to the church. But she hadn't seen or heard anything.

So the murder had taken place later than 10pm, and before 7am, as that was when Carmen had unlocked the church, hoping for some quiet time to pray and gather her thoughts before the madness of the mermaid hunters descended upon her. Although I'd already talked to her about the missing mermaid statue, Matt had also taken an official statement from her about it. However, we were no closer to finding out when it had been taken, or by who – or even how, because the ledge it normally lived on was high up. I'd initially thought the thief could've used the organist's chair, but Matt had tried to stand on it himself, and had discovered that it was on castors, small wheels that had been very well oiled and which, consequently, all rolled in different directions and wouldn't stay still. To stand on that chair was to take one's life into one's own hands. The church's pews looked like they were sturdy enough to stand on, but that meant that they were too heavy to be easily moved.

I yawned and checked my watch. Reading witness statements and doing paperwork had always been my least favourite part of being a police officer. I had hoped that being a detective would be more exciting.

'Are we keeping you?' asked Nathan, sardonically.

'Er…well actually, I *do* need to pop to the supermarket at some point,' I said. 'I'm catering a birthday party tomorrow.'

'But we're in the middle of a murder investigation,' said Nathan. Matt diplomatically picked up a file.

'I'm just going over there to … do … something,' he said, and scarpered. Coward.

'I know. And you know ordinarily I'd be all over it, but I've got a business to run as well,' I said. 'It's a hundredth birthday party, over at the retirement village.'

'But—'

'He's a lovely old fella. He could be your grandad.' Nathan opened his mouth to protest again. '*He could be your grandad*,' I said again, emphatically.

'But you're on the payroll now,' said Nathan. 'You can't just…'

'Well, yeah, but what about when this case is finished and you lot *aren't* paying me anymore, until the next one?'

'"You lot"?' Nathan sounded irritated. 'I'm not "you lot".'

'You know what I mean. I need to keep my business running for the times when, you know, nobody's getting themselves murdered. Which is most of the time, thankfully.'

'Hmm.'

'What does "hmm" mean?'

'This wasn't an issue last time.'

'No, because last time I helped you out no one had been bumped off, and I didn't have any catering work.'

Nathan sighed. 'We didn't really think this through, did we? How it would work if something came up and you had other work booked in.'

'No,' I said, a sinking feeling invading the pit of my stomach. 'Look, I thought my days in the service were over. I've put everything into my catering business, and it's just starting to pay off. I didn't know I'd get called up to help at the same time I had a job booked. And I *do* love police work – most of it…'

'Apart from the paperwork. Tell me about it.' Nathan looked around, then discreetly scooched his chair over and took my hand. 'We'll work it out, okay? Just tell me this is the only thing you've got booked in for the foreseeable future.'

'Umm… I've got a wedding, not next Saturday but the one after…'

'We'll just have to catch this mermaid before then, in that case.' He looked up at the clock. 'Go on, then. These octogenarians aren't going to feed themselves, are they?'

'He's a centenarian, actually, and he's still perfectly capable of feeding himself, but I get what you mean.' I stood up, pushing my chair under the desk and picking up my bag. 'Are you sure this is okay?'

'Would you stay if I said it wasn't?' He stood up as well. 'Don't answer that, that wasn't fair of me. Matt can do all the donkey work I was going to give you, can't you Matt?' He raised his voice so the DS could hear.

'Eeyore,' said Matt. We laughed. 'Nah, I don't mind as long as you bring us a bit of cake.'

'I'll do my best,' I said gratefully, and escaped.

I had the party's buffet menu and the shopping list already worked out and saved on my phone, so I went straight to the supermarket. I pushed the trolley around the aisles thoughtfully, selecting the ingredients almost on automatic. Were there stormy seas on the horizon (to borrow some fishing imagery) for me and Nathan?

Working together in the past had been so much fun, and I'd expected things to carry on just the same now that I was officially allowed to stick my nose in. And the morning's investigation *had* been fun. But there was this whole business with, well, my business. It had only taken off properly over the last eight months or so. Could I really still run a successful catering company at the same time as being an auxiliary detective? It would have been easier if they'd just taken me back on a permanent part-time basis, because then I would have had regular hours that I could've worked my catering jobs around. But they didn't need someone permanent, they needed someone who could help out when a big case came up, and when that happened I had to be available 24/7. Only, how could I guarantee that? Tomorrow's party was a case in point. The customer was only going to be a hundred years old once. I could hardly ask him to move his birthday just to suit me. And weddings! I'd been getting a lot of weddings, particularly over the summer months; I couldn't tell someone twenty-four hours before their big day that I'd have to cancel because someone had been murdered...

But if I packed in the catering, I'd just be sitting around waiting for the next dead body to show up, and with it the next CID posting. If they even needed the extra help, because some stations were bigger than others and had enough permanent staff, and others just didn't want an outsider poking her oar in.

I dumped a packet of frozen puff pastry into the trolley and sighed. Was I going to have to choose? Catering or detective work? There were good reasons why I'd left the service in the first place, promises I'd made to Daisy, and Mum had been relieved too when I'd quit the Metropolitan Police and moved back. Penstowan CID was nowhere near as dangerous as being a uniformed officer on the streets of London, but still – no police work was without risk. My own father, who just shy of his retirement had been supposedly confined to desk duties, had died chasing teenage car thieves down the A39.

The main thing, I thought, was that it couldn't affect my relationship with Nathan. I wouldn't let it. I'd spent most of my adult life putting my career first, and much good it had done me – although of course I had still somehow ended up with an amazing daughter. And a dog…

The amazing daughter, the dog and my mum were all at home when I got in. Daisy came to help me with the shopping bags without me even asking (I said she was amazing, didn't I?). Mum nosed through them as I unpacked.

'Got anything interesting for dinner?' she asked, tossing aside my party buffet ingredients.

'Nope,' I said. 'All this is for the birthday party I'm doing tomorrow. We're having gruel.'

'My favourite,' said Daisy, pulling a face. 'Are there maggots in it?'

'Yes, and snails out of the garden. Extra protein, innit.' Germaine barked. 'Oh settle down, Germaine! I'm joking. I thought we'd have tomato and veggie pasta with lots of cheese, and some nice bread.'

'I think Germaine would prefer the snails,' said Daisy.

'So would I,' murmured Mum.

'Oi! I heard that, and it can be arranged…'

I put all the buffet stuff to one side – I would have to cook some of it tonight, and finish preparing the rest of it tomorrow morning – and set to work on the pasta sauce. I chopped some onions, garlic and mushrooms. I threw them into a deep pan for Daisy to gently fry in olive oil. She took a deep breath in.

'That already smells delicious,' she said.

I chopped up half a red pepper that had been languishing in the bottom of the fridge for a while, and a courgette, and added them to Daisy's pan, then started on a large carrot. I didn't peel it (a lot of the goodness is in the skin), just scrubbed it clean and then grated it. Most shop-bought pasta sauces have a surprising amount of sugar in them to balance out the acidity of the tomatoes, but the carrot would add natural sweetness.

'Nathan not with you?' asked Mum.

'Yeah, I told him to wait in the car,' I said. She scoffed.

'All right, Miss Sarky! I just thought you'd be working the same hours as him, now you're in CID.'

'I'm an *auxiliary*,' I pointed out. 'Anyway, I told you, I've got this party. Nathan let me finish a bit early.'

'That's nice of him.'

'Yeah…' He hadn't really had much choice, had he? If he'd put his foot down and told me to stay I'd still have left, because yeah, *technically* he was in charge of me, but he was my boyfriend and he knew I had other commitments I couldn't just drop. I suddenly felt really bad, like I was playing truant. I should be back at the station with the others…

'Mum, are you daydreaming again?' Daisy was watching me, waiting for the carrot. I pulled myself together.

'No, I was contemplating. Totally different thing.' I scraped the carrot into the pan, then poured in some vegetable stock, adding a really good squeeze of tomato purée. 'Here,' I said, taking the spoon from Daisy. 'You grate some cheese. You know I can't do it without half of it ending up in my stomach…'

I stirred the pan to make sure everything was

combined, added a twist of rock salt and some pepper, then put the lid on to let it simmer. What else could I add? This was a great recipe for using up whatever leftover veg was wilting in the crisper drawer of the fridge. There was half a head of broccoli that had gone a bit soft and bendy. I shaved off the tops of the florets, leaving a large pile of what looked a bit like green rice, then added that to the pan. I hate throwing away food, so I'm always looking for recipes that let me use up odds and ends, but even I had to admit the broccoli stalk was past its best, so it ended up in the compost bin.

We put some large pasta shells on to cook, and just before they were ready I tipped the tomato and veggie sauce into the blender and pulsed it until it was smooth and thick, the perfect consistency for coating pasta. The sauce went back into the deep frying pan, then the drained pasta went into that. I mixed it all round, then put the pan on the kitchen table. A bowl of grated cheese (not parmesan, which would have been more authentically Italian, but a strong cheddar which tasted just as good) and a ciabatta loaf from the supermarket completed the meal. I was just wondering whether to put some aside for Nathan when he walked in. I smiled at him anxiously. Why was I anxious, for goodness sake? It was *Nathan*.

'Hi babe, I wasn't sure what time you'd be back,' I

said, thinking, *I'd have known if I'd stayed at the station.* Nathan shrugged, giving me a slightly uncertain smile of his own.

'There's only so much you can do while you're waiting for forensics and phone logs, isn't there?' He leant in and kissed me on the cheek, then pulled back to look at the food. 'That smells amazing. I'm starving.'

We helped ourselves to dinner, Mum grumbling about eating 'rabbit food', an epithet she immediately assigned to any meal not containing meat even if she actually really enjoyed it. As I sat there with the steaming, comforting bowl of cheesy pasta in front of me, I almost managed to ignore the weird underlying feeling of guilt and anxiety that had sneaked up on me earlier that day.

After dinner, Mum corralled Daisy into helping her clear up so Nathan and I could shower and change out of our work clothes. As I watched him dry himself off I wondered if I should say something, but he beat me to it.

'So you didn't actually miss much,' he said, pulling on some tracksuit bottoms and a T-shirt. 'We got a hit on Tyler's mobile.'

'You know where he went?'

'Yeah, but it's not particularly helpful. It looks like he went down to the harbour just after eight o'clock and stayed there until eleven. Then there was another hit on the tower near the church about fifteen minutes later that puts him near the stones.'

'Could he have been in the pub up till then?'

Nathan shook his head. 'Matt went down to the Admiral and asked around, something we probably should have done when we were there earlier but it didn't occur to me at the time.'

'Nor me. There's the other pub up on the cliffs, or is that out of the cell tower's radius?'

'Technically, it is within the radius of the one on the edge of the harbour, but in reality the signal up there's pretty weak, so I think it's more likely he was near the boats. Matt went and asked in there too, anyway, but all he got was a load of gossip and nonsense about the bloody mermaid.' Nathan rolled his eyes. 'It's bad enough when no one has any idea who could've done it, but it's even worse when they all keep telling you it's a flipping mythical creature.'

'Could he have been at someone's house?' I asked. 'There's a row of old fishermen's cottages actually on the edge of the harbour.'

'Maybe. Although from what we've been able to find out, most of them are holiday lets now, and half of them are empty. It seems holidaymakers like fishing villages, but not the smell of fish.'

'Could've been having an assignation with the mysterious woman Terry told us about.'

'*Speculated* about. He didn't know for sure, did he? And if there were any rumours about that I reckon Matt would've heard about them when he was asking around in the pub.' Nathan shook his head. 'He's going to pop back later and ask anyone who might have been drinking in there last night, but the landlords of both pubs seem pretty certain they'd have seen Tyler if he was in there, and they didn't.'

'Maybe he went to check on his boat?'

'For three hours? He didn't make any phone calls or texts, or if he did he deleted them afterwards, because they're not on his phone – Viv Tyler gave us the code so we could have a look. We're still waiting to get a log of his calls from the phone company, so something might still show up. Otherwise I don't know what he would've been doing all that time.'

'Lying low,' I said, thinking aloud. 'He must've had a meeting lined up with someone at the stones, because it's not somewhere you'd randomly decide to go in the middle of the night. He didn't want his wife to know about it, so he told her he was going fishing, went and sat on his boat, knowing she wouldn't come down and check on him, then went off to meet whoever at eleven.'

'And they killed him,' said Nathan. He sat down on

the bed and looked up at me, smiling. 'This is more like it.'

'What?'

'You and me, swapping theories, putting ourselves in the victim's shoes.' He reached out and grabbed my hand, tugging me down next to him. 'You coming out with outlandish rubbish and me disproving it—'

'Cheeky bugger!' I said, but he just laughed and kissed me, and my indignation evaporated as quickly as it had appeared.

Chapter Six

'So, how's it going, working with Nathan?' Debbie unpacked a Tupperware container of prawn cocktail vol au vents and arranged them on a ceramic platter.

'Great,' I said, carefully avoiding her gaze as I buttered thinly sliced white bread, which would be made into egg and cress sandwiches. Everything on today's menu was soft, nothing requiring too much chewing, and very traditional: vol au vents, a variety of sandwiches with the crusts cut off, quiche, a bit of salad (lettuce, cucumber and tomato – none of your fancy schmancy rocket or micro greens here, thank you very much!). My mum wasn't quite the same generation as the majority of today's guests, but they'd all grown up eating much the same things, so I'd tried out a few new ideas on her first, to see if they were likely to go down well at an oldies' get-together. It had not gone according to plan.

'What's this?' Mum had asked suspiciously, poking at the sea bass ceviche I had made. 'It's raw.'

'It's fresh fish, thinly sliced and marinaded in lime juice, lemon zest, peppercorns, a bit of chilli. It's not raw, it's cured.'

'Cured? Poor thing still looks sick to me.'

So the elders of Penstowan were not ready for ceviche. Vol au vents it was. I looked up and Debbie was watching me.

'Yeah? It's going okay?' she asked.

'Of course,' I said. 'Why wouldn't it be?'

'Well, he's in charge of you now. He's a DCI and you're a lowly DS. A *probationary* DS at that.' She shook her head and opened another Tupperware container. 'I love Callum to bits, but I don't think I could work with him, not if he kept trying to tell me what to do.'

I snorted. 'Nathan knows better than to do that,' I said, but despite the way Nathan and I had left things the night before I felt uneasy. She was right. He *was* in charge of me, and basically everyone else at the station, as he was usually the highest-ranking officer there. The day before, when I'd asked to leave early – anyone else, he probably would've refused (unless it was a family emergency or something; he was the senior investigating officer, not a monster). The first twenty-four hours after a crime can be crucial, because the trail hasn't had time to grow cold, so it would be all hands on deck back at the station and at the crime scene now. All hands apart from mine, which were here, buttering bread.

'Ain't you finished yet?' said Mum, bustling into the kitchen. She was here to help serve the buffet; some of the residents weren't quite steady enough on their feet to come up and help themselves to food, so she was going to assist them. I suspected that she was there more for the social aspect and to help herself to the sausage rolls, but I didn't mind; it meant I didn't need to pay her.

'We'd be finished quicker if there was someone else to help,' said Debbie, meaningfully. She rolled her eyes at me. I laughed.

'Ignore her, Debs. Mother, we're nearly done. You can start by taking some of those plates out and putting them on the table, if people are getting ready to die of hunger.'

'It's a hundredth birthday party,' said Mum. 'You can't go around making jokes about people dying in case someone does…'

The lounge, where the party was being held, was lovely and cool after the heat of the kitchen (cooking during a heatwave can be an unpleasant experience, unless you're a fan of saunas). It looked like the management had bought every single fan they could get their hands on – no wonder Wonnacotts, the electrical shop in town, had run out. It was also surprisingly full for a work day, but then most of the guests looked to be of retirement age, and for those that weren't, a relative's centenary was a special enough reason for a day off. Amongst those in attendance was one of my dad's old colleagues.

'Sergeant Adams!' I said, reaching out to hug my old friend. He laughed.

'Not "Sergeant" anymore,' he said. 'It's just Harry these days.'

'Okay, "Harry", but you'll always be Sergeant Adams to me. The station ain't the same without you there.'

He smiled. 'Kind of you to say so. I did have everything running smoothly. That new desk sergeant woman better not have mucked up my system.'

'No, of course she hasn't,' I said, diplomatically refraining from passing on the gossip Nathan had told me: how Sergeant Sally White had rearranged *everything* because no one could make head nor tail of how Harry had done things. I looked the ex-sergeant up and down, and did a double take. 'Is it me, or have you got younger?' He'd always looked ancient to me as a kid, and I still thought of him as a little old man, but he could only have been in his sixties.

'You know what, I feel like I have. Peggy put me on

this diet, and o' course, I didn't like the sound of *that*. The Mediterranean diet, she calls it. You heard of it?'

'Oh yeah, fish, veg, olive oil, all that kind of thing.'

'Yep. Well, blow me down, but proper tasty it is. Lost loads of weight, cut down on the jelly babies—' For as long as I could remember, Harry Adams had always had a packet of jelly babies or wine gums or midget gems in his pocket, which he would dip into throughout the day. 'Got me diabetes under control. And we joined the National Trust so we could go and look at some of them big houses and walk round the gardens. I've even started planting up me own veggie patch! Never thought I'd get into gardening but I enjoy it.'

'Being a man of leisure suits you,' I said. He nodded.

'It really does. They offered me retirement three times before I took it. They only let me stay on because they was short-staffed, and they didn't think I could do much damage tied to a desk.' That wasn't what Sally White had said. 'And I couldn't imagine meself being anything other than a copper. You know what's it like. Without the job, what are you?' He shook his head, chuckling. 'Well, turns out there's plenty of stuff to be other than a copper. But then you know that.' He nodded towards the buffet table. 'Good to have another string to your bow.'

'Yeah,' I said. 'So anyway, what brings you to this party?'

'Old Bill, the birthday boy, he's my uncle. My mum's brother. He used to look after me when I was little and take me out fishing. He didn't have any kids of his own, so my mum used to say he wanted me to follow in his footsteps, and she thought he was going to leave me his boat.' He laughed. 'Dunno about him leaving me *anything*, the old boy will outlive all of us.'

'You never fancied being a fisherman?'

'Lord, no. When I went out with him as a lad, I'd be chundering over the side before we'd even made it out of the harbour. Proper landlubber, I am.'

We turned to look over at the birthday boy as a roar of laughter erupted from his direction. Old Bill might well have been old, but he still had a hearty (and slightly dirty) laugh. I recognised Jago Thomas and the elderly man who lived next door to Terry Barraclough in the geriatric but raucous group.

'Jago'll be passing on the gossip, then,' said Harry. I looked at him, eyebrows raised. 'About the mermaid killing Mick Tyler. Oh yeah, I heard it. Load of rubbish.'

'Thank God someone in this town has some sense,' I said. 'Of course it's rubbish. But that other bloke – Walter, is it? – he thinks it's comeuppance. He thinks the fishermen have brought it upon themselves by fishing where they're not supposed to, like in the story.'

'Wally Finch hasn't got the brains he was born with.

And how would he know where they've been fishing, anyway? He never leaves the house, except to walk that dog of his.' Harry spotted someone across the other side of the room, waving to him. 'Sorry, I'd better go and mingle. There's cousins here I never knew I had.' He lowered his voice. 'Between you and me, I think I preferred not knowing some of 'em.' He winked and left.

I went over to the buffet table and cleared a couple of empty plates. The guests were hoovering up the vol au vents, and there was barely a ham and cucumber sandwich left. I needed to make space for the cake, which the birthday boy's family had ordered from Rowe's bakery. I'd been a bit miffed when they hadn't hired me to do that as well, but now I was thankful; I would have struggled to find the time to do it. I turned round and there was Walter Finch right behind me, reaching for a slice of quiche.

'Hello, Mr Finch,' I said politely. He screwed up his face, trying to place me. I helped him out. 'Jodie Parker. *DS* Parker. My colleague and I spoke to you yesterday outside Terry Barraclough's house.'

'Oh yeah, that's right. What you doing here? Moonlighting, are you?'

'Something like that.' I picked up the plate of quiche and held it closer to him so he could select a piece more easily. 'I wonder, do you mind if I ask you something?'

'Depends what it is,' he said.

'Yesterday you said something about the mermaid being back because the fishermen have been fishing where they shouldn't have been.' I put the plate back and turned to him again with a smile. 'Can I ask what makes you say that? Have you seen something?'

'Oh yes, indeed I have,' he said, almost indignant. 'They been fishing over at Kevrinva Bay. I seen 'em. They's protected waters round there.' Kevrinva Bay was a little further north along the coast. The waters there were home to a fascinating array of weird and wonderful sea creatures, sponges, sea fan corals, and anemones; and at low tide the beautiful but hard to access beach was covered in rock pools full of sea snails, shore crabs, and dark green seaweed that swayed gently in the shallow water. I'd been there on many a school trip, and it had been drummed into every child in Penstowan that this was not a place where you disturbed the wildlife, whether that was by trampling through the rock pools or fishing in the sea itself.

'You've seen them? Can I ask how?'

'Me and Tess like to go for walks early in the morning, and that's when they were out there.'

'Tess is your dog?' It would have been nice to have another pair of human eyes to confirm his story.

He chuckled. 'I'm too old for a lady friend. Yes, she's

my dog. I normally walk her round the streets near the harbour, but there's nowhere for her to have a good run, so a couple of times a week I take her up on the cliffs and let her off the lead.'

'That's quite a walk.'

'I drive us there. I don't like driving anymore, so I go when it's still nice and early, and there's not many other cars on the road. Maniacs, a lot of them round here, specially the delivery drivers in their vans. And the size of some of them big jeep things! They're not right for the narrow roads round here. Had a couple of near misses with them, coming round a corner too fast, even at that time of day.'

'They're terrible,' I agreed, encouragingly. 'So the last time you saw someone fishing… When would that have been?'

'Last week sometime. Thursday or Friday morning? Seen 'em other days and all, mind, on and off. Normally about six o'clock.' He smiled ruefully. 'All them years, getting up early to catch the tide, and I'm still doing it now. Most mornings I'm awake by five. When it's hot like this, I get up and make a flask of tea, then me and Tess get in the car and head out.'

'Good idea. Neither of you wants to be out and about when it's this hot,' I said. 'So, what exactly did you see? Do you know whose boat it was?'

'No, 'fraid not. It were quite a way out – it looked like they were heading back out to sea. And my eyesight's not what it used to be, so I couldn't see the name or number.' He looked around, almost furtively, then back to me. 'I'll tell you whose it wasn't, though. It weren't Mick Tyler's boat.'

'No?' That tied in with what Terry Barraclough had told us, that the boat had been out of action.

'Nope. Tyler's boat's got a red hull. This one was blue and white.'

'Right…' That sounded promising.

'O' course, half the boats in Penstowan harbour have got blue and white hulls.'

'Oh.' Not quite so promising, after all. 'Anything else you can tell me about it? The size of it? The condition?'

'Not really. From where I was it looked like one of the bigger boats, one that could stay out overnight. Not one of them tourist day-trip ones.'

'You mean the sort that have a kitchen and maybe a sleeping area or something downstairs?'

'Below deck,' Walter Finch corrected me. 'Yes, I think so. Nothing fancy, just a place for the crew to have something to eat or have a rest. But like I said, my eyesight ain't good anymore.' He brandished his plate. 'Now if you don't mind, I'm gonna sit down and eat this bit o' quiche before they bring the birthday cake out.'

So Old Bill had his cake, and his guests picked the buffet table clean, and all the while I could hear snatches of gossip about Mick Tyler's death and the supposed return of the mermaid. I was pleased to note that most of the guests thought it was absolute rubbish, but there was still a fair number who were convinced the vengeful sea creature was behind the murder, most of whom were old fishermen. I shook my head in bemused disbelief as one elderly gentleman tried to convince his younger, sceptical relatives that the mermaid was real, citing the fact that he'd gone out to sea nearly every day for almost forty-five years and had never, ever seen her; because, of course, she was trapped in the stone statue in the church. You couldn't argue with *that* logic, could you? I caught the eye of a younger woman who had to be his daughter, and we shared an eye roll and a grin. But it wasn't just the old folk; I overheard Davey Trelawney's son, Jack, who worked at the retirement home doing maintenance and groundskeeping (and who probably wasn't meant to be at the party at all), telling a group of residents about the night he'd seen the mermaid sitting on some boulders at the foot of Elephant Rock. I knew exactly which night that was, because he'd been arrested for driving home under the influence of alcohol and a hefty amount of MDMA. Davey had had some choice words for him, words that Sergeant – I mean, *Harry* – Adams had passed on to my mum. And then she'd passed them on to me, and the rest of her Wednesday morning coffee group. I thought I'd probably have seen a mythical creature too, if I'd taken as many drugs as Jack Trelawney had.

I didn't believe Walter Finch's assertion that the mermaid had come back to right some wrongs in the slightest. But what about his sighting of a boat where it really shouldn't have been? His eyes might be failing him, but surely he couldn't have imagined that.

I cleared the empty plates off the buffet table and stacked them in the home's dishwasher, apart from a few big platters and bowls that belonged to me. I usually washed them up at the venue if I could, so they wouldn't stink out the van, but today I just packed them up and carried them out to Gwyneth. They could hardly make her smell worse; they might even take the edge off that faint but lingering odour of haddock. But mainly I wanted to get away as soon as possible, because I had a detour planned before I made my way home. Mum was staying behind to talk to a friend of hers who had just moved into an apartment in the same retirement complex; she'd been tempted to buy one herself after Nathan moved in, but we'd discussed it and had decided to build a granny flat in our garden for her instead, and I got the feeling she wanted to double check that it had been the right decision. Quite what we would do if she changed her mind – the builders having already laid the concrete for the foundations – I didn't know.

'Right, that's me done,' said Debbie, taking off her apron and folding it up. 'That went all right, didn't it?'

'Yes, they all seemed to enjoy it,' I said vaguely. She peered at me closely.

'Oh aye,' she said. 'What you planning?'

'What?'

'You've got that look in your eyes. You're gonna go off and do something, aren't you? Remember you're a copper now, you don't need to skulk about, you're allowed to do whatever you want.'

I laughed. 'Not quite.'

'Oi oi!' Tony poked his head around the door of the kitchen. 'Blast, have I missed all the food?'

'Yeah, you're too late,' I said. 'What you doing here anyway?'

'Carmen wanted to drop off a present. She pops in and does a service here every Sunday, so she knows the birthday boy. I was just giving her a lift—' Debbie and I exchanged looks. 'What's that look for?'

We both giggled. 'You dropping Carmen off. Ain't she got a car?' asked Debbie.

'Or did you "just happen" to be passing when she came out?' I said. Debbie snorted.

'Did you stay over last night?'

'Debbie!' I cried, pretending to be shocked. 'Her a woman of the cloth and all!'

Tony looked at us scornfully. 'Listen to the two of you! Jodie, you're no better than your mum.'

'You didn't, then? Never mind.' Debbie snorted again, which set me off. Tony just stood there, watching us, then shook his head and left.

'Tony – come on, we were just kidding!' I called after him.

'Oh leave him,' said Debbie. 'He's got it bad. I didn't even think he was religious.'

'He's not. Which is a good point. Can you even go out with a vicar if you're a godless heathen?' I tried to look serious, but we both started giggling again, harder this time. Debbie swatted me on the arm.

'Stop making me laugh. Poor Tony,' she said. She pulled herself together. 'Right, I'm off before we upset anyone else. Be careful.'

'With what?'

'With whatever it is you're about to do.'

Chapter Seven

'And you actually called me first? I'm impressed.'

Nathan and I stood in the car park, looking out to sea. We were about a mile and a half along the coast from Kevrinva Bay, at one of the entrances to the North Cornwall and Devon coastal path, which led from Penstowan to Appledore, thirty-odd miles away.

'You can thank Debbie for that,' I said. 'And I remembered that the last time I came here I was about twelve and it was hard work getting down to the beach then, so it'll probably be even harder now.'

'Yes, you have to be careful at your age,' said Nathan. I swung for him but he leapt back. 'Wow, you can still move fast when you have to,' he said, grinning.

'You wait. With age comes experience, and cunning. I'll get you when you least expect it...'

We left the car park. Instead of turning east to follow the coastal path we went straight on, between two concrete posts which marked the entrance to the Kevrinva conservation trail. It meandered through a few stunted trees, which had been bent and shaped by the strong sea winds that battered the coast in the winter, and then began to slope steeply downwards.

I have never been very good with heights, and in several places the path narrowed, scrubby plants and shrubs clinging to the cliff face on one side, and dizzying drops down to the rocks below on others. I slowed down, inching forward and clinging onto exposed tree roots whilst trying not to look at the jagged stone below us. At least it was cooler here; or was it terror that was making me suddenly cold?

'You all right, babe?' Nathan had got a little way ahead of me, but, realising I wasn't right behind him, had stopped to look back.

'Yeah...' I said. 'Actually, no, not really. But I will be...'

He waited, a hand stretched out towards me, but I couldn't let go of the tree roots to grab it. I sidled down the path, thanking God I'd worn trainers with grippy soles, Nathan watching and encouraging me all the way, until the path widened out again, and the slope became less pronounced. I let out a deep breath.

'Well done,' said Nathan.

'Thank you. I'm trying not to think about climbing back up...'

We made it down to the beach in one piece. It was still covered in rock pools, just as it had been the last time I'd been there. I gazed into them in childish delight, stepping across the smaller puddles and skirting around the large ones. *I should bring Daisy here,* I thought. I couldn't believe I hadn't thought of it already.

'So what exactly are we looking for?' asked Nathan. I stopped next to a large rock and sat on it, removing my shoes and socks so I could dangle my feet in the water.

'Okay, so Walter Finch saw a boat out there—' I waved my hand vaguely out to sea. 'He's adamant that they were heading out of the bay, where they're not allowed to fish.'

'Right...'

'All the fishermen know they can't fish here, and if they're found doing it they face big fines. I Googled it before I rang you. The waters are protected because of the reef and all the different marine species that live on it, but it's also a nursery for the seals.'

'I thought they lived on Seal Island?' Nathan frowned. 'Hence the name...'

'They do, but the island's basically just a big steep rock sticking out of the sea, so they give birth here. They come into the bay because it's quiet and sheltered, and they can easily get up onto the beach. And the pups stay here until they're big enough to fend for themselves and get out to sea. Birthing season starts in late August down here, and carries on through autumn and winter. We ought to come back here in a few weeks, we might see some babies. Anyway… the fishermen avoid it, because there have been occasions when seal pups have been caught in their nets and it's tragic and they get into a lot of trouble.' I looked at Nathan thoughtfully. 'Now I'm thinking about it, that's probably how the whole mermaid story started. Someone probably caught a seal way back, so they all agreed not to fish here. Maybe if you've drunk enough, or you've been out at sea for a long time, a seal could look like a mermaid…'

'Anyway…' said Nathan, too polite to tell me to stick to the subject.

'Yes, sorry. Anyway, maybe the boat wasn't here fishing. Maybe it was dropping something off.'

'Drugs?'

'Probably. Or it could be anything. This whole coast has a long tradition of smugglers and wreckers.'

'Wreckers?'

'When times were hard, people used to stand on the cliff top with a lantern in stormy weather, luring the boats into the rocks. And after they sank, any cargo the ships were carrying would get washed up on the beach. Along with the bodies of the poor sailors.'

'Nice.'

'Yeah... That was before they built the lighthouse at Trevose Head, of course. Now their descendants get through the hard times by charging tourists a tenner for a box of fudge with a picture of a thatched cottage on it.'

Nathan laughed. 'I've bought a few of those boxes... So you think the boat could've picked something up out at sea, and then brought it here to drop it off?'

'Yeah, from another boat, or maybe something attached to a buoy and left floating in the water until they picked it up. They could've met up with someone in a dingy and handed it over, or they could even have attached it to another buoy closer to shore, for someone to swim out to.'

'Both of those would work,' said Nathan, staring out at the water as if hoping to see whatever this illicit cargo was, bobbing up and down between the waves.

'Hardly anyone comes down here,' I said. 'That path isn't very well known – I think DEFRA or the environment agency or whoever wanted to get it closed off, but all the local council would do was spend more money advertising the actual coastal path, so hikers tend to come and do that instead. So we might be able to find footprints, or see if a boat's been dragged out or something…'

'When did Walter say he saw this boat?'

'He reckons it was Thursday or Friday morning, which links in with what Viv Tyler said about Mick's penultimate fishing trip. I know it's a long shot, but we haven't had any storms or really high spring tides since then, so hopefully if there is any evidence it won't all have been washed away.'

'It's worth a look, anyway,' agreed Nathan. 'I always enjoyed beachcombing as a kid…'

We moved along the beach, peering closely at the sand and the rock pools, looking for anything that seemed out of place. I sighed as I bent down to pick up a small piece of plastic that had been washed up; it had probably once been a plastic bottle of some sort, tossed into the trash and ending up, like so much other rubbish, in the ocean, where it had been battered and broken down into tiny pieces. I'd read in a horrifying article somewhere that a growing percentage of what looked like grains of sand on many of the world's beaches were actually tiny pieces of plastic, plastic that also ended up in fish, which then finally ended up in us… I always tried to pick up any rubbish I found on the beach and take it home, where it would end up in landfill, but what else could you do?

I straightened up and turned to look at the sea. The tide was still out a long way, but it looked to be on the turn.

'The tide will start coming in soon,' I said to Nathan. 'We've still got a while, but maybe we should split up and cover more ground.'

'Good idea,' said Nathan, 'although I'm not holding out much hope of finding anything.' I had to admit I wasn't, either.

Nathan headed west along the beach, back towards Penstowan, while I turned east. We both resumed our search of the sand above the tide line; anything below that probably would have been obliterated as the waves came in. I was almost ready to give up when I spotted something. An imprint in the dry sand, long and thin, with a pattern repeated along it.

'Nath!' I called. He looked up from his own search and I waved him over.

'What is it?'

I pointed at the imprint. 'What do you think made that track? It looks like the edge of a car tyre to me, or maybe a boat trailer.' I followed the line in the sand made by the tide; smooth and still slightly damp on one side, dry, powdery and golden on the other. 'They've driven along the beach, sticking to the impacted sand so as not to get bogged down in it, but they've had to swerve—' I looked around, then gestured to a large protruding rock a few metres away. 'They've swerved to avoid that rock, and the wheel's crossed over the tide line...' There was another print a bit further on. 'There!'

'They've either swerved again, or *that's* the front wheel and *that's* the back,' said Nathan.

'Which would make it a car, probably a jeep or four-wheel-drive of some sort, rather than a boat trailer,' I said. 'Most boat trailers have a small wheel at the front, like a castor, and two bigger ones with tyres on at the back. And they'd be pulling it along by hand, which would be really tricky down here.'

'But how would you get a car on the beach?' Nathan looked around, but the only way down was the steep path we'd navigated. 'Or a trailer, for that matter.'

I nodded further along the beach. 'Look at that headland. With the tide out this far you can walk around it. I wonder if you can get round to the next bay?'

'We'd better have a look, then,' said Nathan. We headed towards the rocky outcrop that jutted out towards the sea, forming the eastern encircling 'arm' of Kevrinva's sheltered bay. At high tide the waves would crash against the foot of the cliff, but now there were rock pools and a surprisingly wide, smooth sand path around it.

'I don't remember it being like that last time I was

here,' I said. 'But then that must've been more than twenty years ago. There's probably been a fair bit of erosion since then, and storms that have shifted the sand about.'

'Beaches are alive, aren't they?' said Nathan. 'Constantly changing.'

We skirted the rock pools and stuck to the sandy path, and it led us all the way around the headland and into the next bay. We got halfway along the narrow but sandy beach in front of us, and then stopped to look around.

'Okay...' said Nathan. 'So you could feasibly drive from this bay into the last one, but how would you get the car down *here*? It doesn't really solve the problem.'

'No,' I said thoughtfully. 'Maybe you could get round into the *next* bay...'

'Maybe you could,' said Nathan. 'But not today. The tide's coming in really quickly now and I don't want to risk getting trapped.'

'No, can you imagine us having to call out Davey Trelawney to haul us up the cliff?' PC Trelawney might be in his late fifties now, but he was still strong as an ox and volunteered with the local rescue team. 'We'd never live it down...'

We hurried back along the beach. The path we'd not long strolled along was already underwater, but thankfully only up to our ankles. I still carried my trainers, socks tucked inside them, in my hands, and I was wearing shorts, so it was actually quite pleasant splashing through the seawater, but Nathan had to roll up his trouser legs and one of them decided to come down before we made it to the other side. He groaned.

'Good job you noticed before it got too deep,' I said. He looked up from the water and grinned.

'We would've had to completely strip off in order to keep our clothes dry,' he said.

'That would be *terrible*.'

'Maybe we should come back later.'

———

Matt was talking to the female PC, Chrissie, when we entered the CID office at Penstowan. He grinned as he took in my outfit.

'Is it Casual Tuesday or something?' he asked. 'I'd have worn my boardies if I'd known.' Chrissie laughed and nudged him. *Hello*, I thought. They were getting a bit pally...

'I thought budgie smugglers were more your style,' she said, and it might just have been the heat, but I could've sworn he blushed.

'I was working in a boiling hot kitchen earlier,' I said. 'But we have just come from the beach.'

Nathan filled Matt in on our discovery. Whether it would actually turn out to be significant, I had no idea. Even if you *could* get a car down there, what would that prove? It could be teenagers mucking about. God knew we had enough boy racers tearing along the country roads, and they'd probably jump at the chance to have a race along the sand.

Chrissie stood patiently while we were talking; she had a file in her hand, which I assumed was the reason she'd come up to CID in the first place (or an excuse to come up and flirt with Matt). But she began to pay more attention as Nathan mentioned Kevrinva, and as we debated on how possible it would be to get a car or boat trailer onto the beach she piped up.

'There's the old boat ramp at Three Sisters,' she said. We all turned to look at her.

'Where's that?' asked Nathan.

'The next bay along from where you were,' said Chrissie. 'The road down to it is really narrow and twisty, and you wouldn't want to meet anyone coming the other way, but you can drive down to the ramp. There's nowhere to park, but there's just enough room to unhitch your trailer, if you've got one, and then do, like, a ten-point turn and drive back up. Me and a couple of friends go kayaking there sometimes.'

'I didn't know you kayaked,' said Matt. She smiled.

'One of the reasons I moved down here. Not much opportunity for water sports in Croydon.'

'Do you reckon you could drive a car down the ramp, onto the beach and then round the next couple of headlands to Kevrinva?' I asked.

'I don't know… We normally go down there at high tide, of course, but then we kayak along the coast to Penstowan beach and back again, and sometimes we're out long enough for the tide to start going out…' Chrissie looked thoughtful. 'I reckon you *could*, but you'd have to time it right with the tide – you wouldn't want to get cut off. And you'd have to have a big four-wheel-drive vehicle to get over the softer bits of sand. An ordinary car's lower down, and it'd get stuck.'

'I wonder if Mick Tyler knew that?' I said to Nathan.

'He should have done,' said Chrissie. 'It was Viv Tyler who told me. That's how I know her. We belong to the same kayaking club.'

Chapter Eight

'Well,' said Nathan, after Chrissie had left, 'that's interesting.'

'It is,' I agreed. 'But I wonder how many other people are in this canoeing club? If they all know about the boat ramp, it doesn't prove anything.'

'But it must narrow it down.' Nathan looked thoughtful. 'It doesn't seem to be common knowledge, I mean you didn't know, and you're—'

'Pretty common,' said Matt, smirking.

'Oi!'

'A local, I *was* going to say,' said Nathan. 'Although…'

'Oh that's right, gang up on me! Just because I didn't bring you any birthday cake.'

'Didn't you?' Matt looked disappointed.

'Nah, those old folks were hoovering it up like there was no tomorrow. Apparently, if you take your false teeth out you can get more sponge in your mouth.' I stopped. 'Although you can't chew it then, of course. You just have to mash it up with your gums...'

'Anyway...' said Nathan, in his *please can we get back to the subject* voice. 'None of this proves Mick Tyler was on that boat, or any other boat in the area, or even in a four-by-four on the beach, when he was supposedly out fishing three nights before his death. But I think we can be pretty certain that wherever he was, and whatever he was doing, he shouldn't have been doing it, and that's what got him killed.'

'Smuggling, you think? Or doinking someone else's wife?'

'*Doinking*?' I said, looking at Matt in disgust. 'Really? How are you single?' I shook my head. 'Hopefully we'll know a bit more about Mr Tyler's extra-curricular activities by this evening. I've got my best spy onto it.'

'Good old Shirley,' said Matt.

'God help us,' said Nathan. 'Right, well until we get Tyler's phone log there's not a lot else we can do. The sun's out. Let's get out of here while there's still a little bit of the afternoon left.'

'You sure, Guv?' asked Matt, although he was already out of his seat and reaching out to turn off his computer.

'Yeah, go on. We'll end up making up for it at some point, we always do. Oh, hang on.' Nathan held out a hand to stop the DS leaving. 'Did Chrissie bring something up for us, or was it a social visit?'

Matt blushed again. Aww... He reached down and picked up a sheet of paper from his desk. 'Yeah, a misper. I've logged it, although there's not much to go on and hopefully the parents are just panicking over nothing.'

'Parents?' I asked, a sick feeling in my stomach. 'Is it a child missing?'

'No, twenty-year-old. Liam Fossett. His parents own the Captains Table, the chip shop on Fore Street?'

'Oh yeah. Go on.' Nathan nodded.

'Student up at UEA – that's Norwich, I think. He's home for the summer holidays. Went out last night and hasn't come home. Not answering his phone.'

'And that's out of character for him?' I asked. On TV shows, they always seem to have the police dismissing missing persons reports until they've been gone at least forty-eight hours, but that's rubbish. If it's out of character or dangerous for someone to be missing – for example, if it's a child, or an elderly or sick person – you can report them as soon as you know they've gone, even if it's only been an hour or so. Matt nodded.

'Yeah. His dad says they have an agreement. They don't care how late it is, or how wasted he is, if he's not coming home or he needs picking up then he rings or texts them so they're not worried if they get up the next day and he's not there. He's never done this before, so they're really concerned.'

'Okay,' said Nathan. 'Are uniform aware? They'll look out for him? Hopefully he's with some girl and the last thing he's thinking about is his mum and dad, but you never know…'

'Yeah, they've been briefed.'

'Then for the moment there's not much more we can do. He'll probably be back home with a raging hangover by the time we clock on tomorrow.'

We left the station. I drove home in Gwyneth – the hot weather really wasn't helping things in the olfactory department – while Nathan followed in his car. In the absence of my usual little helper, Daisy – she was still out with a big group of her friends, and I wasn't expecting her home until it started to get dark – he helped me unload everything from the van and carry it inside.

'There you are!' Mum pounced on us the minute we were through the door. 'I was starting to wonder if the two of you had eloped.'

'You see that thing on the table over there?' I said, pointing to the hall console table. 'That's called a telephone. If you pick it up and dial a number, you can talk to me…'

'All right, Miss Sarky Knickers. You'll be smiling on the other side of your face when you hear what I've found out about your victim.'

'Really?' Nathan and I both stopped in our tracks. She wrinkled her nose.

'Blimey, that must be what you had the egg sandwiches in. Get all that in the dishwasher, and then I'll have a nice cup of tea.'

'Oh, you will, will you?'

'Yeah, in a proper posh cup and all, not a mug. Goes right through me these days if I drink that much. Oh, and a couple of them Nobhob biscuits while you're at it. I'll be in here.' Mum disappeared into the living room. Nathan and I swapped bemused looks.

'It's not too late to cancel the builders and buy her a retirement flat, is it?' I said.

'Or we could just elope,' suggested Nathan. I wasn't sure how to answer that, so I just laughed and did as my mum had told me.

'Right, here you go,' I said, passing her a cup of tea. Nathan gave her a little bow and presented her with a china plate full of oaty biscuits.

'Your Hobnobs, m'lady,' he said gallantly, and she giggled like a schoolgirl.

'Ooh, thanks ever so,' she said, batting her eyelashes.

'Oh behave yourself, Mother.' I sat in the chair

opposite her, with Nathan perched on the arm. 'So come on then.'

'You want me to "spill the tea"?' she asked, raising her cup. Nathan looked alarmed. I rolled my eyes.

'She means the gossip. Yes, we do.'

'Okay, so…' She leant forward, and we watched with bated breath as tea slopped over the rim of her cup and into the saucer, but it didn't go any further. 'I asked around at the party if anyone had heard about Mick Tyler having a fancy woman. And … nothing.' She sat back, a satisfied smile on her face. I gritted my teeth.

'Is that it?'

'Oh, no. No, I asked everyone – they all know everyone, you know what us oldies are like, what with the Wednesday morning coffee club grapevine and the old fishermen's network. And no one had heard any rumours about him having an extra bit of skirt on the go.'

'So he wasn't "doinking" anyone else's wife,' said Nathan, in a low voice.

'Nope, devoted to his wife and them kiddies, everyone says so. So then I says, times have been hard, how was he managing with just the tourist boat trips and that? Two little kiddies is expensive.'

'Did they say he'd started going out fishing again?' asked Nathan. She shook her head.

'No. Couple of them said they had no idea, must be

on the benefits or something. But then one of the old fishing lads said whatever he was doing, he must be doing all right because he'd done a lot of work on his boat. They said it had been falling apart – even when his dad had it he'd always been tinkering with it to keep it running – but Mick was able to pay for proper parts and repairs. Said it'd been running fine until the other day, when something blew.'

'Who said that?'

'Alf Barraclough. His sons work with Mick.' She dunked a Hobnob. 'Or used to.'

'Right, yes. Did Alf think there was anything dodgy about this part blowing? Did he think maybe the boat had been sabotaged or something?' It hadn't occurred to me before, but maybe this wasn't the first time someone had tried to kill Mick Tyler. It had just been the first successful one.

'Oh no, said it was just one of them things, easy to fix, their Terry was just waiting for the part. And yes, before you ask, the Barracloughs and Mick Tyler all got on well, no bad blood or arguments or anything like that.'

'Okay…' Nathan looked thoughtful. 'So no one knows what he was up to?'

'Ah, no, but…' Mum had left her biscuit in her tea for a dangerously long time. She hoiked it up into her mouth before it had a chance to disintegrate. 'Alf said we should go and have a chat with Stuart Mitchell, down at the harbour.'

'Who's Stuart Mitchell?' asked Nathan.

'He owns half the fishing fleet, what's left of it,' I said. 'What's he got to do with anything?'

'A lot of the blokes go to him for business advice. He's about the only one down there who's doing really well. He's bought up several boats when they were going out of business, and then taken on the previous owners as skippers, so they get a salary while he takes any profit.'

'So, what? Did Tyler go and see him?'

'Alf reckons he did. He didn't sell him his boat or anything, but maybe Mitchell gave him some advice that turned his business around. Whatever it was, it looked to Alf like it was working, although he didn't think his boys were getting any more work out of him.' She picked up another biscuit. 'He reckoned maybe Stuart Mitchell showed him a few swerves, like.'

'Swerves?'

'Tax swerves. Fiddling the books or something. I dunno.'

I stood up. 'I think we need to talk to Stuart Mitchell, don't you?'

'Can I finish me tea first?' asked Mum. I rolled my eyes.

'Not you…'

Nathan stood up too, but he reached out and took me by the shoulders, turning me to face him. 'Yes, we do, but not tonight.'

'No? But—'

'No. First off, we've been at work all day. You've been on your feet all morning, cooking. We could both do with being fresh when we talk to him.'

'Okay…' I said. Deep down I was relieved because I was knackered, I just didn't like admitting to it.

'And secondly, I'd prefer to interview him at his place of work, not his home. Get a look at his fishing empire.' Nathan grinned. 'We can ask him if he's seen any mermaids around the harbour.'

'And get a look at his boats.'

'Exactly.' He pulled me in for a quick kiss – a quick, chaste kiss, as my mum was watching us as she dunked her third biscuit. 'Now go and have a shower while I make you some dinner.'

'I'm not sure if I should be offended because you think I smell, but hey, if you're making dinner, I'll overlook it.'

I went upstairs to shower and change into a pair of yoga pants and a loose T-shirt; it was still warm, but my legs had started to get a bit chilly in those shorts. I followed the smell of dinner cooking downstairs, and began to lay the table with knives and forks; two sets, because Daisy was out and Mum had stuffed her face with party food earlier, not to mention biscuits.

I felt a pang as I laid out the cutlery, thinking of the missing person's report that had come in just as we'd left. Liam Fossett. I didn't know him, but I'd been to school with both of his parents and I'd been to their fish and chip shop many times. I'd probably spoken to Liam there, helping out when he was home from university, without even realising it. I hoped they were laying a place at the table for him this evening, and that their earlier fears had been a false alarm.

I heard my mobile phone ringing in the distance; I'd left it upstairs. I ran up to the bedroom and caught it just before it went to voicemail. Daisy.

'Hi, sweetheart,' I said, panting slightly. 'Everything okay? You having a good time?'

'Yeah, we're all at Rani's watching a movie.' Rani was a school friend who was having a birthday that day. Fifteen years old! Daisy would be fifteen in a few months, too. Where were the years going? 'We were going to order pizza, but Rani's mum made this *amazing* Indian meal, oh my God it was *lush*—' I smiled to myself; my daughter had inherited my love of food, as well as my nose for gossip. 'So anyway, Rani said we can all sleepover. Everyone else is staying, can I?'

I was suddenly seized with the impulse to order her home, safe, where I could keep an eye on her. There'd been a murder; the killer could still be on the loose. There was a young man – a boy, really, not that much older than her – missing. The world was full of danger, and it was my duty to protect her.

I took a deep breath. It was also my duty to make sure she became independent, and had friends, and enjoyed life. So I just said, 'Is Rani's mum okay with this? Having a house full of teenage girls is hard work.'

'Yeah, she says it's fine.' Daisy sounded pretty confident in her assertion, and I trusted her to be honest with me at least seventy-five per cent of the time (she was a teenager, and if she wasn't getting up to a few things behind my back I would have been slightly disappointed, as long as I never heard about them), but I still thought it worth checking.

'Let me have a quick word with her.'

I got back to the kitchen just as Nathan started serving up. It was only fish fingers, baked beans and oven chips, but any meal cooked by someone else is a treat.

'Do I need to save some for Daisy?' he asked.

'No, she just called, she's sleeping over.'

'Right…' he said, frowning.

'What's the matter?'

'I just… I'd just feel better if she was here, you know, what with everything that's going on.'

I smiled, took the two plates of food from him and put them on the kitchen table, then reached up to cup his face in my hands. 'Aww, babe. It's so sweet of you to worry about her.'

'Of course I do, she's—' He hesitated. 'I mean, she's practically my daughter…' I pulled his face towards me and gave him a huge smacker on the lips. He looked astonished. 'What?'

'You're more bothered about her than her own father is.' I sat down in front of my plate of food, Nathan following suit. 'I have to admit, I thought about ordering her to come home too,' I said, reaching out for the salt and pepper. 'That Fossett boy's only five years older than she is. But part of being a parent is knowing when to give them some freedom. She's sensible and streetwise. She's with a big group of friends, and she's at someone's house. Rani's mum's there. She knows that if she needs or wants to come home, even if it's in the middle of the night, all she has to do is call me.' I felt a pang as I remembered Matt's words earlier; Liam's parents had the same arrangement with him. 'The world is full of danger – dangerous situations and dangerous people. I hope that she never has to deal with them, but I have to make sure she could if she had to.'

Nathan sighed. 'I know. I'm just not used to being responsible for anyone else. I mean, I know technically she's *your* responsibility, but…'

'You make a great dad,' I said, the words leaving my mouth before I had a chance to stop them. I didn't want him to think I was hinting, either about him adopting her, or about us having a baby together. I was forty-three years old. If we'd met when I was younger, then yes, I probably would be thinking along those lines, but I wasn't sure I wanted to go through either pregnancy or having a baby in the house again at my age. I shoved a piece of fish finger in my mouth quickly, to stop myself saying any more on the subject. 'Anyway,' I said, as I finished chewing, 'you're worrying now, and she's only at a sleepover. Just you wait til she starts going clubbing.'

———

We went to sleep early that night, after checking in with Daisy by text to make sure she was still okay. My eyes were shut and I was asleep almost as my head hit the pillow.

I was woken with a start just after midnight by the sound of Nathan's phone ringing. I sat up, trying to shake the sleep from my brain as I watched him take the call, trying to make sense of his side of the conversation.

My first thought was that it was Daisy, wanting to come home, but she would've rung me, not him.

'Bloody hell,' said Nathan, to whoever was calling. He turned to look at me, his face grim. 'Yeah, we'll be there as soon as we can.' He disconnected the call. 'They've found Liam Fossett...'

Chapter Nine

We drove through the darkened streets towards town, turning off before we reached the one-way system and onto a housing estate that had sprung up about ten years ago. Rows of identical houses lined the streets. My mum had always dismissed them as 'boxes', with tiny back gardens and no character, but they were affordable and had all the mod cons a family would need.

No need to guess which one we were heading for. Three patrol cars were parked outside, and several uniformed officers stood nearby, talking to neighbours and making sure no one breached the crime scene. Incident tape had already been unfurled across the front lawn, tied at one end to the ornamental lamppost decorating a neighbour's garden and at the other wrapped around what was probably a telecoms or power junction box. An ambulance passed us, lights flashing, as we pulled up as close to the house as we could get.

Matt was already on the scene. He held up the tape for us to duck under.

'You got here quick,' said Nathan.

'I was already in town, in the pub,' said Matt. Nathan raised an eyebrow. 'It's all right, I'm sober. When you live on a farm miles away you're always the designated driver...' There was a box of latex gloves and hazmat overalls at the front door. We stopped to put them on.

'We didn't bother with this at Tyler's crime scene,' I said.

'No, but it was outdoors and it was already pretty compromised,' said Matt. 'Forensics will be a bit different here.'

'So what have we got?' asked Nathan, as we stepped through the front door. A pane of glass in the window next to it had been smashed, and shards littered the floor.

'The homeowners came home from a weekend away, long drive, two little ones asleep in the car.' Matt nodded back out to the street, but there was no telling which car he was referring to. 'Dad came up to open the front door first, so they could carry them in without waking them up, sees the break-in, and thank God left them in the car so he could investigate.'

The house was neat and tidy, tastefully if inexpensively furnished. There were pictures on the wall of two smiling children, a boy and a girl. Matt led us down the hallway to the kitchen, as his words suddenly sparked something in my memory.

'They'd been away for the weekend? The dad, he's not Ewan Barraclough, is he?'

Matt looked back at me, surprised. 'Yeah, that's him. How…?'

'When we interviewed Terry Barraclough, he said his brother had taken the family away for a few days somewhere,' I said, and Nathan nodded. 'I didn't think they were meant to be back for another day, though.'

'No,' said Nathan thoughtfully. 'Where are they now?'

'Neighbours over the road took them in.' He stopped in the doorway. 'In there. Careful, there's stuff all over the floor.'

A wooden dining chair lay on its side. Next to it, on the linoleum, was a smear of blood and what looked like a tooth. On the kitchen counter, a couple of knives and a meat tenderiser – a metal mallet with a serrated surface – were laid out. The knives were still clean and shiny, which was some relief, but the tenderiser had obviously been recently used. I swallowed hard.

'Oh my God,' I said. 'Poor Liam. What did the paramedics say?'

'That if he'd been left any longer he would've been dead.' Matt looked grim. 'He's still not out of the woods, hence we're treating this as a potential murder scene. He's unconscious, and it looked like they broke a couple of his fingers.'

'They tortured him?' I said, feeling sick. Nathan nodded.

'Looks that way. Did any of the neighbours hear anything? I'm assuming this must've happened sometime late Monday night?'

'Davey Trelawney spoke to some of them before I got here. The neighbour on one side is elderly and hard of hearing, and the bloke on the other side is on medication which makes him go out like a light. The two houses opposite were having a rowdy barbecue for someone's birthday in their back garden and making loads of noise until pretty late. We even got a complaint about it, but when a patrol swung by it'd gone quiet.'

'So they might actually have heard the smash and thought it was the noisy neighbours,' I said.

'Yes.'

'Where's Mr Barraclough now? We need to find out why Liam came or was brought here, and how he's linked to Mick Tyler...'

. . .

Ewan Barraclough was the spitting image of his brother; blond, tanned and muscular, you could tell he spent his days working outdoors. His neighbour showed us into the living room, where he was nursing a large glass of whisky. His hand shook as he took a sip of it.

'Ewan Barraclough? I'm DCI Withers, this is DS Parker. I'm sorry you've had such a shock.' Nathan smiled sympathetically. 'Not the homecoming you were expecting?'

'You could say that. How is he?'

'He's okay,' I said, hoping he was. 'He's in good hands. How's Mrs Barraclough, and the children? I hope they haven't been too shaken by this.'

'Lou's upset, of course she is. The kids don't know what's going on.' He sighed. 'That poor boy. What the hell was he doing in my house?'

'That's what we're trying to find out. Do you know him?'

'Liam? Yeah, of course. He's been helping out down at the harbour over the holidays,' said Ewan. 'Trying to pay off his student loan.'

'Helping out who?'

'Well, anyone who'll pay him really, but mostly Stuart

Mitchell.' Interesting. That was the second time today we'd heard that name.

'Doing what?'

Ewan shrugged. 'Just stuff. Posting letters, picking stuff up, delivering things. Errands.'

'Errands?' Nathan and I exchanged glances.

'What about going out on the boats?' I asked. 'Does he ever go out fishing? Do the odd night shift or something?'

'Yeah, I think so. I don't really know. You'd have to ask Stuart.'

'Okay. And you don't have any idea why he would come here? Has he been to your house before?'

'Yeah, a couple of times. I was a bit of a gamer before we had the kids. I had a few different consoles, proper gaming chair and all that. Not got time for it now, or room. It'd been in a box in the garage for two years. So at the start of the summer I decided to sell it. He came round to have a look and ended up buying all of it off me.'

'Not that worried about paying off his student loan, then,' I said, and Ewan laughed softly.

'To be honest I ended up giving him most of it for nothing. It's all well out of date now. I knew he couldn't really afford it, but I could see how much he wanted it. It made me feel good, letting him have it.' His smile faded. 'I hope he gets to play with it again.'

'We spoke to your brother, Terry, about the death of Mick Tyler,' I said. Ewan nodded.

'Yeah, I know. He called and told me. We weren't supposed to come back until tomorrow, but Lou and Viv have always been close, and she wanted to come back early to support her.'

'Well, it's a good job you did,' said Nathan, 'because you just might have saved that boy's life.'

Ewan shook his head. 'If I'd been here, he wouldn't have ended up in this mess in the first place.'

'Maybe not,' I said, 'but it might've been you being carted off in an ambulance instead. My colleague, DS Turner, said you'd had a long drive home?'

'Yeah, we were visiting Lou's parents in Durham. It's meant to be about seven hours away, but when you've got little ones and you have to keep stopping for food and toilet breaks, it's nearer nine hours on the road.'

'Why did you choose this weekend to go away?' I asked.

'It was Lou's dad's birthday on Saturday, so he had a party for it.' Ewan grimaced. 'Bloody long way to go for a bit of birthday cake, but Lou misses them, so we thought we'd make a week of it.' His expression suddenly sharpened. 'Is that you asking for my alibi?

Asking why I went away the same time someone killed Mick?'

'We're trying to eliminate anyone connected to Mr Tyler at this point,' said Nathan, diplomatically. 'Your brother mentioned the possibility that he might have been having an affair...?'

Ewan shook his head angrily. 'Yeah, I know, and he shouldn't have. I know he fancied himself as a bit of a player in his younger days, but not now. He'd never cheat on Viv.'

'Then where do you think he was, on the nights when he asked you and Terry to cover for him?'

'I don't know,' said Ewan, but he was unconvincing. I smiled gently at him.

'Look, we don't want to drag his name through the mud. If he was up to anything a bit dodgy it hardly matters now, does it? He can't get into trouble for it. But it could lead us to whoever killed him, and whoever did this to Liam.'

'You think they're linked?' Ewan looked surprised.

'One murder and one attempted murder within a few hours of each other, here in Penstowan? It's likely, don't you think?'

Ewan smiled grimly. 'Maybe it was the mermaid, after all. Terry said people were talking about the statue going missing and coming up with all sorts of ridiculous theories about her drowning sailors.'

'Well, unless she's changed her MO to include torturing people with a meat tenderiser, I'd say it's probably not her, wouldn't you?' Nathan shook his head. 'Forget what other people are saying, what do *you* think happened to Mick Tyler? It sounds like you knew him better than most.'

'I knew he was struggling for money for a while, and then all of a sudden he wasn't,' said Ewan. 'When I asked him how come he was suddenly managing to pay the bills, he said it was best I didn't know.'

'What did he mean by that, do you think?'

'When Terry and I were younger, we got into some trouble with the police. Nothing serious – we got caught shoplifting.' He grinned suddenly and turned to me. 'It was your dad, actually. He put the fear of God into us, then took us home and told our dad. We were expecting him to go ballistic and beat the crap out of us.' He must've seen the look on my face, because he quickly added, 'Not that he'd done anything like that before – he wasn't abusive or anything, he never hit us. But he didn't say anything. Didn't ground us. Didn't punish us. Just looked at us like he'd never been so disappointed in his life.'

'Oh God, that's worse,' I said.

'Exactly,' said Ewan. 'It would've been easier if he'd given us a clout round the ear, but to disappoint him... That was the end of our very short-lived life of crime. We've never been tempted to do anything like that again. I even own up when someone undercharges me, or gives me too much change.'

'And Mick knew that,' I said. 'So he didn't want to tell you what he was doing in case you either judged him for it—'

'Which I wouldn't have done,' said Ewan.

'—or you tried to stop him,' I finished. 'Okay. So let's assume for the moment he *was* doing something illegal. What do you think it could've been?'

'I dunno,' said Ewan. Again, he was unconvincing, but I got the feeling we could push and push and he still wouldn't share his suspicions with us, in case they were unfounded. He and Mick had obviously been very close. 'Honestly, I don't know. I've not seen any signs of crime down at the harbour or anything.'

'No... Thank you for your time, Mr Barraclough. We'll leave you to try and get some sleep,' said Nathan, and we left.

I waited until we were outside before I turned to Nathan. 'Well, that settles it then. There's *definitely* shady stuff going down at the harbour.'

'You noticed that too? I thought you would…' We both turned as Matt joined us.

'I'm on the way to the hospital now,' he said. 'Unless you wanted to…?'

'No, you can handle it,' said Nathan. 'Keep us posted on Liam's condition, let us know if anything changes. And tread carefully with his parents, they'll be in shock.'

'Will do, Guv. Oh, and Chrissie's going to get us a list of the friends he was with before he went missing on Saturday night,' said Matt. 'Uniform talked to a couple of them earlier, when we were still treating him as a missing person, so we'll need to talk to them again.'

'I didn't know Chrissie was on duty,' I said, looking around to spot her, but Matt shook his head.

'Nah, she was in the pub earlier when I got the call about Liam,' he said. Nathan grinned. 'What? It's a small town—'

'With a lot of pubs. Lucky she was in the same one as you,' said Nathan. Matt rolled his eyes.

'You're as bad as she is. I'll talk to you later.'

We watched him go. I stifled a yawn; it was almost two in the morning.

'So what do we do now?' I asked.

'Now we go home and go to bed.'

'What? But you know what they say! "Crime never

sleeps".' I stifled another massive yawn, and tried to ignore my watery eyes. Nathan laughed.

'No, but coppers do. Come on, we've got an appointment with Stuart Mitchell in the morning, and we need to be fresh for it.'

'We've got an appointment?' I said, following him across the road to the car.

'Yes, he just doesn't know about it yet.'

Chapter Ten

'Yeah, course I knew Mick Tyler.' Stuart Mitchell spoke without turning to look at me and Nathan, not taking his eyes off the boat in front of him. Three men in waterproof dungarees and T-shirts were sloshing water over the deck, cleaning up after a night's fishing. I resisted the urge to reach out and tap him on the shoulder to make him look at us while he was speaking. Rude! But then, I thought, he was quite possibly mixed up in something illegal that had led to the murder of one man and the torture of another, so I should hardly expect nice manners.

We'd got up at eight that morning; later than usual, but I was glad of the lie-in after being out at the scene of Liam Fossett's assault until the early hours. I wasn't used to late nights anymore, particularly on what I still thought of as a 'school night' despite it being the holidays. These days I was normally tucked up in bed by ten o'clock.

'Can you tell us the nature of your relationship with Mr Tyler?' asked Nathan. He sounded very polite, which meant he didn't like Mitchell any more than I did.

'"Relationship"?' Mitchell snorted. 'What do you mean, "relationship"? That sounds like the sort of question you should be asking Terry Barraclough. I reckon Mick was just his type.'

'Are you trying to suggest that he was killed in a gay lovers' tiff?' I said, scornfully. So he was a homophobe as well as (potential) drug smuggler, was he? Good to know up front. Nathan gave me a *calm down, ignore him* gesture.

'You know what I'm asking. Were you friends? Colleagues?'

Mitchell shrugged. 'We weren't neither, really. We weren't enemies—' finally he *did* turn round, the sun glinting off his mirrored sunglasses '—but we weren't all matey. I spoke to him if we were both waiting to get served at the pub, that sort of thing, but we didn't exactly socialise.'

'How about work?' I asked. 'Did he ever work for you?'

'Why would he? He's got his own boat.' He shook his head. 'Can't get over someone killing him like that.'

'We've heard that Mr Tyler came to see you for some business advice,' said Nathan. 'Can you tell us about that?'

Mitchell paused for a moment. 'There's not really a lot to tell you.' Nathan and I looked at him, waiting, neither of us speaking, so he was forced to carry on in order to fill the awkward silence. I have no idea if that works anywhere else in the world, but in England most of us will do anything to avoid an awkward silence, including giving away information we didn't intend to. 'Look, he came to see me—'

'When?'

'I dunno – six months ago? A while back. He said he was struggling a bit with the business side of things, and asked if I could give him any advice.'

'And did you?'

'Not a lot I could tell him. Fishing's my business, not tourist charters.' He turned away again. 'That's my fleet out there – I've got nine boats. Very different sort of business to Mick and his pleasure cruises...'

'Apparently, though, you do have a bit of a reputation for helping people out,' said Nathan. 'I'm assuming that's why Mr Tyler came to you. And it seemed to help, because his friends and family reckon the business started doing better after that.' He paused. 'Or he had a lot more money all of a sudden, anyway.'

Mitchell shook his head. 'Nothing to do with me.'

'Yet you do seem to be the shining star of the Penstowan fishing industry,' I mused. 'Pretty much the only one making a success of it.'

He turned to look at me, and I got the impression that he was sizing me up, only I couldn't tell because of those blasted mirrored sunglasses. I do like to see a suspect's eyes while they're being questioned; they often give a lot away. But Mitchell wasn't going to be any help there.

'PC whatever your name was—'

'Detective Sergeant Parker,' I corrected him, calmly. He knew full well what my rank was, he was just trying to annoy me.

'Do you know how my business got so successful? It ain't through luck, or being ruthless or anything like that. It's through planning, being sensible and being able to see what's coming. My family's had boats at Penstowan Harbour for hundreds of years. That stupid mermaid story? My great-great-great-grandfather was the bloke in that story, give or take a great—'

'The boy who caught the mermaid?' asked Nathan.

'No,' I said, 'the one who started it all off by fishing where they weren't supposed to. John Hawken.'

Mitchell raised an eyebrow. 'Oh, so you do know about me. Yep, I'm a Hawken, way back on my great-grandmother's side. I know these waters like the back of my hand. *That's* why I'm successful. I know the best spots. My dad knew where to fish when the usual places were running low. You can't just fish in the same spot for years and years. But the main thing is, I know where to sell my fish once I've got 'em.'

'And where would that be?'

'There used to be fishing harbours all along this coast. They all had their own small fleets. Now there's no fish but loads of tourists. And loads of pubs and restaurants wanting to feed them.'

'The Rick Stein effect,' I said. The popular chef had moved to Padstow many years ago and set up a restaurant, which had brought new life – and a plethora of other restaurants – to the town, as well as the rest of the North Cornwall coast.

Mitchell nodded. 'Yep. Padstow's got a fully working harbour, but all those other places, where do you think they get their fresh fish from?'

'You?' asked Nathan, but it was clearly a rhetorical question.

'Not just the restaurants, the fish and chip shops too. I saw the growth in these fancy pubs and that, and whenever a new place opened, or changed hands, I was straight in there, getting contracts with them to supply all their fish.' He smiled, looking very satisfied with himself. 'And yeah, it got to the point where I couldn't keep up with demand, so when I saw some of the independent fishermen here struggling, I offered to buy their boats. Kept 'em on as crew, gave 'em a decent wage, but still left me enough to make a good profit from my customers. It also had the knock-on effect of taking out my competitors.'

'Is that why Tyler came to see you?' I asked. 'He was after a job?'

'Yeah. He wanted me to buy his boat, but I said no. You've got to know when to expand and when to sit tight, and now's not the right time to get any bigger. When your overheads start outstripping your profit, you don't want to add more to your wage bill or anything like that.'

'So how was he suddenly making more money? What do you think changed?' Nathan looked at him closely.

'I have no idea.' Mitchell watched his crew finish cleaning the boat, with a definite 'case closed' attitude.

'Okay. One more thing,' said Nathan. 'I understand Liam Fossett has been working for you?'

'Liam? Yeah, good kid. He's meant to be here now, actually.' He turned to us with a casualness that didn't look completely genuine to me. 'What's he done?'

'You haven't heard? He's in hospital,' I said. Mitchell's forced casualness disappeared abruptly.

'What? Has he had an accident?'

'Only if he tied himself to a chair, broke his own fingers with a meat tenderiser and then smashed out a tooth "by accident",' I said. Mitchell whipped off his sunglasses, his face paling under the healthy tan.

'What? But that's not—' he stuttered, and I thought for a moment he was going to say more, but he stopped himself. 'Oh God, that's terrible. Poor lad. Did he say who did it?'

'Not yet. He wasn't in any condition to make a statement,' said Nathan. 'But we will be talking to him later today. Can you think of anyone who might have a grudge against him? Or is there anything that he might've been involved in, that could've led to this?'

'No – no, he...' Mitchell looked genuinely shocked. But more than that, he looked frightened. 'No, he was – is – a good lad. I'm sorry to hear that he's in a bad way.' He swallowed hard. 'Is he allowed visitors?'

'Family only at the moment,' I said. 'Until we get a chance to talk to him.'

'Of course.' Mitchell put his sunglasses back on. I got the impression they were like armour; something for him to hide behind. 'Please pass on my condolences to his parents.'

'He's not dead, Stuart,' I said pointedly, and we left.

. . .

'So, what did you make of that?' asked Nathan, as we headed back to the car. He stopped at the driver's door and looked back towards the harbour, where Stuart Mitchell had gone into the small weatherboarded building that was the hub of his maritime empire. I wondered what he was doing; making a few phone calls, I would have bet.

'He wasn't expecting that news about Liam,' I said. 'As soon as we said his name he looked alarmed, but he definitely wasn't expecting to hear that he was in hospital.'

'Nope, that's what I thought. He was expecting to hear he was in trouble, not in a coma.'

'Talking of which, are there any uniforms at the hospital?'

'No,' said Nathan, 'but I think I'll get someone down there, keep an eye on him.' He turned back to me. 'I didn't like the way he asked about visitors, did you?'

'No, I didn't…' We both watched Mitchell's office for a moment longer, but he didn't appear. We got in the car and drove back to the station.

We arrived just as PC Chrissie was escorting a young man out of the station. She stopped and put a hand out to make her companion halt as well, then called to us.

'Guv? You got a minute?'

'Of course,' said Nathan. She turned to the young man.

'This is DCI Withers, and DS Parker. Can you tell them what you just told me?'

He nodded and I stepped forward to open the station door. 'Let's go back inside for a minute, shall we?'

We walked through the foyer to an informal interview room. It still felt weird to me, having the run of the station; I'd been here so many times when my dad had been the officer in charge, and I'd been thoroughly spoilt by whoever was on the desk (usually my old friend, Sergeant Adams, who would entertain me and feed me jelly babies until my dad was ready to leave or I felt sick, whichever came first), but I'd never really seen more than the foyer and my dad's old office.

We all sat down. Chrissie smiled at the young man.

'Thanks for doing this, Ryan,' she said. 'This is Ryan Horrocks, a friend of Liam's. He was with Liam on Monday night. We had a chat the other day, didn't we, Ryan? When we were looking for Liam. He just came in and gave a statement, but I thought you might want to go over it with him?' She passed over a sheet of paper to Nathan, who scanned it quickly.

'That's a good idea,' I said, giving Ryan a reassuring smile. 'If we've got any questions it saves you coming in again.'

Ryan swallowed nervously. From Chrissie's demeanour I got the impression he didn't have anything to be nervous about, but that seems to be the effect the police have on a lot of people, even the most innocent.

'So Ryan, I see here that you were in the pub with Liam and some other lads on Monday night,' said Nathan, passing the statement over to me. I glanced down at it.

'You were in the King's Arms?' I asked. He nodded. The pub was in the middle of town, a fair distance away from where Liam had ended up at Ewan Barraclough's house. It wasn't even on his way home; the fish and chip shop he lived above with his parents was five minutes away from the King's Arms, in the other direction.

'What time did you leave?' asked Nathan, although it was on the paper in front of us.

'We left about ten,' said Ryan. 'We were going to bed—'

Nathan looked confused. 'You mean you were going home?' he asked.

'What? No, to bed.'

Nathan looked even more confused. 'At someone *else's* house?'

'What?' Ryan looked from Nathan to me to Chrissie and back again, like we were being dim.

'Bed,' said Chrissie. 'It's a club in Bude.'

'So *that's* not a confusing name at all, then,' I murmured. Ryan smiled.

'When it first opened I got locked out of the house. I told me mum I was going to Bed, and she thought I meant was going to *bed*, so when she went up she put the dead lock on the front door. Only I wasn't going to bed, I was going to Bed, and when I came home at three o'clock in the morning I couldn't get in. So now when I'm going out, I make sure she knows whether I'm going to bed or Bed.'

Nathan and I exchanged looks. This whole conversation was making my head hurt.

'Okayyyy…' said Nathan. 'Did you get a taxi, or was one of you driving?'

'Taxi. We all wanted a drink.'

'Who did you use?' I asked. 'Magda?' Magda Trevarrow, wife of Rob the mechanic, ran the local taxi firm, which seemed to consist of her and any random driver she could pull off the street to do a shift. To be fair there wasn't a lot of business for her in Penstowan; being so remote, everyone either knew how to drive or had just resigned themselves to never leaving town again.

'Yeah. You know what it's like round here, you have to book in advance or you can never get one. I rang and booked it a few days before. You can check with her,' said Ryan.

'We will. So what happened?'

'We'd left the pub and we were waiting for the taxi, when Liam got a phone call and said change of plan, he wasn't coming.'

'Do you know who it was?'

Ryan shook his head. 'No. We thought it must be a girl. Booty call or something.'

'Why do you say that?'

'Because it had to be something good for him to change his mind.' He looked at us like it was obvious, but he could see by our own expressions that it wasn't. 'Mermaid night at the club, wasn't it? Big party to celebrate the start of the festival. Free entry to all the girls dressed up as mermaids...'

'Wall-to-wall skimpily dressed young ladies?'

Ryan blushed and nodded. Nathan smiled.

'Yeah, I think that would've appealed to me too at your age... So does Liam get a lot of booty calls?' Nathan kept his voice very even, but I knew he was thinking the same as me – that it hadn't been a booty call that night, and maybe not any other night.

'Yeah. Proper player he thought he was.' Ryan's smile faded. 'We wound him up about it, but he wouldn't tell us who she was. I should've asked him when it was just the two of us, he might have told me then.'

'Do you remember any other times he got a call like that?'

'Yeah. A few weeks ago, there was a European Cup qualifier on, so we went to watch it in the pub. He got a call just before kick-off, said he had to leave at half-time. I was a bit pissed off to be honest. I don't see him that much since he went to university, and it was supposed to be us catching up, watching the footie and that. He missed the whole second half.' Ryan looked thoughtful. 'He got another one last week, on Thursday.'

'You're sure it was last Thursday?' Nathan asked. Mick Tyler had supposedly gone out fishing that night, but if he genuinely had, it wasn't with his usual crew.

'Yeah, I remember it because we were at a gig in Exeter.'

'Did he cut short his night out with you again?'

'No. He didn't say much to the person on the other end, but he looked pissed off. He rang someone else straight after and I got the impression he'd sorted it out with them, because he was fine after that. I didn't hear what they were talking about, though.' Ryan frowned. 'Actually, when he got that call on Monday he didn't look too happy then, either. I even said, "You don't look very happy for a bloke what's on a promise." I should've known something was up.'

I reached over and patted his arm. 'Don't blame

yourself. It's really easy to look back and think there were signs you should've spotted, but why would you? It's not your fault.'

Chrissie showed Ryan out as Nathan and I made our way up to the CID office. Nathan accosted a DC who was just putting the phone down.

'Sunil, do we have Liam Fossett's phone?'

'Yes, Guv. Matt dropped it off after he left the hospital last night, I think it's on his desk. He said Liam's mother had given him the passcode so we could have a look at his call history.'

'Good. Any word on Liam's condition?'

The DC nodded towards the phone. 'Matt said the doctor was supposed to be checking on him this morning, so I just rang to see if there was any change.'

'What did they say?'

'He's in a medically induced coma. There's some swelling on his brain, which they believe will go down, but until it does they're keeping him asleep.'

'Poor kid. Good work, Sunil.' The young DC almost glowed at the praise. Nathan wasn't that much older than most of the officers under him, but he was highly regarded and respected, and they all wanted to impress him. Not me, though; I was happy enough with just seducing him at every opportunity.

I found the phone on Matt's desk, enveloped in a

plastic evidence bag. A Post-It note with a six-digit number was stuck to the outside of the bag. I held it up. 'Shall we?'

The phone had been found in Liam's pocket. The screen was cracked, a casualty either of the beating itself or from when Liam had hit the kitchen floor tiles. There was no reason to suggest his assailant had touched it, but we were still careful to touch it ourselves as little as possible.

I scrolled through the call history, frowning. I looked up at Nathan. 'Babe – um, Guv—' No, that felt *really* wrong. 'Nath, there's nothing on here to show that Liam received a phone call on Monday night.'

'Nothing around ten?' Nathan bent over the phone screen, watching me scroll down. 'Nothing earlier? Ryan might've got the time wrong.'

'No, nothing. Look.' I pointed. 'The last call he got was from Ryan, just before seven. Less than a minute long. That was probably them arranging to meet in the pub first.' I grinned. 'I'm amazed they spoke for *that* long, most kids that age text rather than call. I don't think Daisy even realises you can actually *speak* to people on a phone.'

'What about any calls he made? Could Ryan have got it wrong and Liam had placed the call himself?'

'Nope. Last one made was to his mum, earlier in the

day, replying to a call he missed from her.' I closed the call history and clicked on the text message icon. 'There's a few text messages from Monday night, looks like it's the other friends they were going clubbing with… Last one was at nine o'clock. Presumably they were all together in the pub after that.' I opened up the call history as something occurred to me, and scrolled way down the list. 'Here,' I said. 'This is last Thursday, when he supposedly got a call during the gig. He didn't receive or make a phone call all day. And if I could be bothered to scroll all the way back to whatever day the football was on, I'm betting he didn't get one then, either.'

'So that means, either Ryan's lying about the calls—'

'Why would he?'

'He wouldn't. Or Liam had a burner phone.' Nathan looked at me. 'Why would he have a burner phone? And what's the betting it was called from *another* burner?'

'County lines,' I said. 'Drug dealing. It make sense, doesn't it? During term times, Liam's the main man at university, distributing the stuff. He could pick up more stock every time he came home for a visit. He might've had a line of his own, in Norwich, using local kids. Then during the holidays, he helps out on the acquisition side of it—'

'Going out for a spot of "night fishing" and picking it

up from someone overseas.' He nodded slowly. 'It's a possibility...'

'It's what we were thinking for Mick Tyler, isn't it? That he was going out in the boat, or someone else's boat, and picking up packages left tied to a buoy, floating just under the surface.'

'Or meeting another boat and doing an exchange, cash for drugs.' Nathan took the phone from me and turned it over in his hands as if looking for something, or maybe hoping it would magically turn into the drug dealer's burner phone, or "line". 'The NCA have told us it's on the rise, but usually a dealer would be using younger kids, or maybe ones who are more vulnerable, forcing them into dealing for them. Liam doesn't really fit that profile.'

'No, but he *was* in debt, wasn't he? According to Ewan Barraclough, anyway. What with tuition fees and living expenses, he could have student loans coming out of his earholes, and he must still have had at least another year to go.'

'All of which sounds feasible, but without that burner phone or Liam coming clean about what he's been up to, it'll be hard to prove.' He sighed. 'Because of course whoever beat him up took his phone with them.'

'Why do you think they tortured him?'

Nathan shrugged. 'Drug deal gone wrong. No honour among thieves. Take your pick.'

'That would explain a beating. But why *torture*?' I shook my head. 'There's more to it than just a deal gone wrong. They wanted information. They wanted to know where someone, or something, is.'

'You think someone's been taking a slice off the top before passing it on?'

'Maybe. They were expecting, I dunno, twenty kilos and they only got eighteen. Or twenty grand and they got shortchanged.'

'And they thought Liam knew where it was.' Nathan smiled grimly. 'Let's hope he wakes up and tells us where it is before they try again.'

Chapter Eleven

'So what now?' I asked.

'Now I think we dig a bit deeper into Stuart Mitchell's business empire,' said Nathan. 'So far, he's the only thing we've got that connects both our victims.'

'He was pretty quick to downplay any connection to Mick Tyler,' I pointed out.

'Did you believe him?'

'God, no.' I laughed. 'But that might just mean that I'm a nasty, suspicious person—'

'Or a copper.'

'Or a copper. Yeah. I mean, it is perfectly feasible that his operation is entirely innocent and he really is just an astute businessman.'

'He certainly has the sunglasses for it,' said Nathan, dryly. 'It's also perfectly feasible that he's part of a smuggling ring, bringing drugs into the country and then arranging for them to be distributed. And of course that could tie in with what old Walter reckons he saw, a boat out in an area off-limits to fishing vessels.'

'I could contact the police in Norwich, see if they have any information on a drug ring operating out of the university,' I suggested. Nathan scoffed loudly.

'Students? Taking drugs? What will you think of next?' We both laughed. 'Good luck with that, I'm sure there'll be a number of them to choose from. Besides, Liam doesn't have any previous, I checked.'

'No criminal record could just mean he hasn't been caught yet. But he could be on the local nick's radar. It's worth—'

I was interrupted by the entrance of Davey Trelawney. One of my dad's old recruits, Davey was built like a moose and was physically incapable of making an entrance without attracting attention. He had a surprisingly calm and gentle nature, despite being strong enough to wrestle a bear to the ground with one hand and open a jar of pickles with the other. Not that I'd seen him do that. Not recently, anyway.

He looked around, then stopped when he saw me and headed over to my desk.

'All right, Jodie? You got a visitor downstairs.'

'A visitor?'

'Yeah, your mum. Looks like she's on the warpath an' all. Wouldn't keep her waiting if I were you.' He chuckled. 'I seen her come in here with that same look on her face a few times for your dad. He never kept her waiting, either.'

'Oh God…'

I left Nathan to it and headed downstairs. I refused to rush; she was my mum, not one of the hardened criminals I'd faced every day when I'd been in uniform. Still, I seemed to get down the stairs and into the foyer quicker than I'd ever done before.

She was pacing up and down, Germaine in her arms. Germaine had never liked being held like that for too long, but as I approached she gave me a resigned look that told me she knew better than to argue with a Parker woman when she was in a mood.

'All right, Mum? Everything okay?' I said. She turned around and held out the dog, leaving me no choice but to take her.

'Here, I've got to go out and I can't be looking after your animals all day,' she said.

'"Animals"? I've only got one. Unless you're counting Nathan,' I said, hoping to appeal to her sense of humour or to her soft spot for him.

'She's *your* responsibility,' she said, almost growling. Germaine growled as well. Oh great, the dog was pissed off with me too. I bent down and released her, keeping hold of her lead, then straightened up to look at Mum. *Don't get into an argument,* I told myself.

'I know she is, Mum. Thank you for looking after her. I didn't know you were going out today, otherwise I'd have arranged a dog sitter. Is Daisy not back from her sleepover yet?' I'd had a text message from her letting me know she was fine and she was staying for breakfast, but other than that I hadn't had a chance to talk to her.

'No, she isn't,' snapped Mum. 'Which you'd have known if you'd been at home.' *Aah,* I thought, *now we're getting to the problem.*

'You know that I'm working at the moment,' I said gently, and she nodded vehemently.

'Oh yes, I know. Despite what you said when you moved down here. No more crime fighting. No more sticking your nose into things.'

'I've been doing that since the trouble at Tony's wedding,' I said. 'You said at the time, you were right behind me. It's what Dad would've done – helped a mate in trouble.'

'Was Mick Tyler your mate?' Mum asked. 'Or that Fossett boy?'

'Well, no, but—'

'I had all this with your dad. He could've retired at sixty, you know. He would never have been anywhere near those boys who stole that car. He'd have still been here, with me.' My dad, who had supposedly been safely ensconced behind a desk in the latter days of his career, had spotted some car thieves on his way home and given chase. The chase had ended in the crash that had taken my dad's life, and with it, I was now realising, part of my mum's, too. She wasn't angry with me (well, yes, she was, *obviously*), she was worried. I pulled her towards me and hugged her, which she resisted with every fibre of her being for about ten seconds, and then she went soft and hugged me back. When she spoke again her words were muffled against my shoulder. 'I know why you helped Tony, love. I even get why you felt you had to help Nathan with the other cases. But that was different, that was – *unofficial*. Nathan could tell you to back off—'

'Yeah, he did try that a few times,' I said. 'It never really worked.'

'You know what I mean. He stopped you getting in too deep. This time – well, it's like Dad all over again. Every time I think I've got you safe, you go out and find another way to make me worry about you.'

'I'm sorry,' I said, feeling terrible. She stood back and took my face in her hands.

'I'm so proud of you,' she said, and I felt tears come to my eyes. 'But I worry about you, and I know I'm not the only one.'

'Daisy does?' Of course she did. I'd worried about my dad, and Penstowan had been a lot smaller and quieter in his day.

'Of course she does. And I know you know how that feels.' She gave me a peck on the cheek. 'Right, sorry but I've got a minibus full of old biddies waiting for me. We're off to Truro for a mooch round the shops and lunch in the pub.'

'Um, what about Germaine…?'

'She's not allowed on the bus. Liz Brownlow – you know her, the one with the wonky ear who always wears too much make-up – reckons she's allergic to dogs. Says they bring her out in hives and make her eyes go all puffy.' Mum cackled, and I knew she was feeling better. 'Daft old trollop, it might be an improvement.'

'But—' I said, helplessly.

'You never heard of police dogs? See you later, sweetheart.' And with that she was gone, and I was left with the dog. Behind me the new desk sergeant, Sally, cleared her throat. I turned round and she pointed at the sign on the wall, smiling sympathetically but firmly. *NO DOGS ALLOWED EXCEPT GUIDE DOGS.*

'She's my emotional support Pomeranian,' I said, and Germaine obligingly lay down with her head on her paws, doing her best 'look at me, I'm so cute!' pose. But it was to no avail. I sighed. 'Okay, I'll take her outside…'

I stood outside the station and called Nathan to explain my sudden disappearance. He sounded a bit miffed, but agreed there was nothing else for it but for me to stay with the dog until I could find someone else to take her. Oh good, so now *he* was annoyed with me as well... I decided to take her for a walk to wear her out, and then I would try to sneak her up to CID; she could sit under my desk, and as long as her infamous gastric problems didn't flare up – on a 'windy' day you could smell her from half a mile away – no one would even know she was there. Hopefully.

I rang Daisy, but she was on a bus just like her grandmother, only this one was taking her and Jade and some of the other girls from the sleepover to Exeter. She reminded me that I'd okayed the trip when she'd asked permission last week. I had, but I'd forgotten.

'You've had a lot on your mind,' she said, and I wasn't sure if her tone of voice was *meant* to make me feel guilty, but it did. I told her to have a nice time and let me know when she was headed home, and hung up.

'Looks like we're stuck with each other,' I told Germaine. We headed up Fore Street, where she abruptly decided to relieve herself, and I was just picking it up when I heard a voice next to me.

'There she is, DS Nosey Parker, cleaning up the streets.' I looked up into Tony's grinning face.

'Oh yeah, it's all glamour being back in the force,' I said.

'I thought you'd be working, what with everything that's been going on?'

'Yeah, I thought that too…' I smiled at him. 'I'm glad I bumped into you, actually. Fancy dog sitting?'

'Nope.'

'Fair enough, I had to ask. I also wanted to say sorry for taking the mickey about you and Carmen yesterday. It was mean.'

He shrugged. 'It's okay.'

'No it isn't, you're my friend and I should be supporting you. Things have just been a bit – weird.'

'Trying to juggle everything?'

'Yeah. I keep thinking I've got all my balls safely in the air, as it were, and then suddenly I get hit by one, and then another, and then another, and suddenly it's raining balls.'

'You sound like you need a cuppa. Got time for one?'

'Only if there's a scone to go with it.'

We walked up Fore Street to Rowe's, café, bakery and purveyors of the finest pasties in Cornwall. There were a couple of tables outside, already full of diners making the most of the sunshine, so we went inside where it was cooler and probably more comfortable for Germaine. The owners knew her, and they liked dogs, so she was duly served with a bowl of water while we waited for our tea.

'Oh Tone,' I said, flopping back in my chair. 'I'm making a terrible bloody mess of everything. Me mum's pissed off with me, Daisy's feeling neglected, I'm letting the team down at work and Nathan's going to get fed up soon with me ducking out all the time. And we're only three days into the investigation.' Germaine made a little growling noise as I accidentally nudged her tail with my foot. 'Oh and Germaine hates me, too.'

'Don't be daft,' said Tony.

'It's true,' I said. 'And I was nasty to you, and that wasn't fair. How are things going with you and Carmen?'

'I have no idea,' he said. 'We get on really well. She's clever, and funny, and she laughs at my jokes—'

'Well *that's* a really good sign, because you're not actually that funny...'

'Oh, ha ha. I do think she likes me, but... I dunno. If she wasn't a vicar I'd have made a move by now.'

'Why does her being a vicar make a difference?'

'You know why. "Are you even allowed to go out with a vicar if you're a heathen" I think is what you said.'

'Ahh, yes. You weren't meant to hear that...'

He sighed. 'You're right, though. Religion is such a massive part of her life, and I respect her views, I just don't share them. My mum used to drag me along to church when I was a nipper and I just thought it was all fairy stories, telling people to be nice to each other. And I knew that a lot of the people who also went to that church *weren't* very nice to each other. A lot of them still ain't.'

'But you are.'

Tony waved my praise away. 'Leave it out—'

'No, Tone, you are. You're probably the nicest person I know. You're a lot nicer than me.'

'Well that bit's true.'

I flicked a sachet of sugar at him. 'You didn't need to agree with that bit. But you're, like, Christian without actually *being* one. You do loads for charity, and for this town. You care about people. You embody all the stuff you're meant to do as a Christian—'

'I do always have fish on a Friday.' He clasped his hands together as if in prayer, and tried (and failed) to look pious. I laughed.

'Saint Anthony of Penstowan.' I reached across the table and touched his hand. 'You deserve to be happy.'

'I'm not *un*happy. I just… I do get lonely sometimes.'

'You and Cheryl are definitely not trying again, then?' Cheryl was his ex-fiancée, and their disastrous wedding had been the catalyst for my amateur sleuthing. He shook his head.

'Nah. We've talked about it, but I think a clean break

is for the best.' He took a sip of tea, then shook his head. 'Anyway, enough about my love life. What are we going to do about your problems?'

'I don't think there's a lot I can do, I just need to help Nathan solve this case quickly,' I said. 'Really quickly, actually, because I've got a wedding coming up in a couple of weeks and I can hardly turn round to the bride and groom and say, "Sorry, I'm working".'

'I was shocked to hear about Liam,' said Tony. 'He's a good kid. Greg and Donna must be going out of their minds with worry.'

'Yeah,' I said, noncommittally. This 'good kid' was possibly a drug dealer. Tony looked at me sharply.

'What's that tone of voice all about?'

'What do you mean?'

'That "yeah". That sounds very much to me like you're hiding something. What is it?'

'I can't tell you, you know that.'

'It sounds to me like you reckon Liam had something to do with whoever beat him up—'

'It wasn't a mugging, Tony,' I said, a hint of exasperation in my voice.

'Oh what, so he brought it on himself?'

'I didn't say that.'

'That's what your face is saying. It didn't take long, did it?'

'What didn't take long?'

'For you to start thinking like a copper again.' Tony sat back in his seat, shaking his head. 'Look at yourself. You know this kid—'

'I don't, actually.'

'Okay, but you know his parents. You and Donna were in all the school plays together! You went to drama club with her. Have you been to see her yet?'

'No,' I said, that now familiar feeling of guilt sweeping over me. 'Matt's been liaising with the family—'

'"Liaising with the family"? She's an old friend of yours! Let me guess, you don't want to face her and tell her you suspect her son of – of what?'

'It's not like that!' I protested loudly. Under the table, Germaine whined, and an elderly couple who were enjoying their elevenses looked over disapprovingly. I lowered my voice. 'He wasn't just beaten up, he was tortured. Why would someone torture him if he wasn't involved in something bad?'

'I don't know!' Tony was getting more and more wound up. 'But you know the family. He's a good kid.' I opened my mouth to speak, but he spoke again before I could get a word out. 'And yeah, I know it probably doesn't look good if you look at the evidence. But when Mel was murdered on my wedding day, and Cheryl disappeared, all the "evidence" pointed to me, didn't it? But you knew me. You knew I wouldn't hurt a fly, let alone someone I loved. Without you, I'd have been banged up for murder. That's why you helping Nathan on all the other cases *worked*. You knew the people involved, or at least you knew that so-called "proof" doesn't always prove anything. Now you're ready to condemn someone who, deep down, you *know* wouldn't be involved in anything bad enough to warrant a beating, because you're thinking like a police officer again. We don't need that. We've got Nathan for that. We need you to think like Jodie again.'

Chapter Twelve

'We need you to think like Jodie again.'

Tony's words echoed in my head as Germaine and I walked back to the police station. Surely I *had* been thinking like Jodie? Being a police officer was part of who I was. It was practically in my DNA; it had never just been a job. Yet I couldn't deny that this investigation, being an official part of it, felt different. Different, and a bit odd.

We wove our way through a crowd of kids dressed up as mermaids, little hands reaching down to pat Germaine's fluffy white body as we passed. I'd almost forgotten that Merrymaid Week was still in full swing, and would be until the closing fireworks on Friday night. The children and the tourists were happy enough, but a feeling of unease seemed to hang over the locals like a grey cloud. Everyone we passed seemed to be talking about Mick Tyler's murder, and 'that poor Fossett boy' – the news had travelled fast. No one had a bad word to say about either of them.

We reached the station and paused (or pawsed, in the dog's case). I couldn't really take her inside, but I couldn't take her home and leave her, because the builders were there today working on the extension for Mum's granny flat, and Germaine had taken an instant and irrational dislike to the foreman, Derek, who was nice if prone to taking his top off and working bare- (and sweaty) chested (which Mum, of course, rather liked). What to do?

On an impulse I headed to the car park at the back of the building. We'd driven to work in my car today, rather than Nathan's. I weighed the car key in my hand for a moment then thought, *sod it.* And thirty seconds later I was in the driver's seat, Germaine strapped in the back in her car harness, and we were heading out of town towards the A30.

We stopped at some traffic lights a couple of miles down the road, and I texted Nathan. *I've taken the car, just gone to follow a lead. Back later.* I didn't specify *what* lead I was following, because I wasn't even sure if it was one;

there was just that niggling feeling that I needed to go and do this. I needed to go and be Jodie again, not DS Parker.

We drove to Exeter, radio on, me singing and Germaine howling along to the music. As we reached the city streets I turned the music off; it was that or wind the windows up, because neither me or Germaine would've passed the auditions for "Cornwall's Got Talent". I turned into the hospital car park and pulled into a space, and it was only then that my next problem hit me. If I couldn't take the dog into a police station I *definitely* wouldn't be allowed to take her into the hospital. I could leave her in the car, but it was a really hot day; I'd have to leave the window wound down a bit, but Germaine had a well-deserved reputation as an escape artist, so if I did that I would be coming back to an empty car (probably with her sitting on the bonnet waiting for me).

As I sat there swearing at myself for not thinking this through properly, an absolute vision in a smart blue dress appeared across the car park. I leapt out before it could disappear again.

'Debbie!' I called. Debbie – for it was she – jumped out of her skin and turned around as Germaine and I trotted over to her. She smiled, but underneath it there was a slightly guilty expression.

'Oh, hi…'

'What are you doing here? You look nice,' I said, studying her dress. She shrugged.

'Oh, you know… Just had a job interview.'

'What? That's brilliant! Why didn't you tell me?' I hoped she *hadn't* told me and I'd forgotten, otherwise that would be another item to add to the rapidly growing list of things to feel guilty about. I hadn't wished her good luck or anything.

'I didn't want you to think I wasn't enjoying working with you on the catering business,' she said. 'I am, but—'

'But it's not what you were trained for.' Debbie had been a nurse working in a hospital up in Manchester when she'd met Callum. 'Debs, I totally get it. I never expected to have you working with me forever, although I'd love it if you decided that was what you wanted. What job is it? Nursing, here?'

'No,' she said, shaking her head. 'I couldn't do this drive every day, not in rush hour. It's in Geriatrics, part-time community nurse. It's a new position based out of one of the doctors' surgeries near Penstowan, although they haven't decided which one yet. I'd be travelling around to old people's homes and clubs and that, giving them health checks, flu vaccinations, and that kind of thing. And it's school hours, which is just what I need.' She looked at me. 'But what are *you* doing here? You're not ill, are you?' Germaine snuffled at her feet, and she laughed. She bent down to make a fuss of her. 'Or are you the patient, Germaine?'

'I'm here to talk to a victim's parents,' I said.

'The Fossetts? Of course. I heard about that. I don't know them, but they do lovely fish and chips.' She nodded at the dog. 'You do realise you can't take her in there, don't you?'

'Yeah, that just occurred to me. I don't suppose…?'

She laughed. 'Aunty Debbie to the rescue. Again. If you ain't careful I'm keeping her.'

'You are an absolute star and I don't deserve you as my friend,' I said, handing her the lead before she changed her mind.

'I wouldn't go that far, but you can buy me a coffee when you're finished.'

'It's a deal.'

Hospitals have never been my favourite place. Are they anyone's? Probably not. But at least I wasn't here as a patient, and I wasn't visiting a loved one. Tony was right; Liam's parents must be going out of their minds with worry.

I asked at reception, flashing my warrant card, and

was given a room number. Into the lift, up three floors, into a beige corridor, and down to the end, where an efficient-looking woman sat at a nurses' station. I got out my warrant card and asked for Liam again, and was taken down another corridor to a private room. Nathan and I had discussed the need to have a uniform outside, but with a limited number of officers it hadn't been possible, so I was pleased that it was something of an epic quest to find him in the hospital maze.

The room door was shut, but there was a window from it out into the corridor. Through the glass I could see Liam lying on the bed, surrounded by machines and monitors, tubes and wires dangling from him. Poor kid. In a chair next to his bed sat his mother, my erstwhile school drama club buddy. She looked absolutely worn out, and old – much older than she actually was. A wave of guilt washed over me. We weren't close friends anymore, but I was investigating the case, and we had been close once. I should've been the one to accompany Liam to hospital the night before. At the very least, I should've been here this morning to talk to his parents.

I knocked gently on the window, and she looked up. For a moment confusion crossed her face and I knew she hadn't recognised me; but then it cleared and she gave me a weak smile. She turned back to her son, patting his hand and saying something to him, and then she got up and headed over to the door. I opened it for her and stood back to let her out.

'Jodie. Thank you for coming,' she said. It seemed to take all her energy to get the words out.

'Oh, Donna...' I said, and tears came to her eyes. I reached out and drew her in for a hug, and we stood there for a moment while she got herself together. She pulled away, dabbing at her eyes with her sleeve, and then looked at me more shrewdly than I would've expected.

'Is this a social or work visit?' she asked. I smiled softly.

'Bit of both. Shall we sit down?' There was a row of chairs along the wall. I led her over to them and we sat down, the plastic hard and unyielding under my bottom.

'Who's done this, Jodie?' she asked me. 'Who would hurt my boy?'

'I don't know,' I admitted. 'Not yet, anyway. But we will find out. If we can find out why, then we should be able to find out who.'

'Is there a why, though? Sometimes bad things just happen to people...'

'Sometimes, yes. But less often than you'd think.' I turned my chair slightly to face her better. 'This wasn't a mugging or random assault or anything like that. It looks to us like whoever did this was trying to get information out of Liam.'

'What information? What could he possibly know that justified doing this to him?' Donna looked bewildered and on the verge of tears again, and I couldn't blame her.

'We don't know. That's what we're trying to find out.' I took a deep breath. I wasn't going to sit here and accuse her son of being a drug dealer and sometime smuggler, not while he was being kept unconscious and hooked up to a load of machines in the next room, but … that *was* what I was asking, wasn't it? 'What's Liam studying at university?'

She looked surprised for a moment. 'Politics and International Relations,' she said, making a face. 'Sounded blooming boring to me when he told me that's what he wanted to do, but he said he wanted to make the world a better place, and politics was the way to do it.'

'It certainly seems to have been politicians who've buggered it up,' I said, and she gave a little laugh.

'That's exactly what Greg said.' She looked around, as if only now realising that her husband wasn't with her. 'He said he was going to get coffee. Do you think he's all right?'

'I passed the coffee shop on the way in,' I said, soothingly, 'and there was a big queue. There always is when you're dying for a cuppa.' *Oops, shouldn't have said 'dying',* I thought. The word felt a bit close to home. 'What about his university friends? Have you met any of them?'

'No. None of them live down this way. He seems to have a lot of friends, though. He took a while to settle in at first, and I think he was quite homesick, so I told him to go and join a few uni clubs.' She gave a small, wistful smile. 'He took me at my word. He joined the student union, some Amnesty International group where they teach English to refugees, and lots of gaming groups – he's really into his gaming. He's very happy there.' She let out a sob, rushing to stifle it. 'I hope he recovers enough to go back.'

'I'm sure he will,' I said, crossing my fingers out of her sight. 'He's in really good hands here. I understand he's been helping out down at the harbour over the holidays?'

'Yeah. He normally helps us in the shop, but I s'pose he's at an age where he wants to be a bit more independent. Stuart Mitchell's been finding him bits and bobs to do on the boats.'

'What sort of bits and bobs?'

'I don't really know. Cleaning and doing a bit of maintenance. Doing odd jobs for him.'

'What about going out on the boats? Has he done any night fishing or anything?'

'No, nothing like that.' She managed a weak laugh. 'I think that would interfere with his social life too much. He has stayed out a few nights, but that's because he's been out with friends. Greg got annoyed with him about it, but I said, he's a teenager, we used to be exactly the same. And at least he tells us who he's staying with.' She noticed my inquisitive look. 'Ryan. Ryan Horrocks. They've been friends since primary school.'

'Right,' I said. Ryan hadn't mentioned Liam staying over, but then to be fair we hadn't asked him. It didn't necessarily mean that Liam had actually spent those nights out on one of Stuart Mitchell's boats, doing something he shouldn't be doing.

'Everything all right?' I looked up to see Liam's dad, Greg, standing in front of us with two takeaway coffees and a worried expression. It cleared somewhat when he realised who I was. 'Jodie! Not seen you for ages. Are you on Liam's case?'

'Yeah,' I said, 'but I wanted to come and check in with you both anyway, make sure you're okay.' *Because Tony made me feel guilty that I hadn't already,* I thought.

'We appreciate it,' said Greg, gruffly. 'But we'd appreciate it more if you found out who did this.'

———————

We talked for a little bit longer, but it felt awkward; it was obvious I was questioning them, rather than just offering my support, and it also felt obvious (to me, anyway) that I – the police – thought that Liam had been involved in something that had led to the beating. Donna answered my questions calmly, almost on automatic; too exhausted with worry to consider why I was asking what I was. But I could see Greg beginning to get angry and frustrated. I really didn't want to make things worse for them, so it wasn't long before I stood up, hugged Donna, and gave them my best wishes for Liam's speedy recovery. I glanced through the window into his room as I left, my heart sinking as I saw all the machinery around his bed; heart monitor, drip, oxygen tube, and a whole host of other things I didn't recognise or have any idea what they were for. I just knew that if my daughter was hooked up to even one of those things, I wouldn't want some bloody nosey copper coming and asking me anything that suggested it was her own fault.

'Okay?' asked Debbie, as I left the hospital. She was sitting on a bench on a grassy area outside the main entrance, Germaine lolling in the shade underneath. I shook my head.

'Not really. Poor kid.'

'You want to talk about it?'

'I can't.' I sighed. 'Come on, let me buy you a coffee and you can tell me about this job you're after instead.'

Chapter Thirteen

A fter coffee, Debbie and I went our separate ways. I still had to work out what to do with Germaine, but then Daisy texted me to say she and Jade were heading home from Exeter themselves (apparently yesterday's birthday girl had turned into today's mean girl, and they'd had enough of her). I told her to wait right there, then drove round to get the two of them. As the bus would take almost twice as long to get back to Penstowan as the car (well over an hour), they were very happy to see me. And I was very happy, because it meant they could take Germaine. And Germaine was very happy too, because she knew she was going to get thoroughly spoilt for the rest of the day.

'You're back, then,' said Nathan, as I sat down at my desk. 'Where's the dog?'

'Moulting white hair all over the furniture at Jade's house,' I said. 'I told Nancy not to buy a dark brown sofa.' I sighed – I felt like I'd been doing a lot of that lately – and leant back in my chair. 'I went to the hospital to talk to Liam's parents.'

'Matt's already done that,' said Nathan, frowning. 'They don't know anything.'

'No, I know…'

'But…?'

'Donna Fossett's an old school friend. I felt like I should go and see her.' I shook my head. 'I know the drug smuggling idea seems like the most plausible motive, but I dunno. Is it *too* plausible?'

'What do you mean? It was your idea, wasn't it?' Nathan pulled his chair over next to mine. 'You can't deny that it all fits. It's not like there's no drug dealers, or users for that matter, in Cornwall. It's the same with a lot of seaside towns, all over the country. It's fine in the summer when all the tourists are down here, but out of season people have to find other income streams, not always legal ones. And you said yourself, there's a proud tradition of smuggling all along this coast.'

'Yeah, I know, and it still wouldn't surprise me if Stuart Mitchell was involved in that. But it's Liam. He doesn't fit the profile.'

'Of course he does. He's a student, trying to pay off his debts,' said Nathan.

'About that… I asked the Fossetts if he was in any debt, and Greg said they have a sit down and a good chat about it every time he comes home. He said the chip shop's doing well enough that Liam hasn't had to take out loads of student loans. They've paid his tuition fees, so that's a big chunk of money he hasn't had to borrow. He had a part-time job last term to pay for food and going out, stuff like that, so all he's really had to borrow is money for accommodation, which being in halls on campus isn't as bad as it could be. Greg said they've always drummed it into him that he should avoid debt as much as possible, so every holiday he comes back and works as hard as he can to pay off what he's borrowed, before he goes back and borrows more.'

'So? That still means he was in debt.'

'Yeah, but not so much that he'd need to do something illegal. This kid is a model student and son. He's never been in trouble. He's doing really well at university, getting his work done rather than just partying every night. The main thing he seems to do in his spare time, other than gaming, is going on political protests and stuff like that.'

'He's a politics student, is he?' Nathan raised a wry

eyebrow. 'You do realise that politicians have been known to take drugs, don't you?'

'Yes, of course. But his mum said he wants to make the world a better place. I don't see how he could square that with drug smuggling.'

Nathan looked at me for a moment like he was going to disagree again, then he smiled. 'This is one of your hunches, isn't it?'

'I suppose it is, yeah. I mean, I know that's not much to go on—'

'On the contrary, I know better than to ignore them.' He chuckled. 'Your blasted hunches have proved me wrong on several occasions. But we do have to follow the proper procedure, okay? No going off on a tangent on your own, not without telling me, anyway. If you think the drug angle is wrong, then find me *another* angle. But until then, we have to follow what looks like the most likely scenario.'

'And the most likely scenario, for both Mick Tyler's death and Liam's assault, is still a drug deal gone wrong.'

He nodded. 'Yes, I think it is. Anyway...' He smiled, then reached over to his own desk, picked up a file and handed it to me. 'For you.'

'What is it?'

'Statements from Ewan Barraclough's neighbours.

Sunil and a couple of the uniforms have been door-knocking, seeing if anyone heard anything, trying to narrow down a time. This is what we've got so far.'

'Anything?'

'I don't know. That's why this is for you.' He laughed at the frown that crossed my face before I could stop it. 'Now you remember why you quit...'

'I don't mind,' I said, although I couldn't deny that reading witness statements was one of my least favourite parts of the job. 'But what about searching Mick Tyler's boat? There could be something on there. And his car. Did anyone find it? We could—'

'We could, but we don't need to. Uniform found his car parked near the church. Matt's with the forensics team now, searching it.'

'Right...'

He laughed again. 'You do realise that for ages I was taking on parts of our previous investigations I really should've been letting Matt handle, just so I could keep you involved? Matt's a DS, he needs to be given more responsibility if he ever wants to make DI. The brass think I have a problem with delegation, but really I just had a problem with you.'

I felt my mouth drop open. 'I'm sorry, I never meant—'

Nathan looked around, but we were alone in the

office now. He reached over and took my hands. 'Don't get me wrong, it was a problem of my own making. A wonderful, funny, sexy problem that I never want to solve...' He leaned in and kissed me. 'But, you know, you're mine now, I don't have to try quite as hard to impress you anymore...'

I swatted him on the arm. 'Don't you take me for granted, DCI Withers!'

'I wouldn't bloody dare. Your mum would have me.' He sat back, still smiling, but not as broadly. 'We're okay, aren't we?'

'What? Of course we are.'

'I know this is weird – me telling you what to do—'

I opened my mouth to answer, but the phone on Nathan's desk rang. *Saved by the bell,* I thought. Nathan answered it.

'DCI Withers... Yes... What? When?... Give me the address, DS Parker and I are on our way.' He put the phone down and turned to me with a grin. 'Forget the witness statements, you and I have something much more interesting to deal with.'

The house was a large 1930s detached, in a street on the outskirts of Penstowan, far away from the smell of fish.

There was a beautifully tended front garden, with a smartly paved driveway leading through it to a garage at the side. A police car was currently parked on it, behind a new-ish Audi.

I knocked on the front door and Davey Trelawney answered.

'Nice house,' I said.

'This is what you get when you ain't on a copper's salary…' He stepped back to let me and Nathan through. 'She's in the kitchen, out the back there.'

We walked down the hallway and through a door that led into a big open-plan extension, where I was immediately struck by kitchen envy. The cabinets were an expensive satin white, with counter tops of black granite flecked with specks of quartz that glittered in a ray of sun from a skylight overhead. Big double oven, eight-ring gas burner… I almost forgot why I was there for a moment. But then I turned and saw the anxious woman sitting at a long wooden table, an old farmhouse style that nonetheless fitted with the modern style of the rest of the room. There were big bi-fold glass doors out into a back garden that was as neat and tidy as the front.

'Mrs Mitchell?' said Nathan politely. She looked up from her phone, her eyes flicking for a split second towards a couple of suitcases that were tucked around the side of the kitchen island before landing back on us.

'DCI Withers, DS Parker. Can you tell us what happened?'

'I already told the other police officer,' she said, waving her arm towards Davey, who had entered behind us. From upstairs there was a loud thump and the sound of giggling.

'Your children?' I asked. She nodded.

'Yes, they've been upstairs the whole time. They have no idea what's going on...'

'Can you tell us what happened?' Nathan asked again. 'I understand you've already spoken to PC Trelawney, but I'd like to hear it from you.'

She looked at her phone again and sighed, then put it down on the table. 'We were about to go out. I was putting some – stuff – in the car, and then I came in here to get something—' her eyes rested on the suitcases again before she could stop herself '—and then I saw a man in our garden. He was breaking into my office. I hid behind the kitchen island so I could keep an eye on him while I phoned the police, only I'd left my mobile on the table. I could hear him throwing stuff around in there and swearing.' I looked out at the garden again; the office was a sturdy-looking weatherboarded summer house, and through the open door I could see a desk with a computer on it. She followed my gaze. 'I run a hand-made costume jewellery business from it, so I thought he was trying to steal my stock or equipment, although it's not really worth much.'

'But he didn't take anything?' asked Nathan, and she shook her head.

'No, that wasn't what he was after. I was scared and I didn't want to move, but I made myself stand up to get my phone, and then the man came out. He was on his own phone and he said something like, "No sign out here, maybe in the house?" And then he turned round and looked straight at me.' She shivered. I reached out and took her hand. 'He came over and banged on the glass, said my husband had something of his that he needed back, could he come in, but I told him to go away because I was calling the police.' She picked up her phone again. 'And then I called you lot, and he swore at me and said I knew what he was after. He banged on the glass again, so hard I thought he would break it, but he left before you got here.'

'That must've been very scary,' I said sympathetically. She nodded. 'Did you get a good look at him? Do you think you could describe him?'

She smiled thinly. 'I can do better than that. I took a photo of him.'

'Well done,' said Nathan. 'That's really quick thinking. Can I see?' She hesitated for a moment, then unlocked her phone and handed it over. As Nathan scanned the photo I turned back to her.

'And do you?'

'Do I what?'

'Do you know what he was looking for?'

'What?' She looked surprised. 'No, no of course not. I thought maybe it was something to do with the fishing business, but Stuart doesn't tell me anything about work.' But she couldn't look me in the eye. I gestured to the suitcases.

'You off somewhere?'

'Yes… Me and the kids are going to stay with my mum for a few days.' Her voice wavered. I squeezed her hand.

'It's Maggie, isn't it? Maggie, have you and Stuart had a fight? Is that it?'

'No!' She was vehement. 'No we haven't, we never fight. He's a good man.' She hesitated. 'But—'

'But what?' Nathan passed the phone back to her. 'I can see you've called him a few times now. Does he often ignore your calls? Or is there a reason why he wouldn't be able to answer?'

She looked from Nathan to me, then down at the table, her eyes filling with tears.

'We can't help you or Stuart unless you talk to us, Maggie,' I said gently. She sniffed and nodded.

'Stuart called me this morning from work, about eleven o'clock.' That was around the time we'd spoken to him. He must've gone straight into his office to use the phone after we left the harbour. 'He told me to pack some stuff and go to my mum's, said he had a few things to sort out first and then he'd join us.'

'And now you can't get hold of him?'

'No, not on his mobile or on the office phone.' She looked at us pleadingly. 'Is it something to do with Mick Tyler, and that poor boy? I heard them talking about it when I went to the shop earlier. I know he was doing some odd jobs for Stuart, but my husband would never hurt anyone.'

'But maybe someone he knows would,' I suggested, and she nodded.

'He did tell me once that some of the people he was dealing with weren't very nice. But that was a while back. I assumed he'd stopped working with them.'

'I'm afraid that might have been wishful thinking,' said Nathan. He looked at me and gestured towards the door. 'DS Parker, can we...?'

I patted Maggie ineffectually on the hand, then stood up and followed Nathan to the other side of the room, where Davey Trelawney was waiting.

'What do you think's happened to Stuart Mitchell?' I asked him, in a low voice.

'Nothing good,' he said. 'Davey, get on the radio and ask them to send someone over to Mitchell's office at the harbour. If they find him, detain him.'

'Will do,' said Davey, and he went out in the hallway to make the call. Nathan turned to me.

'You know what this looks like…'

I sighed. 'Drugs. I know. Something went down on Thursday night, they didn't get the shipment they were expecting and now they're trying to find where it went. They killed Mick Tyler trying to find out where it was, they almost killed Liam doing the same, and now…'

'And now they might have Stuart Mitchell.' Nathan shook his head. 'I don't like this. Whoever this bloke was, he must've seen her car on the driveway. He knew people were in the house and he didn't care.'

'Maggie's had a lucky escape,' I said, and he nodded.

'Yeah, and her kids…' We both turned back to look at her. She was on the phone again, obviously trying to contact her husband. We rejoined her.

'Where does your mum live?' I asked.

'Barnstaple. Not far, but…' *But the people Stuart Mitchell had upset wouldn't be able to find them there.*

'Okay,' said Nathan. 'PC Trelawney—' Davey had just joined us '—he'll stay with you while you finish packing, and then I think it's probably a good idea if you go and stay with her for the moment as planned. Make sure you give him her address, so we know where to find you.'

Maggie went pale. 'You think that man might come back?'

'Probably not,' I said, 'but if he thinks whatever it is he was looking for is here, he might. And it would be safer for your children if you're not in the house.'

'Oh my God...'

'We'll send a patrol round to keep an eye on things,' said Nathan. 'It would be good if we could catch them in the act, but my feeling is he'll realise we're onto him and steer clear. Better to be safe than sorry.'

'Yes, I suppose so... But what about Stuart?'

'It could be something as simple as him being out of mobile range. You know what the signal's like down here,' I said. 'You never know, he might already be on his way to your mum's and you're worrying about nothing.'

'Yes, you're right,' she said, but she looked as unconvinced as I was.

Chapter Fourteen

W e sat in the car outside the Mitchells' house for a few minutes, watching as Maggie Mitchell went back and forth packing her own car with the suitcases and some kids' toys. Nathan held up his phone.

'Here,' he said, showing me a photograph of a big, burly man with a scowling face. He passed it to me so I could get a closer look. 'The Mitchells' intruder. Good-looking bloke, isn't he?'

'A real keeper,' I said. It was a little blurred, probably because Maggie's hand had shaken while she hurriedly took it, but even out of focus the look of fury in the man's eyes was obvious. He was clean shaven with closely cropped hair and a square jaw. He was probably in his forties, but he was one of those people where it's hard to tell; he could've been ten years younger, but he'd seen a bit of trouble and it showed on his face. A violent nature always made people look hard-faced and older than they were.

'Do you recognise him?' asked Nathan.

'No… I'm not saying I know everyone round here, but I reckon I know all the troublemakers by sight,' I said. I passed the phone back. 'I think I'd remember that face, anyway. In films, bad guys always *look* like bad guys, don't they? That's what he looks like. He looks like a Cockney gangster from a Guy Ritchie film.'

Nathan laughed. 'He does. Looking like that he had two choices, go into acting or become a thug.'

'And you don't have to audition to be a thug.'

Nathan's phone rang. 'Hi, Matt… Yep… Put a call out on it… That was good thinking…Okay, thanks.' He rang off. 'Uniform went down to the harbour. Mitchell's office is all locked up, no sign of any disturbance. Chrissie spoke to a couple of the lads down there, they said it's unusual for him to leave during the day but they didn't see anyone hanging around. His car's gone.'

'But nobody's been able to get hold of him?'

'Nope. Chrissie got a list of all the boats registered to Mitchell's company from the harbour master while she was there. Most of them seem to be moored up, and they'll keep an eye out for the others coming back, make sure he's not on any of them. Matt's back at the station, he's trying to trace Mitchell's mobile and he's put a call out on the car. If he's on route to his mother-in-law's, Traffic will find him.'

'But if that *is* where he's heading, he should be there by now.'

'Unless he went somewhere else first.'

'Or someone carjacked him,' I said. 'Or he's done a runner.'

Nathan nodded. 'Yeah. We won't know until we find his car.'

We watched through the windscreen as Maggie loaded her kids into the car and set off, followed by Davey Trelawney in his patrol car. Nathan gave them a brief wave, then said, 'Let's head back to the station. Matt's got something to show us.'

Back in the office, I was relieved to see that Sunil was back at his desk, going through the witness statements that had previously been earmarked for me. Lucky escape... Matt was on the computer. He looked up as we approached and picked up a plastic bag that had been lying next to the keyboard. 'Look what I found...'

It was a cheap pre-paid mobile phone.

'A burner? Where was that, in Mick Tyler's car?' asked Nathan.

'Yeah, on the passenger seat, shoved down between the seat and back cushions,' said Matt. 'It's been dusted for fingerprints so we'll soon know for certain if it's Tyler's, but I reckon it must be. Can't get into it though, so I got the number off the SIM card and sent off for a warrant for the call logs.'

'Nice one,' said Nathan, taking the bag from his DS and turning it slowly to look at the phone.

'That would explain why there was apparently no phone activity from Tyler on the night he died,' I said. 'There was nothing on his personal phone, but maybe he was using this instead to arrange where to meet up with his killer.'

'And that makes it even more likely that Liam Fossett had a burner, too,' said Nathan. 'I'm betting Mitchell has one as well. That's how they communicate with each other, without it being traced back to them.'

'Liam must've had his on him, the night he was assaulted,' I said. 'Ryan said he received a call, but there's nothing on his phone.'

'They called his burner,' said Matt, nodding. 'And then after they finished torturing him, they took it—'

'Because it could lead us to them,' finished Nathan. 'Once we get Tyler's call and text records, track down every number he's ever called or texted from it.'

'They'll probably all be burner phones too,' I pointed out.

'I know. But maybe someone got sloppy. We can

hope.' Nathan yawned and stretched out, his yawn setting me off as well. Matt laughed.

'State of you two...'

Nathan looked at his watch. 'Let's go home. There's nothing else we can do now, unless Traffic find Mitchell or his car, and they can always call us. It'll take at least twenty-four hours for Tyler's phone records to come through.'

My phone beeped with a text message. I quickly opened it, read it and sighed.

'Can't we stay here until then? Daisy took Germaine home before the builders knocked off, even though I warned her not to, and she just ate the builder's sweaty T-shirt after he took it off and left it lying around. The dog ate the T-shirt, that is, not Daisy. Anyway, he's not a happy man.'

But I couldn't put off going home forever. We headed back to find Mum had inserted herself between Derek the bare-chested bricklayer and my naughty (but cute) Pomeranian, and it looked like she was only about seven seconds and two double entendres away from being accused of sexual harassment. I wasn't sure if she was attempting to help, or just taking advantage of having a half-naked man in front of her for the first time in years. Daisy wrestled the soggy garment from Germaine's jaws while my shameless mother cooed over Derek's muscles in a way that was completely inappropriate for a woman of her age. Derek snatched up the chewed rag and held it up to his chest, but it was no longer up to the job. Nathan looked from him to my salivating dog and mother, and then to the tattered T-shirt and sighed.

'Would you like to borrow one of mine?' he said. Derek nodded and followed him upstairs almost at a run.

'Oh for goodness sake, Mother!' I said, exasperated. 'What are you like? That poor man.' She shrugged, completely unabashed.

'I didn't mean anything by it, I were just trying to make him laugh,' she said.

'Laugh? He looked terrified. And how did Germaine get anywhere near the builders in the first place?'

'Daisy was supposed to be keeping an eye on her,' said Mum. Daisy looked furious.

'No I wasn't, you were! I told you I was looking something up on the internet!'

'I didn't hear you.'

'But—'

I held my hand up. 'It doesn't matter. We *all* need to keep an eye on her when the builders are around. Today it was only a T-shirt, but what would happen if she took a chunk out of Derek's leg? They'd make us get her put down.' Germaine, who had calmed down completely now the builder had left the room, lay on the floor by my feet with a little whine and put her paws over her eyes. I felt a surge of guilt; I should've been here, looking after her, not dumping the dog on anyone who'd take her. Just one more item on the long list of things I was currently feeling bad about.

Daisy picked Germaine up and gave her a big fussing, which the dog didn't really enjoy, but as Daisy was pretty much the person she loved most in this world she put up with it.

'See?' said Mum. 'No real harm done.'

'I dunno, did you see the state of his T-shirt?' asked Daisy.

'I'm more concerned about the potential effect on Germaine's digestive system. Have you *seen* how much that man sweats?' I pulled a face and we all giggled, but I still felt like the worst mum (and dog mum) in the world.

We got through the rest of the evening without disaster. I made chicken escalopes with a chorizo crumb for dinner, bashing out chicken fillets until they were roughly a couple of centimetres thick and then coating them in flour, then egg, then breadcrumbs with a large chunk of spicy chorizo salami grated into them, along with rock salt, freshly ground pepper, and a pinch of ground cumin and coriander. Daisy had been about to give Germaine the tiny bit of chorizo that was left over (I couldn't grate all of it, for fear of grating my fingers as well), but I stopped her just in time; it was an extremely hot and spicy salami, and I didn't think it would be a good accompaniment to sweaty builder's T-shirt... I pan fried the chicken pieces for a couple of minutes on both sides to get the coating golden and crispy, then finished them off in the oven; they only took about ten minutes to cook all the way through, as they were so thin. I served them with mashed potatoes and cauliflower cheese, and let me tell you, if you haven't eaten mash with cheese sauce on it you haven't lived. Afterwards I curled up on the sofa, Nathan on one side, Daisy on the other, watching a new Netflix show we'd started bingeing the week before. Mum fell asleep in her chair almost immediately, and we laughed (quietly, so as not to disturb her) as Nathan put the subtitles on so we could still 'hear' the dialogue over her snoring; she sounded like a hippo with a deviated septum. Later I cuddled up to Nathan in bed as he turned the light out, and fell asleep thinking about how much I loved spending time with my little family, even when we weren't really doing anything.

• • •

The next morning it was back to the station, and back to the boring job of combing through the witness statements, though luckily for me Sunil had done most of them. Neither Stuart Mitchell or his car had turned up anywhere overnight; a quick call to Maggie Mitchell confirmed that he still hadn't made it to her mum's house, as they'd arranged, and it seemed pretty certain now either that he'd done a runner and left her somewhere safe (which was a possibility), or that something bad had happened to him; the person (or people) who had killed Mick Tyler and put Liam Fossett in hospital had got to him, too. But whether that meant he was dead, there was no way of knowing. Not until we found his body.

The call records for Tyler's burner phone still hadn't come through. Liam was still in a medically induced coma, although the doctors were pleased with his progress and told me that the swelling on his brain had come down significantly, and they were confident that he would pull through. That piece of good news lifted the whole station's spirits. It was always hard to lose 'one of our own', a local, but to lose one so young was doubly tragic. I hoped Tyler's would be the only funeral for Carmen to preside over, but until we found Mitchell…

My phone rang just as Nathan was in the middle of updating the rest of the team. I apologised and quickly declined it, looking at the caller display as I did. Nina. Was she calling me about our lunch next week, or had the awful picture of me dressed as the evil mermaid gone viral on the council's social media accounts? Either way, I was sure she'd realise I was working and call me back later.

My phone beeped as she left me a voicemail message. As Nathan finished the briefing I took myself out into the corridor to listen to it.

'Jodie, it's Nina. Please call me back as soon as you get this, it's urgent, I'm really worried about Glen.' Glen was her younger brother, I remembered; he'd been several years below us at school. It sounded like Nina was trying very hard to stay calm and speak clearly, but the panic and alarm in her voice were evident even over the fuzzy mobile signal.

I called her straight back, and five minutes later I was on my way to Glen Falconer's house.

Chapter Fifteen

Nina was waiting outside with a worried expression on her face. I jumped out of the car and reached out to hug her.

'Don't worry, I'm sure he's fine,' I said, but she shook her head.

'If he's fine, why's he avoiding me?' she asked, which I couldn't really answer. Instead I pointed to the front door.

'Have you been in?'

'No, I was waiting for you.' She took a deep breath, then took a door key from her pocket, inserting it into the lock. She hesitated. 'Just in case he'd ... you know...'

The door swung open with an ominous creak. In normal circumstances it probably wouldn't have felt ominous, but with everything going on at that moment we were all on edge. Nina's fear was rubbing off on me as well.

'How many times have you called him?' I asked.

'Five times since Saturday. The first time he answered and said he was fine, but under the weather so he wouldn't be around much. So of course I popped round to see if he needed anything, but he didn't answer so I thought he was sleeping. I've called him four times since then, and no answer.' She looked at me, concern writ large across her face. 'I do worry about him, after he left the army and split up with his girlfriend and everything. I hate to think of him being on his own.'

'Has he been depressed?' I was starting to dread what we might find. She nodded.

'He found it hard when he first came back, you know, getting used to being a civilian again, but I thought he'd turned a corner. He'd been getting some work down at the harbour—'

I tried not to react as my heart leapt into my mouth. 'At the harbour? Who was he working for?'

'He was getting some work on the boats, I don't know who with.' She looked at me curiously. 'Is that relevant?'

'I'm not sure… Come on.' I pushed the door open and led the way in. The house felt empty, but not deserted; the sort of empty you get when someone has just quickly popped out for something. 'Glen?' I called, not expecting an answer. I didn't get one.

'Glen!' called Nina, moving deeper into the house. We walked through the living room, into the kitchen, then up the stairs to the two small bedrooms and the bathroom. No sign of him.

We headed back to the kitchen and I started to look around. Glen wasn't here, that much was obvious, but it looked to me like this wasn't a planned absence. There was an unopened bottle of milk in the fridge, with a day left to go on the use by date. Leftovers in a Tupperware container that still resembled food, rather than a decomposing mess, although I wasn't sure I'd want to eat it. He wouldn't have bought groceries or kept leftovers if he'd not intended to be there.

There were two mugs by the sink, the remains of a half-drunk cup of tea in one. I pointed to them.

'Wherever he is now, it looks like he had company last time he was here,' I said. Nina looked doubtful.

'He probably just couldn't be bothered to wash up,' she said, but the kitchen was tidy and well organised; there were no other dirty plates or mugs waiting to be washed. Everything, from the collection of cooking oils by the hob to the magnetic knife rack (with every knife present and lined up according to length), was neatly arranged, with a place for everything and everything in its place – probably a habit he'd learnt while in the armed forces.

'Does he like to cook?' I asked, and she nodded, surprised.

'How can you tell?'

'Not many bachelors have extra virgin olive oil, and coconut oil, *and* ground nut oil, *and* rapeseed oil…'

She managed a soft laugh. 'I forgot, you're a detective now.'

'That's why I'm here.' I looked around. I could not shake the feeling that he'd just stepped out (probably to buy *more* cooking oil) and would be back in a minute. 'They left in a hurry,' I murmured.

'What?'

'Glen left in a hurry, otherwise he would've washed up. This is not the house of a man who leaves stuff in the sink unless he really has to. He had someone here, gave them a cup of tea while he… I don't know, did something, then they both left in a rush.' I looked around again. 'Is anything missing?'

'I don't know…'

'Let's have a look upstairs again, see if any of his clothes are missing.'

'Okay,' said Nina, 'although I'm not sure I'd know even if there were.'

We went back to Glen's neat bedroom. Nina opened a

wardrobe. There were still clothes hanging there, not that many, but then maybe Glen didn't have that many to start off with; a lot of men didn't. I opened a bedside drawer, though, and it was empty. So was the one under that.

'He's taken his kit bag,' said Nina. I turned round to see her staring at the top of the wardrobe. 'He had his old Army kit bag up there, and it's gone.'

'Whatever was in here's gone too,' I said, indicating the drawers.

'That's where he keeps his pants and socks,' said Nina. 'I think there might be a couple of T-shirts and that missing, too.'

'So he made some tea, left his companion downstairs while he came up here and packed a few things, then they both left,' I said. 'I didn't think to ask, is his car outside?'

'No, but he normally parks it in the garage,' she said. 'I haven't got a key for that, though.'

'We'll have to see if we can get in,' I started, but I was interrupted by Nina's phone ringing. She took it from her pocket and looked at the number, frowning.

'Hello?' she said, uncertainly. Her face cleared as the person on the other end spoke, and she looked up at me. 'Glen! Thank God, I was getting worried—'

'Put it on speakerphone, but don't tell him I'm here,' I

said quietly. She hesitated. 'Look, I'm here as a friend, not a police officer.' She still looked a little uncertain, but nodded and pressed a button on her phone so I could hear.

'Where are you calling from? I didn't recognise your number,' she said.

'No, it's a new phone,' said Glen. He had a deep voice, which surprised me whenever I heard it, because I still thought of him as the annoying ten-year-old who was always trying to hang around when I was over at their house. But right now, underneath it, tension. 'I dropped my old one and it broke, that's why I haven't returned your calls until now.'

'Oh, right,' said Nina. 'So are you feeling better? Where are you?'

'Yeah, I'm fine, still trying to shake this virus or whatever it is. I've been staying in bed most of the time, just resting.' Even without seeing his face, I could imagine the shifty expression he'd be wearing. Nina and her brother had always been close, and I didn't think lying to her would've come easy to Glen.

'Is that where you are now? In bed?' Nina looked at me as she spoke, waiting to catch him out.

'Yeah.'

'Well that's weird, Glen, because that's where we're

standing right now,' I said. 'In fact, I'm sitting on your bed, and you're definitely not in it.'

There was a shocked silence, and I thought for a minute he'd hung up. *Dammit*, I thought. I'd hoped he was calling because he needed help; had I blown it?

'Who's there with you?' he said, and Nina and I shared a relieved glance.

'You remember my friend Jodie?'

'Jodie? She's a bloody copper—'

'No I'm not,' I said, and then wondered why I'd said that. 'I mean, I am, but I'm here as a friend. What's going on, Glen? Are you in trouble?'

'No... No, of course I'm not,' he said, but that tension was still there.

'Are you sure? Nina's worried about you. We both are. There's a lot of stuff going on here at the moment, and if it's got anything to do with you, you could be in danger.'

'What sort of stuff?' He sounded *really* anxious now.

'Have you heard about Mick Tyler?' I asked.

'Why, what's happened to him?'

'He's dead. Someone drowned him in a water trough.'

'What? Shit, I—' I heard him gulp down the phone. 'I didn't know that. I'm sorry. Oh my God...'

'And then there's Liam Fossett. Somebody tortured him and left him for dead.'

'*Liam*? But he wasn't even – he's just a kid. Is he okay?'

'Just about. And then of course there's Stuart Mitchell.' Nina looked at me in surprise. The news about Tyler and Liam had spread all around the town by now, but Mitchell's disappearance hadn't made the grapevine yet.

'What's happened to Stuart?' As an ex-soldier Glen must've been used to being in high-pressure situations, but his voice still betrayed shock. Shock, and fear.

'Disappeared. No one knows where he is,' I said casually. 'Of course, with what's happened to Mick and Liam, it doesn't look good for him, does it?' There was a pause again, but I knew Glen hadn't hung up as I could still hear his ragged breathing. 'Glen, if you know anything, anything at all—'

'No, no, I don't know…'

'Please, Glen,' said Nina, her eyes full of worried tears. 'Tell us. Jodie will help you, won't you?' She turned to me, pleading. I nodded.

'Of course I will. Look, I'm not trying to pin any of this on you, mate. At this point I just want to make sure no one else gets hurt, or worse. Just tell us what's going on. Or better still, come back and talk to us so we can keep you safe.'

'I have to go,' said Glen flatly.

'No! Don't hang up!' cried Nina.

'I have to. I'm safe, all right? But I won't be if I come home. I love you, sis.'

'Glen—'

The line went dead. Nina looked at me and then burst into tears. I pulled her into a hug. 'He's okay,' I said, although I didn't know that for certain. 'He says he's safe, and he knows how to look after himself. And now of course—' I indicated the phone in her hand '—we have a number for him.' She immediately went to redial but I gently put my hand over hers and stopped her. 'He won't answer, not now. Give it a day or two, let him have time to think. You're such a close family, he won't be able to ignore you forever. *He* called *you* today, remember?' She nodded, wiping at her eyes with her free hand. 'Come on,' I said. 'Let's go and have a cup of tea.'

I took her home, where we had a mug of tea and I let her talk about her brother. Without having to pry too much, I discovered that Glen had been back in Penstowan for almost six months, his life having been turned upside down somewhat after an injury saw him invalided out of the Army, and a long-term relationship had ended. He'd been picking up odd jobs here and there, including some down at the harbour; however not, by the sound of it, for Stuart Mitchell. He knew a lot of the fishermen down there, having gone to school with a fair few of them, and he'd been helping out with boat repairs (he was a trained mechanic), even occasionally covering for sick crew members, although according to Nina he wasn't much of a fisherman. If he *was* involved in whatever operation Mitchell and Tyler had been running, I thought, his lack of fishing skills would not have been a problem…

I left her holding the phone in her hand, staring at it as if willing it to ring again, and I knew she'd be redialling her brother the minute I'd left.

———

I found Nathan in the office, staring thoughtfully at the murder board.

Now, I'm sure you've watched stuff like *CSI*-wherever on the telly, or at least one of the numerous highly popular American cop shows out there. They're full of impossibly handsome, square-jawed leading men, normally white with the odd black or Latino sidekick thrown in for comic relief or 'buddy' stuff. The female detectives manage to run around in ridiculously high heels without ever twisting an ankle or getting blisters on their little toes, plus they're always tall and skinny; they look like they'd blow over in a strong wind (particularly in those heels), yet they're able to tackle bad guys who are built like Sherman tanks with a couple of ninja-style high kicks and a flick of their long hair. For the record, I don't know *any* female coppers, uniform or otherwise, who would even think about wearing high heels to work, and as for the karate kicks, I've always been more fond of the rugby-tackle-around-the-knees-then-sit-on-them approach when it comes to apprehending suspects. It ain't pretty (or dignified), but it works. It also makes you less likely to be sued for breaking someone's nose when your high heel flies off mid-kick and smacks them in the face.

The other thing shows like *CSI* have are high-tech offices, where fingerprints can be traced in seconds by highly sophisticated computer software. In real life, some poor bugger has to sit in front of a screen and scroll through the database, comparing records (you can narrow down the search by looking for certain characteristics, but it all comes down to a real person being able to match that fingerprint found on the murder weapon to one on the database). And of course, they have murder boards. Big, shiny, glass boards (all the better for fancy lighting and cool camera shots) for the impossibly attractive detectives to write on or, better still, interactive ones, where all they have to do is wave their hand authoritatively across and all the information pops up, usually in a bright colour (again, because it looks cool on camera).

So was that the kind of technology Penstowan's finest got to work with? Was it heck. Nathan stood in front of an old whiteboard. It was on wheels, because most of the time it lived in the stationery cupboard, and only got wheeled out when CID had a particularly tough or complicated case to crack; although apparently it had also been used to work out the seating plan for Sunil's wedding a few months ago, because a few faint circles with names like 'Aunty Priya' and 'Uncle Pradeep' still lingered, just like the residual resentment of the family feud that had meant they couldn't be seated on the same table as cousin Sanjay. Families, huh? Nathan might not have had *CSI*-style tech to hand, but he had managed to get creative by writing 'VICTIMS' in red marker pen and 'SUSPECTS' in black. If things got much more complicated, he'd have to break out the blue one.

'Everything okay?' he asked, looking round. 'Is your friend all right?'

'Not really,' I said. 'I think the mermaid has struck again...'

'What?' Nathan looked shocked. 'Who else has died?'

'Well, no one,' I admitted, 'I just said that for dramatic

effect. But there's definitely a link.' I told him about Glen, about the abandoned mugs in the kitchen, and about the phone call.

'Sounds to me like he could *be* the mermaid,' said Nathan.

'What, Glen? Nah.'

'He's ex-Army,' Nathan pointed out. 'Trained to kill. He would definitely be capable of torturing Tyler and Liam—'

'Physically, yes. But it wouldn't be in his nature.'

'And of course he's conveniently made himself scarce after the murder and assault, and the disappearance of Stuart Mitchell.'

'For starters, he disappeared long before Mitchell did. And you didn't hear his voice. He sounded scared, and genuinely shocked and upset when I told him about Tyler and Liam.'

'Hmm…' Nathan turned back to the board, tapping a marker pen against his teeth. 'So is he a victim, or is he a suspect?'

'I don't know. You might need another column on the board. And another colour pen…'

Nathan grinned as he reached down to a nearby desk, where a packet of marker pens lay. He picked up a green one and took the lid off, hesitated for a moment and then wrote '?' on the board, with GLEN FALCONER underneath.

'Right,' he said, recapping the pen. 'If he's a victim, or potential victim and that's why he's done a runner, why is he in danger? What's he done?'

'Nicked drugs off whoever killed Tyler. How's this for a theory?' I took the pen from him and drew a boat on the board. 'He's been working at the harbour. Tyler goes out on a drug run for Stuart Mitchell, the Wednesday night before he was murdered.' I wrote 'T' inside a circle above the boat. 'Now, he normally has Liam Fossett helping him, but Liam was at a concert and had already told him he couldn't do that run. So who else is nosing around, needing money?'

'Glen Falconer.'

'Exactly!' I drew an 'F' above the boat. 'So they do this drug pick-up…' I added a bag full of pills to my drawing. 'Maybe Glen doesn't quite know what he's getting into and when he sees the amount of drugs – or maybe we've got it round the wrong way, they're dropping off drugs and picking up money—' A couple of pound signs joined the bag of pills.

'Whatever,' said Nathan, too polite as ever to tell me to get to the point.

'Whatever, he sees it, gets greedy and when they get to dry land he nicks it and does a runner.' I drew an arrow leading from the 'F'. I'd never had the chance to use a murder board before and I was enjoying myself. 'Knowing Mitchell and whoever he's in bed with will come after him, he uses his Army skills to disappear...' The arrow trailed into the white wilderness of the board, ending at another '?'.

'Okay...' said Nathan. 'Very artistic. But if that's the case, why torture Tyler? Tyler would be pissed off with Glen dropping him in it. If I was Tyler I'd have dobbed Glen in to the bad guys like a shot, to save my own skin. And Liam—'

'Liam might not even have known who was taking his place,' I said. 'That's why the torture didn't work. He couldn't tell them who'd taken the drugs because he wasn't there and he didn't know.'

'Okay, now *that* makes sense.' Nathan nodded. 'But there's still other questions.'

'*Lots* of other questions. Like who's behind all this.'

'Yeah, I don't mean that, I mean from what you've learnt today. Was there really someone else in the kitchen with him while Glen was packing some clothes? Who? Did they go with him, or are they still in Penstowan?' He gave me a crooked smile. 'I don't suppose there was a lipstick print on one of the mugs in a distinctive shade or anything...?'

'Not many fishermen wear lipstick, Nath. Not during the week, anyway.'

'Who says it was a fisherman? Who says it was even a man?' He looked at the white board again. 'Maybe Tyler's murder wasn't about drugs at all. Nina said that Glen's relationship broke up, yeah? Do you know why?'

'Nope. Didn't ask.'

'And Terry Barraclough suggested that Mick Tyler was cheating on his wife—'

'Which Ewan Barraclough strongly refuted,' I said. 'And it sounds to me like Ewan and his family socialised with Mick and his lot far more than Terry did. I reckon he probably has a clearer idea of what the Tylers' marriage was like.'

'Okay, but hear me out. What if Tyler was – how did Matt put it?'

'Doinking.'

'Oh God, yes. What if Tyler was "doinking" Glen's girlfriend and he found out, and then he killed him?'

'And then she went back to his house?' I scoffed. 'Come on Nath, that's a bit of a stretch, even for you.' He laughed.

'Even for me? Cheeky mare.' He shook his head. 'No, you're right. I'm just trying to work out who this mysterious companion of his was. If we can work that out, they might lead us to Glen. And he might lead us to the murderer.'

'He definitely knows who's behind this,' I said. The phone on the desk next to me rang. I picked it up; it still took me a spilt second to remind myself how to answer. 'DS Parker.'

'Jodie? It's Ewan Barraclough.'

'Oh, hi Ewan,' I said, loudly, so Nathan would hear. He stopped staring at the murder board and hovered next to me instead. 'Everything all right? What can I do for you?'

'Yeah, we were just wondering if your lot have finished with our kitchen? Me and Lou have been staying with Terry because we don't want the kids knowing what happened, but we're keen to get back.'

'Hang on, let me check.' I covered the phone's mouthpiece. 'Have Forensics and Scene of Crime finished with Liam's crime scene?'

'Yes,' said Nathan. 'They called while you were out, they're all done.'

'Ewan? Yeah, they're all done.'

'Cool.' Ewan paused. 'Will there still be – will it—'

'There could still be blood stains and some mess at the scene,' I said, softly. 'The forensics team will have swabbed the blood and taken away some evidence, like the kitchen tools used by Liam's attacker, but they won't have cleared up all the mess. I'm sorry.'

'Right, okay…'

'My advice, go back on your own and have a look at it, see what you think. If it's bad, we can put you in touch with some specialist crime scene cleaners.'

'Okay, thank you.'

'While I've got you,' I said, 'have you had any thoughts about why Liam chose your house to come to?'

Ewen sighed. 'Actually, I have.'

'Go on.'

'I told you he came round to buy my old gaming stuff, yeah? Well, we were looking at it in the garage, when he spotted my punch bag.'

'Punch bag? You a boxer?'

'Kick boxer. I represented the UK in the under 21s European championships when I was younger. Came second two years running.'

'You were good, then?'

'Yeah. Still am. Liam and I were joking about it, and I said if he ever needed back up to give me a call.'

'You think that's why he came to you?' I asked.

'Yeah, I reckon so.' Ewan sounded upset. 'Poor kid. He needed my help and I weren't there to give it to him.'

Chapter Sixteen

I t had been an eventful morning. I left Nathan on the phone, updating the Superintendent of the Devon and Cornwall Constabulary on the case. I had the horrible feeling he'd be updating them on how I was getting on, too, as the whole idea of having a casual, 'floating' CID officer was part of a trial, and I wasn't sure I really wanted to hear that part of the conversation. So instead I volunteered to do the 'bun run' and headed to Rowe's to get lunch for me and Nathan, and for a couple of other officers who were by now back in the office.

'Jodie!' I stopped in my tracks and looked across the road, which was bustling at this time of day and of the holiday season. Carmen was on the other pavement, but she waved and joined me. 'Hello! I thought it was you.'

'Hello, Vicar.'

She smiled. 'Oh no, Carmen, please. I'm off duty.'

'I didn't think vicars were ever really off duty.'

'No, just like police officers.'

I laughed. 'That's true. We have more in common than I thought. Everything okay?'

'Oh yes, I just wondered how you were getting on with the investigation?' She frowned. 'Only if you can tell me, of course.'

'We've got a few leads to follow,' I said diplomatically, although I wasn't sure we had. 'Any sign of your stone mermaid? Obviously we've not really had a chance to look into that…'

'No, no, I wouldn't expect you to. That poor Fossett boy! Quite shocking.' She shook her head. 'I do wish whoever took the statue hadn't, though. I'm a little bit over Jago Thomas and his blasted mermaid stories. Not just him, either.'

'I can imagine. The older generation of Cornish are very superstitious, fishermen even more so. But you can tell Jago and his friends that we are very confident the Siren isn't behind any of the attacks, not unless she's drastically changed her M.O.'

'Well that's good to know,' said Carmen. 'I was starting to get nervous around the font.'

I laughed. 'I think you'll be safe to carry on baptising people in it. Well, I'm just off to get lunch for everyone…'

'Are you going to Rowe's? Me too.' We carried on up Fore Street, Carmen's long stride forcing me to trot a bit to keep up. I had the feeling she wanted to say something to me, but she didn't. I began to feel a little awkward.

We joined the queue at the counter, sharing a roll of the eyes at the man at the front who couldn't decide between a sausage roll and a pasty, and then a cheese and pickle roll or a ham and tomato one. Carmen turned to me.

'I was thinking,' she said. 'I know the Fossetts aren't religious – they don't come to church, anyway – but I was thinking maybe I should go and see them. Tony said you and Liam's mum used to be quite close. What do you think? Would they appreciate a visit or would I annoy them?'

I smiled at her. 'I can't imagine you annoying anyone, Vic – Carmen. I'm not religious, but if my daughter was in hospital and that poorly, I'd be touched to know that others were thinking of us.'

'That's what I was hoping.' She smiled. 'I wouldn't get all preachy or start praying or anything – not unless they wanted me to. I'm not one for trying to force my religion onto anyone.'

'No...' I said. The queue shuffled forward, the indecisive man finally making his choices and heading for a table. Only now at the counter there was a family of six, with four children under the age of ten, all of whom wanted different things, none of which their parents approved of. I hoped no one back at the station was starving. 'Can I ask you something?' I turned to Carmen, thinking of Tony and how I needed to make it up to him for being mean to him at the party on Tuesday. 'You're a vicar, right? Which means you can date and get married. You can have a boyfriend.'

'Or a girlfriend,' she said. 'My church is very inclusive.'

'Oh, cool,' I said, thinking it would be just like Tony to fall for someone who wasn't into men. 'I'm not propositioning you, by the way.'

'With your handsome policeman boyfriend? I should think not.'

Phew, I thought. She did like men after all. 'So what I was going to ask is, can you only date Christian men? Only most of us round here are godless heathens, so that wouldn't give you a lot of choice.'

The queue shuffled forward again, serenaded by the screams of one of the toddlers who hadn't been allowed to have a massive slice of fruit cake on the completely unfair grounds that he didn't like it and wouldn't eat it.

Carmen laughed. 'Going by the congregation who actually turn up on a Sunday, the purely Christian dating pool is almost exclusively married or widowed and over seventy-five.'

'So does that mean you could date someone who didn't share your religion?'

'Well, dating someone who followed *another* religion would be tricky. Christianity, Islam and Judaism do share a lot of common ground, but there are too many differences in the way we observe our faiths. And being with an atheist would be even harder, I think.'

'But what about a normal person?' I said. She laughed. 'Oh dear, I didn't mean it to come out like that. I don't mean you're abnormal for being religious. I just meant that a lot of us are too busy getting on with our lives to even think about some big invisible father figure in the sky.'

'That's not *quite* how we see God—'

'You know what I mean, though. It's not like we're not spiritual or anything. I mean, sometimes I can just stand there and look up at the stars, or at the sea, and this feeling of peace and, I dunno, of being at one with the universe or something comes over me. Would you be able to date someone like that? Someone who was a good person, they just didn't go to church.'

She looked thoughtful, and a small smile crossed her lips as she spoke again. 'You know, I had never really considered dating someone who didn't share my religious views before. But I do believe that you can embody Christian values and be a good person without ever reading the Bible. If a man was kind and considerate, if he cared about people, was compassionate towards his fellow humans and actually tried to make a difference to the community...' She looked positively swoony at this point. She shook herself. 'Well, I think we'd have enough in common to maybe make it work.'

'And if he made you laugh,' I added, and her smile broadened.

'Oh yes. A man who could make me laugh...'

There was muttering in the queue behind us, and I realised it was now us holding everybody up. I picked up the CID lunch order, said goodbye to Carmen and set off back to the station, stopping only to take out my mobile phone and text Tony: *Ask Carmen out RIGHT NOW!*

Back in the office, I doled out the sandwiches as I passed the other officers' desks and headed over to where Nathan and Matt were sitting, deep in discussion.

'Here you go, babe,' I said, passing Nathan a ham and cheese sandwich. I'd given up trying not to call him that; it just felt like second nature. Matt looked up with a grin.

'What about me?'

'You ain't a babe. Not to me, anyway.' I tossed him a slightly warm and greasy paper bag. 'But I bought an extra sausage roll in case you were back.'

'Aww, cheers mate,' he said, tucking into it enthusiastically.

'If we could get back to what we were doing before Hurricane Jodie arrived…'

'Sorry,' I said, rolling another chair over and plonking myself down. 'What have I missed?' Matt swallowed a lump of flaky pastry.

'Mick Tyler's burner phone records came back,' he said. 'We were just going through them.'

I rolled a bit closer and looked at the printout on the desk in front of us.

'He's made and received a fair number of calls, but all from the same three numbers,' I said. Nathan nodded.

'Yep. Although actually there's four numbers, if you go back to the beginning. Look…' He picked up the sheet and made his way over to the murder board. Matt and I exchanged looks and followed him, Matt leaving a trail of crumbs behind him.

Nathan spun the murder board around and began to write on the clean side. 'So, the phone was first activated back in March.' He wrote down Tyler's phone number.

'Five months ago,' I said. 'Which is around the time he went to see Stuart Mitchell.'

'For the first three months, he made and received several calls, normally once a month, or maybe three-weekly, to these two numbers.' He wrote two more numbers down, both of them only differing from the first by a couple of digits.

'They're from the same batch of SIMs,' I said. 'Look, the numbers are practically the same. You know what that looks like?'

'A drug dealing ring,' said Matt. 'The kingpin buys a batch of burner phones or SIMs, then as he recruits new people he gives them out.'

'That's exactly what it looks like,' said Nathan. 'Which backs up our earlier theory, doesn't it? So the calls follow this pattern. This number – let's call this Phone A – calls Tyler, who then calls Phone B—' Nathan pointed to the third number. 'Although on another occasion, Phone B rings Tyler. And then there's a gap of about ten hours, after which he calls Phone A again. And then nothing for another three or four weeks.'

'Hmm…' I said. 'So Phone A is our Kingpin, calling Tyler to tell him about a job. Maybe he calls Phone B as well. Tyler and Phone B – maybe Liam? – then talk to each other to arrange the trip out to the bay.'

'Then Tyler rings Kingpin back to tell him when the

job's done.' Nathan stood back and compared the sheet of phone calls to the board. 'Yeah, I reckon that's right. Only Phone B can't be Liam, because Liam would've been at university during this period.'

'Of course… What are the other numbers?'

'Well, a couple of months ago, Phone B disappeared from the equation, to be replaced by…' He wrote another number on the board, again, a phone number that was very similar to the others.

'Phone C,' said Matt. 'And this time Phone C *could* be Liam, because it ties in with him coming back for the holidays. Universities finish for the summer earlier than schools, so he would have been back in Penstowan around the time Phone C first appears.'

'Okay…' I said. 'Does Phone B appear in the records again?'

'No. So maybe that's someone who used to work for Mitchell, but later moved away.'

'Or got banged up,' I said. 'We should probably look to see if Mitchell has any known associates who got put away around that time.'

'Yes,' said Nathan. 'Good thinking. They might not have anything to do with Tyler's murder, but at least they might be able to throw some light on who did.'

'Okay. You said there were four numbers in total? Where's the other one?'

Nathan wrote on the board again, adding Phone D. 'This one only appears once. Phone A called Tyler on Saturday morning. They had quite a long conversation. And then Phone D rang him Sunday night, at seven fifteen. Nowhere near as long.'

'Just long enough to arrange a time and place to meet?' I said. Nathan nodded.

'Yeah, that's what I'm thinking. Phone A, who seems to be the one making the deals, maybe he's heard from the end customer – the person whose drugs they're bringing in. And the end customer has just realised there's stuff missing from the shipment, and *he's* rung Phone A to complain. So of course A rings the skipper who was responsible for picking the shipment up and asks him what the hell's going on. Tyler's protesting, he doesn't know, or perhaps he's dobbing in Glen Falconer, if he is involved. But they can't get hold of Glen because he's scarpered. So that evening Phone D, who's either the end customer or someone hired by him, calls to arrange a meeting that night at the stone circle to "talk", or maybe he thinks Tyler will give him the rest of his drugs. Who knows.'

'And the owner of Phone D kills him.'

'Yep.' Nathan sighed. 'All of this works, of course, but I'd really like to establish a link between the players. At the moment all we have is hearsay that Tyler and

Mitchell spoke about *something* all those months ago that suddenly got his finances out of the red. And we know that Liam was helping out at the harbour, but other than that there's no proof he was ever on a fishing trip.'

'No... Can I see?' I held my hand out for the printed list of phone calls. I ran my eyes down the list until I got to the date I was looking for. 'Okay, see here, on Thursday night? Tyler had a call from Phone C. Ryan said Liam had a call that evening while they were at a gig, and that Liam rang someone else immediately. So that was Liam ringing to tell Tyler that he couldn't go out on the boat that night.'

'So where does Glen Falconer come into all this?' asked Matt.

'Viv Tyler said Mick would never go out on the boat at night on his own. And depending on how they pick the shipment up, it might take two of them to do it. Say Liam is his usual crew, but he's not around to help. Glen was taking on odd jobs down at the harbour, and I reckon he would've been in the same year as Mick at school, so they would definitely know each other. Mick knows Glen could do with the money and he trusts him to keep quiet, so he persuades him to take Liam's place, maybe just for that night. Or maybe he's thinking Glen can take over permanently once Liam's back at uni.'

'But Glen's an idiot and helps himself to the shipment,' added Matt.

'Yeah,' I said, but I felt uncomfortable. Glen wasn't an idiot. I didn't know him that well, not anymore; I remembered him as Nina's irritating little brother, but now I thought of it he hadn't really been irritating at all, in fact he'd been rather sweet. And Nina had moaned about him, but we'd made a point of including him in our games when we could. And he'd sounded shocked and upset on the phone...

'We've got the records for Tyler's own phone, haven't we?' I said.

'Yeah, on my desk,' said Nathan. 'You thought of something?'

'Possibly...' I looked at Tyler's last few phone calls, then quickly called Nina. She answered straight away.

'Have you found him?' she asked breathlessly. I kicked myself for raising her hopes; I should've just texted her my request.

'No, sweetheart, I'm sorry. But we are looking into it. Can you give me his phone numbers? The old one and the one he called you on today?' I wrote down the digits and said goodbye, with a promise that we would find Glen as soon as we could. I hoped it was a promise I could keep.

'What's that all about?' asked Nathan. I held up the post-it note with Glen's numbers on it.

'Here. On Thursday morning Tyler rang Glen, from his own phone. He could've been arranging to meet him that evening, because he already knew Liam wasn't going to be there. Ryan said Liam was pissed off when he got the phone call, remember? Because he'd already told them he wasn't available. So he rang Tyler, who reassured him it was fine because he'd already arranged Glen to cover for him.'

Nathan looked at the printout. 'That makes sense…'

'And then Tyler rings Glen again on Saturday morning, after the phone call with Phone A. He's warning him that the owner of the shipment knows there's something missing, and they want it back. Maybe he's telling Glen to hand it over. Or maybe he's telling him to run.'

'That's the day he went missing?'

'We think so. It's certainly the last time up until this morning that Nina managed to speak to him.'

'It does fit,' said Matt. 'But why would Liam protect Glen? They were torturing the poor sod. Surely he would've told them he wasn't on the boat with Tyler that night, and would've told them it was Glen?'

'Tyler might not have told Liam who it was,' said

Nathan. 'He might not even have told Mitchell. Think about it. Mitchell would need to know that whoever was doing these drug runs was trustworthy. He wouldn't necessarily have known Glen well enough. He might've stopped Tyler using him, and he might even have insisted that he went out on the boat on his own rather than use someone who didn't have Mitchell's seal of approval.'

'So when the end customer – let's call him Mr Big—' started Matt.

'Or Ms Big,' I pointed out. Nathan laughed. 'What? Women can be just as evil and ruthless as men.'

'Can't argue with that,' said Matt. 'Okay, so when this Big person asks Mitchell – who I'm assuming is Phone A?' Nathan and I both nodded. 'They ask Mitchell who was on the boat, and he tells them it was Tyler and Liam.'

'Yeah. So they start with Tyler, and when they don't get any joy out of him, they torture Liam.'

'And all the time they're looking in the wrong place, because Glen has got whatever it is they're looking for, and he's nowhere to be found,' I said.

'So now we know – or we think we know – *why* Tyler was murdered, but we still need to find out who did it.' Nathan drew a big question mark on the board. 'We need a link…'

'So what do we do next?' I asked.

'*Find* that link, of course.' He grinned. 'Easy… Matt,

go back to the phone company and tell them we need call records and any other information they can give us for those other burner phones. We'll need the same for Glen Falconer's phones, both of them, but it looks like they're on another network, so you'll need to get another warrant first. Sunil?' The DC was sitting nearby and had been listening in to our conversation. He jumped up eagerly.

'Yes, Guv?'

'Get onto the tech lads. We need a trace put on Stuart Mitchell and Glen Falconer's phones, both their registered and unregistered ones. I'm fully expecting all of them to be turned off, but let's at least see where they were the last time they were active, it'll give us somewhere to start looking.' He turned back to the board. 'This is the one I'm really interested in, though.' He pointed to the phone number we'd dubbed 'D'.

'The killer,' said Matt. Nathan nodded.

'I think so. I think it'll be turned off like the others, though.' He fixed Sunil with a serious look. 'I want this one monitored 24/7. Set up an alert. I want to know the minute it comes back on again.'

'You think it will?'

'If Glen has what they're looking for, then they'll probably try to contact him at some point.'

'What about me?' I asked.

'Find Glen. He's ex-Army, isn't he? He could be using his survival skills to camp out somewhere, in which case he's pretty much off-grid. But the armed forces are like a family – they stick together. Trawl through his social media and emails, call Nina again, find out if there are any old army mates that he's kept in contact with who might cover for him. The easiest place for him to hide would be with one of them. If he genuinely didn't know about Tyler's death and Liam's assault until this morning, then he's been under the impression the only people he's hiding from are the bad guys, not us, so maybe he was a bit less careful than he should have been.'

'On it,' I said. Matt and Sunil wandered back to their desks, leaving the two of us. Nathan looked at me and smiled quizzically as I sighed and clutched at my heart.

'What?'

'You're just so *dreamy* when you're in charge,' I said. He laughed.

'That's wildly inappropriate in the office, DS Parker. But you can say it again when we get home.'

'You think that's inappropriate? Babe, you ain't heard nothing yet. In fact I—' But before I could go any further, the phone on the next desk rang. Nathan answered it.

'DCI Withers. Yes?… Where?… We're on our way.'

Tracking down Glen would have to wait.

Chapter Seventeen

W e already knew that Stuart Mitchell hadn't made it to his mother-in-law's house, but at least we knew now where his car was. Nathan and I got out of our own car and headed over to the uniformed officer standing next to the Toyota 4x4.

'DCI Withers, DS Parker,' said Nathan, flashing him his warrant card. I followed suit. 'You're out of Barnstaple, yeah?'

'Yes, sir. PC McKenzie.'

'What have we got?'

'We were looking for the car after you put the call out yesterday afternoon, but there was no sign of it. And then a couple of hours ago one of the homeowners reported it as abandoned.' The PC nodded towards a house. It was part of a small new housing development just off Meddon Street in Bideford. It was almost identical to its neighbours, very clean and neat, apart from a couple of wheelie bins in the driveway. 'They complained it was taking up one of their allocated parking spaces and wanted it towed.' He gestured at the bins. 'Thank God it's bin day tomorrow, otherwise they'd have left it longer.'

We left PC McKenzie with the car and headed for the house.

'I wonder why Mitchell left it here?' I said.

'Maybe he knows someone in the area,' mused Nathan. 'Maybe he dumped it and borrowed someone else's car. Or—'

'You the police?' The woman suddenly in front of us on the doorstep made both of us jump; she must've been peering through the front room curtains and seen us approaching. Nathan recovered first.

'Oh! Yes. DCI Withers, DS Parker… Was it you who reported the car over there?'

'Yes. I came outside to put my bins out. That's where I always put them. I was really annoyed when I saw it was still there.'

'*Still* there?' I asked. 'You noticed it before?'

'Yeah, yesterday. I told them they couldn't leave it there, but they both completely ignored me, like I was invisible or something…'

'Both? There was more than one person in the car?' Nathan and I exchanged glances.

'One of them was in that car. The other pulled up behind him, right across our driveway, that's how I noticed them. I was going out later and I wouldn't have been able to get my car out of the garage. They've built these houses so close together—'

I interrupted before she could go into a long rant about the failings of modern urban development. 'What happened then?'

'The bloke in the other car – the one across my drive – he jumped out first.' She paused. 'Actually, now I think about it there must've been two of them in that car, coz he got out the side nearest the house…'

'The passenger side? Did you get a good look at him?' She'd obviously been watching out of the window, so I was hoping she had.

'Oh yeah, he reminded me of that footballer – you know, the one who was in that film—'

'Vinnie Jones?' suggested Nathan. She nodded.

'Yeah, that's him. Didn't look happy, either. Wouldn't want to meet him down a dark alley, you know what I mean?'

'I know exactly what you mean. This him?' I asked. I took out my phone and found the photograph of Maggie Mitchell's garden intruder, which Nathan had forwarded to everyone in the team, and held it up for her to look at.

'That's him! Looks like a right piece of work, doesn't he?'

'He certainly does. What did he do?'

'He got out and went over to the Toyota. The bloke inside looked like he was bricking it, to be honest. The first bloke tried to open the door, but it was locked. He banged on the window and told him to get out of the car.'

'And did he?'

'Not at first. The other one went round to the front of the car and leant on the windscreen – like this—' She held her arms out, her palms flat, and leant forward. 'He had his hands on the glass and he was leaning in, staring at him, saying he couldn't stay in there forever.'

'So he was pretty aggressive, then?' said Nathan. Why on earth hadn't she called the police?

'Yeah. I was just wondering if I should call you lot when Simon over at number twenty-four came out with his dog. He didn't say anything to them, just looked over, and then the big bloke laughed and said they were old friends and just larking about. And then the other one got out of the car and said it was fine, but it still looked a bit awkward to me.'

'Can you describe the Toyota driver?' asked Nathan.

'Hmm… I dunno, I was looking at the other one more. He had short, dark hair. Didn't get a good look at his face because he had sunglasses on, those big-mirrored ones. Looked like he thought he was a bit flash.' Stuart Mitchell had been wearing mirrored sunglasses the last time we'd seen him, and he definitely fancied himself.

'Okay… Then what happened?'

'Both of them went and got in the big bloke's car. I came out to tell them they couldn't leave the other one there because it's residents only parking, but they completely ignored me and drove off.' She looked from Nathan to me and back again. 'I was annoyed, but I was busy and I had to go out and I forgot about it, and then I was annoyed again when I got home and it was still in the space, but I had my kids with me then and I just got distracted. But now I'm thinking about it, it wasn't good. Do you think I should've called you lot then?'

YES!!! I wanted to say, but I didn't. Most of us have probably seen things that didn't seem quite right at the time, but not wanted or been confident enough to get involved. And what if we called the police and it was all an innocent mistake? No one likes making a fuss. Best to stay out of it… Unless you were the victim, of course.

'We're here now,' said Nathan. 'The car will have to stay there for the moment, I'm afraid, until I can get a crime team out to look at it.'

'Really?' She went from looking guilty to looking annoyed in about five seconds. 'But my bins—'

'We have reason to believe the man in the Toyota was taken against his will,' said Nathan.

'You mean he was kidnapped?' And now she looked shocked. 'Oh my God...'

'Your bins will have to go somewhere else,' I said.

PC McKenzie gave us a cheery wave as we drove off. We pulled out back onto Meddon Street and Nathan glanced over at me.

'So, what do you think?'

'Stuart Mitchell's in big trouble,' I said. He nodded. 'But he does still have at least one decent bone in his body.'

'What makes you say that?' Nathan sounded surprised.

'Look at what happened. Or what I *think* happened. He's finished up at the harbour and he's on his way to his mother-in-law's to lie low. But then he realises he's being followed by Big Boy and his mate.'

'They obviously think he's got the missing drugs with him, or can lead them to wherever they're hidden,' said Nathan.

'Yeah. But he doesn't know where they are; as far as he was concerned, Mick Tyler or Liam must've had them, but they're out of the picture and the drugs are still missing.' I paused as Nathan pulled over to let an oncoming car pass – it was a very narrow road, like many in this part of the country. 'He *could* try to lose them but he doesn't want to risk leading them to his family, so he pulls into the side street where they're bound to find him. He doesn't even try to run.'

'That makes sense,' agreed Nathan. 'He put his family first. Shame he didn't feel quite as paternalistic towards Liam.'

'Yeah… Anyway, when Big Boy – we have *got* to find out this bloke's name, I can't keep calling him that – when he comes over and bangs on the door, and starts attracting people's attention, Mitchell knows he has to go with him because the last thing he wants is for someone like the dog walker or Bin Woman to call the cops.'

'Because then everything comes out, and at the very least he's serving time for drug trafficking.'

'And at worst, for being an accessory after the fact for Mick Tyler's murder,' I said. 'Do you think Forensics will be able to get fingerprints off the car?'

Nathan shrugged. 'I don't know. It's definitely worth a try. Big Boy grabbed the door handle to get Mitchell out, but it'll be difficult to get prints off something that shape. Our best bet is the windscreen. And I'm not one to judge on appearances, but if that bloke doesn't have a criminal record I'll eat my hat.'

'You haven't got a hat.'

'All right, one of yours. The one with the bobble on it.'

We got back to the station and were immediately mobbed by Matt and Sunil. Nathan held up his hand to stop them both talking at once and led them over to his desk.

'I gather from all the excitement you've both come up with something?' I said. Sunil nodded.

'Yes,' said Matt. 'Lots, actually.'

'Okay. Hit me with it,' said Nathan. 'One at a time…'

'All of those phones seem to be turned off, just like you said, Guv,' said Sunil. 'But I was able to check where and when they were last on.' He pointed to the numbers on the murder board. 'We know about Tyler, obviously, and this other one – Phone B – has been off for ages, so we concentrated on the others. Phone C, which we believed was Liam's, last pinged on Monday night at 11.55pm, which is probably around the time of the attack. It's been turned off since then.'

'The attacker took it off him and left him for dead,' I said. Nathan nodded.

'Yeah, sounds like it. Sunil, you said "believed" it was Liam's phone…?' he asked. Matt grinned.

'We *believed* it before, but now we know it. The original warrant was for Tyler's burner and all associated numbers, so they had all the call records and account informationready, they were just waiting for us to ask for it,' he said. 'They didn't have much in the way of account information as all the phones were unregistered, paid for in cash. And all the credit top-ups were paid for in cash as well.' He paused. 'Except for one.'

'They used a credit card?' Nathan looked incredulous.

'Liam used his debit card to pay for a top-up. Maybe he was in a hurry and forgot, or he got to the till and realised he didn't have enough cash.'

'He's just a kid,' I said. 'He's not a criminal mastermind. He probably didn't realise that he was supposed to play it cloak-and-dagger.' I sighed. 'Silly sod, getting caught up in this.'

'Makes it easier for us, though,' said Nathan. He picked up a marker pen and wrote on the murder board under the phone numbers. *Phone C = Liam Fossett*. 'That only leaves Phone A, which I think we can assume is Mitchell's –' Nathan wrote on the board again, *Phone A = Stuart Mitchell '–* and Phone D – the killer's.' *Phone D = killer*.

'Big Boy,' I said. Matt and Sunil exchanged looks. 'Maggie Mitchell's intruder, who also appears to be

Stuart Mitchell's abductor. And yes, I know that's a terrible nickname.'

Sunil looked at his list of phone numbers. 'Phone D was last active yesterday afternoon...' I peered over his shoulder.

'That's about forty-five minutes before we spoke to Maggie Mitchell. Around the time her intruder was in the garden, on his phone.'

Nathan nodded, then rubbed out 'killer' and wrote, *Phone D = Big Boy/Thug*. I may have imagined it but I could've sworn that he cringed as he wrote 'Big Boy'.

'What about phone calls?' said Nathan. 'Did Liam get a phone call on Monday night, as Ryan said?'

'Yes, just before 10pm. From Phone A.'

'Stuart Mitchell rang him?'

'Yes. Mitchell made a phone call on Monday afternoon to another unidentified number – different network, so I'm still chasing that. They had quite a long conversation. That number called him back later for a much more brief chat, then Phone D—'

'Big Boy,' I said. Matt shook his head.

'Nope, I am *not* calling him that. The killer called him later that night, at 9.50pm. Then Mitchell called Liam, and called the killer back straight afterwards.'

'He was throwing Liam under the bus,' said Nathan.

'Yeah,' I said. 'Imagine you're Mitchell. Your client

has told you there's drugs missing from their shipment, so you give them the name of the boat skipper. Tyler. You hear the next day that Tyler's been murdered, which is a shock but at least that's the end of it. Only you don't hear from your client. Mitchell rings up the client to check they're good, and he tells him Tyler didn't have the drugs and Mitchell still owes him. So then he gives them the name of the other person who was supposed to be on that drug run. Only unbeknown to him, Liam wasn't on it.' I shook my head. 'You'd have to be pretty cold to hand over a kid like Liam, knowing that the last person you did that to ended up dead.'

'Yep,' said Nathan. 'Mitchell tells Liam he needs to meet him to discuss what happened to Tyler, Liam agrees, but when he gets there it's not Mitchell he's meeting, it's the killer.' We all paused for a moment, thinking about poor Liam in hospital. He might've made a big mistake working for and trusting Mitchell, but he was young, and he didn't deserve the beating he'd had.

'Anything from Mitchell's phone after Monday night?' I asked.

'Yeah. He made a call on Wednesday morning, at 11.05am.'

'That's just after we spoke to him,' I said to Nathan. 'Who was it to?'

'That unidentified number again.'

'He heard from us that Liam had been tortured and immediately called the client,' I said. 'He must've been hoping that no news was good news and it was all over, and then when he heard from us he rang them to find out what the hell was going on.'

'And they told him they were still waiting for him to come up with the drugs,' said Nathan. 'So he rang his wife and told her to leave town. They were going into hiding until he could work out what had happened.'

'He had no other names to give them,' said Matt.

'Mitchell's phone last pinged at twenty-five past eleven yesterday,' said Sunil. 'In Bideford, where you found the car. And it's been turned off ever since.'

'Bugger,' I said. 'So we can't trace any of them? What about Glen?'

'His registered phone last pinged on Saturday afternoon, on the A303 at Sparkford, near Wincanton,' said Sunil. 'And then his new burner phone was activated at the same spot. I think he stopped at the services at Sparkford and bought the new phone before turning off his old one.'

'And then the burner got turned off too?'

'Well… I'm not sure. It pinged at Sparkford, then near Wincanton. Then nothing for a whole day, then it pinged again near Wincanton on Wednesday, then nothing until this morning, presumably when he called his sister.'

'Maybe he didn't turn it off,' said Nathan. 'He thought that if anyone was trying to track him, they'd be looking for his registered phone, hence buying the burner. He could just have been out of range.'

I nodded. 'Somerset's like Cornwall – some parts of it are very rural. Mobile phone coverage is probably pretty patchy outside of the main towns. He must've been staying somewhere without a signal, and then gone into Wincanton for something. Where was he this morning?'

'Wilton, on the outskirts of Salisbury.'

'Salisbury?' I said. 'There's a massive Army base in Salisbury, isn't there?'

'Yes,' said Nathan. 'Is that where he was based?'

'No idea, but it makes sense that he might have friends in the area. Do we have his call records?'

'Not yet,' said Matt. 'I had to get a new warrant and that, but I told them it was urgent so hopefully we'll have them in the morning.'

'Wherever Glen Falconer is now, we need to find him before anyone else does...'

Chapter Eighteen

I t was late in the afternoon by now. Trawling Glen's social media and contacting his old regiment could be done from home, so we headed back to see how things were going with the builders and whether they'd had any more harassment from the dog. Or from Mum.

To my relief they'd spent the day without any incident. I took off my shoes the minute I was through the door – I normally live in jeans and trainers, so going a few days having to look smart and wear proper shoes felt like punishment – and sighed gratefully as I popped my slippers on. I groaned.

'Oh my God, that feels so good,' I said. 'Is it really sad that I've been looking forward to putting my slippers on for the last two hours?'

'No, of course not,' said Nathan, grinning and nodding his head.

'This is what happens when you go out with an older woman.'

'Mum, is that you?' Daisy called from the kitchen.

'No, it's burglars,' I said. She stuck her head round the door.

'Did you get my tail?'

'What tail?' Germaine chose that moment to rush up to me, yapping excitedly and wagging her own tail. 'Get down, sweetheart, let me get in the door first. Daisy, what are you talking about?'

'You've forgotten, haven't you?'

'I don't know what you're talking about, so yeah, looks like it…'

Daisy sighed. 'You said you'd go to Holsworthy to pick up the rest of my costume.' I slapped myself on the forehead. Tomorrow – unbelievably – was Friday and the last day of Merrymaid Week already. It was amazing how fast a murder investigation could make time fly. It would be carnival night, culminating in a big firework display and a contest for best mermaid costume. I obviously wouldn't be entering with my terrible, ugly (and somewhat slutty) mermaid outfit from Monday, which I'd ripped as I'd taken off, but Daisy had been working on something which she described as a 'Gothic feminist reimagining of the Siren myth' (her words, not mine). The tail had proved too tricky for her to sew herself, so the mother of one of her school friends, who lived out near Holsworthy, had agreed to make it for her. I groaned again, not in podiatric pleasure this time.

'Oh sweetheart, I'm so sorry, I *did* forget. We've been so busy...'

'It's the holidays,' said Nathan. 'You've been around all day, couldn't you have got the bus there?'

Daisy rolled her eyes. 'What, you think this is Liverpool or somewhere?' Nathan was actually from Crosby, which he described geographically as 'Liverpool on Sea'. I loved his accent, although he did his best to downplay it when he was working, and we only really heard him in his full Scouse glory when he was overexcited or a bit tipsy. 'We don't have *buses* here! Honestly.'

Nathan held his hands up. 'Pardon me for suggesting such a thing.'

'Actually there *is* a bus, three times a day, which you could've got if you'd got out of bed early enough,' I pointed out. I did feel bad, because she'd always been able to rely on me, but at the same time she was at an age now where there were things she could do herself. I'd been happy to run around after her ever since we'd moved to Penstowan, probably over-compensating for the times in London when she'd had to go to a child minder, or I'd had to work a late shift and not tucked her up for the night, or her useless father had failed to turn up to see her yet again; but I couldn't do that *and* run a business *and* be a part-time copper. I couldn't do everything. Oh great, there was that guilt again. 'Anyway,' I said, trying to control it, 'if you'd rung and reminded me I'd either have found the time, or paid Magda to go and pick it up for you in her taxi.'

'I never used to have to remind you,' she said, looking a bit pouty.

'It'll have to wait until tomorrow now,' I said, but Nathan cleared his throat.

'Um, we might have a trip to Salisbury on the cards, depending on what we find out this evening,' he said.

'And I need it tonight, because I've got to sew it onto the rest of the costume...'

'Bloody hell!' I snapped, and then regretted it, because it wasn't Daisy's fault, or Nathan's, or even mine really when you got down to it; it was just one of those things. And it had been my choice to move somewhere without much in the way of public transport or nearby amenities, other than the shops and cafes on Fore Street. I sighed and took my slippers off. It wasn't as if it was even that far, only about twenty minutes each way. 'Fine, let's go and get it now before I sit down, or I won't get up again. You can come with me and just dive into your friend's house and get it, okay?' Daisy nodded, then went off to text her friend to tell her we were on our way. Nathan slipped his arms around me and gave me a kiss on the forehead.

'And breathe…'

'Sorry.' I took a deep breath as instructed, but it didn't stop me feeling tired. And I still had to cook dinner and then look into Glen's possible whereabouts when I got back.

'I'll order a takeaway,' said Nathan. So that was one less thing on the To Do list…

By the time I'd driven Daisy to Holsworthy and back, changed into my lounging-around clothes and tucked into takeaway pizza (which was nice enough, but not as nice as my homemade ones, I thought), I finally started to unwind. And then nod off.

Nathan nudged me. 'Uh oh, no you don't! We've got work to do.'

'Fine,' I said, dragging myself upright. 'In that case I'm going to need tea. Lots of tea…'

We set ourselves up in the kitchen. Mum was in the living room, watching her soaps, while Daisy had taken herself upstairs to finish her costume. Apart from mentioning the whole 'Gothic feminist' idea behind it, she'd been very secretive about this costume. Part of me dreaded to think what she had come up with, and hoped I wouldn't have to stop her actually leaving the house in it.

'Okay,' I said, logging into my laptop. 'What are we looking at first? Social media?'

'Yeah,' said Nathan. 'If he spent time away from the rest of the family while he was in the army, chances are he'll have a Facebook account or something, just to keep in touch with them. And maybe call Nina, see if she can tell you what regiment he was in.'

'No need,' I said, turning the screen to face him. I'd already found Glen's Facebook page, and his cover photo showed a regimental badge.

'That was easy,' said Nathan.

'About time *something* about this case was,' I said. 'I'd rather not call Nina again about any of this, if we can avoid it. The next time I talk to her I want it to be with good news.'

'Fair enough. I'll look up the regiment, you stay on there and see if he talks to any of his old army buddies.'

I trawled through Glen's posts. They were all either family photos and get-togethers, or stuff to do with the army; memories of postings abroad, with Glen posing in his uniform next to armoured cars and tanks. I remembered Nina saying he'd been a mechanic; these were obviously the sort of vehicles he'd worked on.

Fixing tired old fishing boats down at the harbour must've been a bit of a comedown for him.

I changed tack, clicking on the Photos tab, and scrolled through all the photos that he'd been tagged in. Lots of him overseas, more armoured vehicles, then lots of him and a nice-looking blonde woman, who I assumed was his ex, smiling happily at the camera. More recent ones of him with Nina and her husband and kids, and one last selfie of him and his ex standing on the South Coast path, the sea in the background.

I stopped. There was a whole thread of photographs here, of Glen with another man who looked to be similar in age, maybe slightly older. Like Glen, he was well built, with short, neat hair, greying at the sides. The way he stood up straight, almost to attention, even though he was clearly off duty and smiling – everything about him screamed 'army', or maybe ex-army.

'Here, Nath,' I said. Nathan looked up from his own computer.

'You found something?'

'Yeah…' He pulled his chair closer so he could see my screen. 'These photos here were posted by a David Sinclair, a few months ago.' There was a picture of Glen, standing in front of an impressive, well-looked-after castle next to a river. 'This is Longford Castle. And then this one…' This one was a selfie of the two men, arms round each other's shoulders in a blokey embrace, with some kind of ancient raised earthworks curving behind them. I hadn't been able to work out the location from either the photo or the comment that came with it, but luckily the next photo was of Glen standing next to a National Trust sign, pointing to it. 'This is Figsbury Ring. Guess where they're near?'

'Salisbury?'

'Yep. Last one. Glen and David having a beer and a barbie in David's garden, all taken over the same weekend.'

'So Sinclair must live near Salisbury? Near enough for a day trip to these places?'

'Yep. And Glen's been there before, so…'

'So he could feasibly have gone there again. Do we know who David Sinclair is to him?'

'Looks ex-army to me,' I said, turning the laptop back to me and clicking on the thread. It took me to Sinclair's own page. I clicked on the 'About' tab, then on 'Work and Education'. 'Here we go. Same regiment as Glen.'

'Bingo!' said Nathan. 'And that's the area his phone was in, last time it pinged. We need to get Sinclair's address and pay him a visit.'

I clicked on another photograph on Sinclair's page. 'Easy peasy. He seems to be very proud of his car, and there are lots of photos of it. All we have to do is run the plate.'

'Nice work.' Nathan shut his laptop, then reached out to close mine. 'That's enough for today. Now, what were you saying earlier about me being dreamy…?'

We set out early the next morning. Matt, who had stayed behind in the office the evening before, supposedly to catch up on some paperwork (I say supposedly, as we'd seen Chrissie clocking in for the evening shift as we'd left), had run David Sinclair's number plate and given us an address in Old Sarum, a pretty-looking village on the outskirts of Salisbury. It was a good hundred and fifty miles away and would take us the best part of three hours to get there, but if Glen was hiding there, and if he could tell us what the hell was going on with Stuart Mitchell, it would be worth it.

'Looks like a nice place,' I said, Googling it on my phone as Nathan drove out of Penstowan, heading along the country roads that would lead to the A30. 'Apparently there's an Iron Age fort with ramparts, traces of a Norman cathedral, interpretative panels and a gift shop.'

'I do love a good interpretative panel and a gift shop,' said Nathan, and I laughed.

'What actually is an interpretative panel?'

'I don't know. I suppose it depends on what your interpretation is…'

We listened to the radio as we drove – a perk of using one of our own cars for work, rather than a patrol vehicle – tuned in to one of those greatest hits stations that seems to only have about fifty songs on constant rotation; listen long enough, and you were sure to hear the same ones all over again. But just because it was work (and we were going to be in the car long enough to hear several of those songs more than once), it didn't mean we couldn't enjoy the road trip together. Nathan sang along to 'Single Ladies', and I wasn't sure whether to be impressed or worried that he knew all the words. He wouldn't be putting Beyoncé out of a job any time soon, though.

I'd driven this stretch of road many times when I'd lived in London, heading down to visit my parents; first on my own, and later with Daisy, but never with Richard, my useless waste-of-space ex. He'd always found some excuse not to come with us. I think at first it was just that he didn't want to spend the weekend with his in-laws in the armpit of nowhere (which was what he'd christened Penstowan after seeing where it was on the map), but later on it gave him the perfect opportunity to cheat on me. I shouldn't have been surprised – when I'd first started seeing him he'd been married to someone else, although I hadn't found that out until I was deep into a relationship with him – but I was. And then all the excuses, all the times he'd had to 'work late', or he couldn't swap shifts and come away with us, they all started to add up. I glanced across at Nathan, who was currently exhorting me to put a ring on it, if I liked it, and smiled. I trusted him, with my life, with my family, and with my heart. The thought of Nathan cheating on me caused me actual physical pain, but at the same time I just knew he wouldn't. Happy people don't cheat, do they? And I knew he was happy.

'Uh uh oh, oh oh oh…' Nathan saw me watching him and stopped singing. 'What? Did I miss out an "uh" or something?'

I laughed. 'On the contrary, I'm very impressed with your knowledge of Destiny's Child lyrics.'

'It's Beyoncé, actually, and if I wasn't driving I'd be doing the dance routine, too.'

'Thank God you're driving, then.'

We got to Sparkford and drove into the services, which consisted of a petrol station and car wash, with a shop attached. Across the car park was a fast food restaurant. We got out and went into the shop, looking around. I nudged Nathan and pointed to the area behind the cash register.

'Look,' I said. 'They don't sell phones, but they do sell pay-as-you-go SIM cards.'

'Glen could've bought one and swapped it with the one in his old phone.'

'Yup. Is it worth asking the cashier if they saw him?'

Nathan shrugged. 'Worth a try, but it was a Saturday afternoon during the holiday season, so they would probably have been busy.'

I approached the cashier and held up my warrant card. 'Hi, can you help me? We're trying to trace this man and we think he came in here on Saturday. Just wondered if you recognised him?' I showed her Glen's Facebook profile photo. She studied it carefully, then nodded slowly.

'Yeah… I think that was him. Big bloke. Looked like an army type. We get lots of them in here, often in uniform…' Her eyes glowed at the thought of it, and I smiled.

'There's something about a uniform, am I right?' I said, and she snorted.

'Not all uniforms. The blokes who work over at Maccy's don't do anything for me,' she said, nodding towards the fast food restaurant. I laughed.

'No, it's not quite the same, is it? Although they can

give you free burgers... So did you talk to this bloke? Did he say where he was going?'

'No, he seemed to be in a bit of a hurry.' She grinned ruefully. 'I did my best but he wasn't interested.'

'His loss,' I said. 'Do you remember what he bought?'

'No, sorry. He kept looking out at his car, though, like he was worried about someone nicking it.'

'Do you have CCTV out on the forecourt?' Nathan asked, stepping forward.

'Yeah, to stop driveaways,' she said.

'Can we see it?'

'I don't have access to it. I could call the manager, see if he'll come in early? He's due in at twelve.'

Nathan and I exchanged looks, weighing up whether we should hang around and wait for the CCTV or just press on in the hope of finding Glen.

'No, don't worry about it,' said Nathan. 'We'll be in later if we need it.'

We got back on the road, after popping into the fast food restaurant for an egg and bacon breakfast muffin – we'd left home without having breakfast, intending to stop somewhere en route, and the smell of bacon, burgers and fries was too much to resist.

'So what's the plan when we get to Sinclair's?' I asked, crumpling the wrapper. The muffin hadn't lasted long. Nathan swallowed the last of his and turned the radio down, silencing the Bee Gees, which was, indeed, a tragedy.

'I think it's best to play it by ear,' he said. 'We'll knock and ask to speak to Glen, like we know he's there, and see what happens.'

'We need him to come back with us,' I said.

'Yeah, if he's still there. He might've moved on by now.'

'What do we do if he has?'

'At this point, no idea.' Nathan smiled grimly. 'Let's just hope he's there.'

We reached one of the (many and slightly confusing) roundabouts on the A36 ring road around Salisbury itself, then turned off onto the A345. We headed up the road towards the old castle and the Old Sarum fort. On our left there was a sports ground and open fields, on our right a row of houses, mostly big detached 1930s houses with the odd pair of semis peppered here and there.

'That one!' I said, pointing. David Sinclair's house was a well-kept semi-detached house, set quite a way back from the road, with a long driveway that led past the house to a garage. The front garden was mostly paved over, but with neatly trimmed topiary box balls in pots to mark out the driveway, and either side of the front door. It looked like the garden of someone who wasn't really into flowers, but liked things to look smart.

It reminded me of Glen's own very neat, everything-in-its-place home.

'No car on the driveway,' said Nathan.

'Might be in the garage,' I said. 'If Glen realises he needs to hide, he might be hiding his car in there.'

'Or they might be out...'

We parked on the road and walked up the driveway. Nathan knocked on the door. I half expected no one to answer, but almost immediately a shape appeared behind the rippled glass panel of the front door, approaching until the door opened and resolving itself into the tanned, well-built form of David Sinclair. He smiled at us in a friendly but somewhat reserved way.

'Oh, hello. Sorry, I told your lot before, no offence but I'm not interested—' He stopped as he clocked our puzzled expressions. 'You're Jehovah's Witnesses, right?'

I snorted. Nathan held up his warrant card. 'Not quite. David Sinclair? Is Glen Falconer here? We'd like to talk to him.'

'So would I,' said Sinclair. He stood back and opened the door wider. 'He's not here. You'd better come in.'

Chapter Nineteen

We sat in Sinclair's living room. It felt very masculine, all leather sofas, black furniture, and hard lines. A few books, mostly non-fiction by the looks of it, sat on shelves, arranged by size. A large, framed black and white photograph of New York above the fireplace was the only decorative touch.

The rest of the house was pretty much the same. I'd asked to use the bathroom when we'd first entered, primarily because I needed a pee but also so I could have a nosey round the bedrooms and make sure Glen really wasn't staying there. Two of the bedrooms were a good size, the third little more than a box room containing a desk. One bedroom was sparsely furnished, containing exercise equipment and a sofa bed, while the main bedroom had grey curtains and a grey duvet cover on the neatly made large double bed. In the bathroom there was a surprising array of skin care products and shaving things, but only one razor, and one toothbrush; no sign of a guest.

Sinclair handed us both mugs of tea, then returned with his own and sat in an armchair opposite us.

'I'm happy to talk about Glen,' he said, 'but I'm not sure how I can help you.'

'How do you know him?' asked Nathan. 'Army comrades?'

'Yeah. We were in the same regiment until he got injured and left.'

'What happened?' Nina had mentioned he was invalided out, but Glen had seemed fit and healthy enough to me on the few occasions I'd seen him since.

'Our regiment's served in Afghanistan, Iraq, Somalia – not always combat roles, but they're dangerous places at the best of times,' said Sinclair. 'He came through it all without a scratch. Then we get back home, some of the lads decide to have a kickabout, Glen goes in for a tackle and ends up tearing his cruciate ligament.'

'Ouch!' I said. 'I've heard of professional footballers doing that. It can be career-ending, can't it?'

'Yeah, sometimes. Glen was on crutches for six months, but it never really healed properly, so there was no way he could go back to active service. In the meantime, I'd decided it was time to slow down a bit – I'm a few years older than him – and I got a posting out here as an instructor.' He gestured vaguely out of the window. 'The army reserves are based just over there. I suggested Glen do the same, but I think Helen – his ex – she'd had enough of being an army girlfriend and persuaded him to leave completely.'

'And then they split up,' I said. He nodded.

'Yeah. Poor sod, his whole life changed over the course of a few months.'

'How did he cope? Did he talk to you about it?'

'Yeah, eventually. I think he struggled with being a civilian at first, but he came to stay with me about three months ago and he seemed to be doing all right.' He looked at me, then at Nathan. 'But now it seems maybe he wasn't?'

'That's what we're trying to find out,' said Nathan. 'When was the last time you spoke to him?'

'He rang me on Saturday night, said he was going to be in the area and could he come and stay at mine for a bit.'

'Did he say why?'

'I didn't actually talk to him, he left me a voicemail. I was away training with the reserves and I didn't get back until yesterday. We were up in the Highlands, and I didn't have a phone signal for most of the trip.' He stared down into his tea, musing. 'He sounded stressed out, though. Like he was trying to sound all nonchalant, but underneath he was panicking a bit.'

'What would he be panicking about?' asked Nathan.

'No idea. Like I said, he seemed fine last time I saw him. But if he was in trouble, I like to think he knows he can talk to me. I think he needed help, not just a place to stay.'

Nathan and I exchanged glances.

'Is there anyone else he would contact, if you weren't around?' I asked.

'No one I know of. We're not exactly encouraged to be touchy-feely in our game. I know he's quite close to his sister…?'

'We'll be sure to talk to her,' said Nathan, although of course we already had. His phone rang, and he checked it. 'Sorry, I have to take this. DS Parker?' He gestured for me to follow, and we headed out into the hallway, shutting the door behind us. 'Go ahead, Matt. You're on speakerphone, Jodie's here too.'

'The call records for both of Glen Falconer's phones just came through,' said Matt. 'He used the burner phone to call Nina, while you were there, Jodie. Straight after that he sent a text message to Stuart Mitchell's burner. Listen to this: "If it's about the Molly, we should talk."'

'"Molly"?' I said. 'You know what that's slang for.'

'Yeah. MDMA. Looks like we were right about the drugs,' said Nathan. I felt my heart sink. I didn't like to think of Nina's little brother, or Liam Fossett, being involved in something like that. 'Did Glen get a response to his text message?'

'No, Mitchell's phone was turned off by then, and it's been off ever since,' said Matt. 'Which is why we've only just learnt about the text now. But Sunil's also been keeping an eye on Glen's location, and his phone has pinged again, once this morning near Wincanton again, and about fifteen minutes ago near Crewkerne.'

'Crewkerne? He's heading west, then,' I said. Nathan nodded.

'Matt, I think we're pretty much done here, so we'll be back about two, half past. Keep checking those records, and keep an eye on Glen's location.' He hung up and looked at me. 'What do you reckon to that, then? "We should talk"?'

'He's planning to hand the drugs back,' I said. 'In Penstowan?'

'Sounds like it, if he really is heading west,' said Nathan. 'The text message suggests he wants rid of whatever he's got now, and in the absence of a reply where else would you go?'

'Back to the scene of the crime,' I said. 'He's probably sticking to all the back roads so he's still out of mobile range most of the time, but he'll have to follow the A30 at some point, and then we'll know for certain where he's heading.'

'Is everything okay?' Sinclair had followed us out into hallway. Nathan frowned and turned to look at him.

'Does the word "Molly" mean anything to you?' he asked.

'Not really. Other than the obvious, that it's a girl's name,' said Sinclair carefully; it was clear he knew the slang term. 'Should it?'

'Being somewhere like Afghanistan, or Somalia, it must be pretty stressful,' said Nathan.

Sinclair shrugged. 'It can be, yes. But it helps being part of a team.'

'Did Glen ever get stressed? What did he do to relax, or to let his hair down?'

Sinclair stared at us. 'What exactly are you asking me, DCI Withers? If Glen or I took drugs?' Nathan didn't answer but held his gaze steadily. Sinclair scoffed.

'Are you serious?' He looked at Nathan with an incredulous expression. 'Do you know how much shit would hit the fan if someone on active service got caught taking drugs? Even when they were off duty? They'd be a danger to the whole base, not just to themselves.'

'They'd get the book thrown at them,' I suggested.

'Not just the book, the whole bloody library. The lads

might have a few beers to wind down, but I really mean a few – anything more was unsafe. We learnt that the hard way.'

'What do you mean?' I asked, glancing at Nathan. Sinclair sighed heavily.

'In Afghanistan, there were a couple of journalists embedded with the regiment. They'd been out there on and off for ages, during the fighting, so they should've known better, but I suppose they got careless because "the war" was supposedly over. They liked to party, but they decided that alcohol wasn't enough.'

'They took drugs? Where did they get them from?'

'Wherever there's an army base in a foreign country – I mean a *real* foreign country, somewhere with a different culture as well as a different language – there's always a group of locals trying to make money out of the troops, selling stuff from back home, telling you they can get you nice girls, alcohol, porn videos, you name it. And drugs, of course.' He shook his head. 'These journalists started buying coke off one of them, just a little bit here and there to start off with, but then they started asking questions, about where it had come from, who was growing it, that sort of thing. Glen was sweet on one of them – this was before he met Helen – and she told him that with the fighting over, they were having to find other things to report on. They were going to do a story on whether or not the troops should even still be there, and what effect we were having on the local community. Were we encouraging the drug trade just by being there to buy their wares? Although that was nonsense, of course, because it was her and her cameraman who were buying it. Anyway… We heard rumours that the local drug lord wasn't very happy with them, but they weren't worried, although they should've been. I think the coke made them feel invincible. And besides that they were always with a bunch of heavily armed soldiers, so who was going to stop them? Except of course they went out one day without us, and we never saw them again.'

'What? What happened?'

'We know that a group of men forced them into a car and drove off, because a local kid who used to come and get sweets off us ran to the base and told us. A team of us went out looking for them. But we followed the trail into a dangerous part of town, and it felt to me like the kidnappers were using them as bait, trying to lure us into an ambush. So we left, and by the time we went back with reinforcements there was no sign of them. We all felt bad about it, but it was their own fault. Glen was pretty upset.'

'Not someone you'd expect to get involved with drugs, then,' I said.

'No, God, the last person. He's a health nut apart

from anything else. He wouldn't put that rubbish into his body.'

'The question,' said Nathan quietly as we left David Sinclair on his doorstep, 'is whether Glen would help sell "that rubbish" to other people...'

―――――――

We hit the road and headed back towards Penstowan. I felt discouraged. It seemed pretty certain now that the little boy I remembered from my play dates with Nina had grown into a drug smuggler, even though it didn't fit with what I knew of him (which wasn't much – we hadn't been *that* close as kids, and I'd seen little of him since both of us had returned to Penstowan). And Liam Fossett; again, I didn't know him that well, but I'd been close to his mum once and it just didn't seem right to me that a child of hers would be involved in something like that. But that didn't necessarily follow, did it? I'd never subscribed to the old 'I blame the parents' myth. I'd got up to all sorts that my mum and dad hadn't known about and probably wouldn't have approved of. But... Most of us get our moral compass from our parents. The things I'd done that mine wouldn't have approved of were *little* things. I *might* have shoplifted a pair of earrings from Top Shop in Truro once when I was a teenager, just for a laugh and a rush of excitement, but I'd never killed anyone. I'd never done anything that would actually *hurt* someone, or potentially cause them harm. And I was pretty certain that Daisy would follow my lead; maybe the odd minor indiscretion (which I'd better not find out about!), but she knew right from wrong, and she knew there was a line that you didn't cross. I would have bet that the Fossetts had pretty much the same line as I did, and I was surprised (or still in denial) that Liam apparently had crossed it, not just once but on a regular basis.

'You're quiet,' said Nathan. 'You okay?'

'Yeah, just thinking… You think you know people, and then they behave in a way that makes you realise you don't.'

'Glen? How well do you actually know him, though? I know you and Nina were pretty close, but he's been away in the army for years. He's not the little boy you remember.'

I smiled in spite of myself. Trust Nathan to know pretty much exactly what was going through my mind. 'I know. I suppose I'm just disappointed. I thought better of him. And the Fossetts will be gutted when they find out that Liam's involved in drug smuggling.'

'Yeah. And it's not like it's just a bit of weed or something—'

I looked at him in mock surprise. 'DCI Withers, I didn't realise you had such a liberal attitude towards smoking pot!' He laughed.

'It's not so much liberal as pragmatic. You know as well as I do that a lot of people grow it round here. They tend to be too relaxed to cause trouble. Closing time on a Saturday outside the Market Arms, now, that's a different story.'

'Tell me about it,' I said. 'I used to *hate* doing the weekend night shift when I was in uniform. I'd spend half the time hosing sick off my shoes or the back of the van. Drunken stag and hen nights were just the worst.'

'Yep. Yet alcohol's legal, and it's still totally acceptable to be plastered in public, isn't it? It's the cause of so many fights, and so many accidents.'

'Criminalise alcohol and legalise cannabis, I reckon,' I said. He snorted.

'It would make our lives easier, wouldn't it? MDMA, though – that's something else. I know loads of people take it every weekend and they're fine, but you never really know what you're taking. If Mitchell's importing MDMA or ecstasy there's no telling what's actually in it.'

'No...' Nathan was right, of course; all the signs pointed to drug smuggling, and it had been me who had initially come up with that scenario, but this was one time where I actually wanted to be wrong. I came out of my reverie as we pulled back into the service station we'd visited earlier.

The same cashier was behind the counter. She smiled as we made our way over.

'Back again?' she said.

'Yeah. If your manager's in we'll have a look at that CCTV, if you don't mind…'

We crowded into the manager's office, which was the size of a broom cupboard. The manager, Dave, a young man in his late twenties suffering from premature balding and bad breath, tapped into his computer and pulled up the footage from the previous Saturday afternoon.

'Shall I leave you to it?' he asked, having studied our warrant cards closely first. 'It's a bit tight in here.'

'Yes, that might be best,' agreed Nathan. I didn't speak, as I was trying not to breathe too heavily. Dave disappeared, shutting the door behind him, and I relaxed.

'Dave's been on the cheese and onion crisps,' I said, waving a hand in front of my nose to disperse the lingering scent of halitosis.

We scrolled through the footage until we spotted Glen's car, an ancient Land Rover of the sort very popular amongst the local farmers, which would've rendered it almost invisible in the rural backwaters of

Cornwall and Somerset even if we'd known to look for it there. It pulled up on the forecourt. Glen got out, stretched, and then started to fill the car with diesel. The fuel cap was on the driver's side, next to the pump, and the CCTV, which was only interested in making sure no one drove off without paying, gave us a view of that side of the car and its number plate. Glen looked in the car a few times as he filled it up, no doubt making sure that his precious cargo – someone else's drugs – was still there.

He went inside the shop. The footage from the interior camera showed nothing unusual, just another customer leaving before Glen entered. Glen glanced outside, again towards the car, then headed for the counter. At the till he stopped and chatted with the cashier as she took his money. He was about to turn away, when as an afterthought he stopped. With another glance out of the window, he turned back and gestured to the mobile phone SIM cards hanging behind the till.

'Just as we thought,' I said. 'This is where he got his new SIM card.'

'Yeah.' We carried on studying the footage, but there was nothing of note. Glen simply paid and left. We switched back to the forecourt camera as he got in and, after a moment, drove away.

'Wait!' I said, as Nathan reached out to stop the footage. 'Go back a bit … just as he drives away he's caught by the other forecourt camera... There!' I tapped the screen and Nathan paused the footage. The Land Rover was fully in shot now, although still at an angle. It was hard to see through the windscreen, but just as it turned there was a slightly clearer view through the passenger side window. 'Is that someone with him?'

On TV cop shows – specifically the ones I mentioned earlier, with the magical fingerprint databases and the fancy glass/digital murder boards – they always manage to zoom in on CCTV footage. It never goes blurry, which is what happens nine and a half times out of ten in real life when you blow up an image, and if it does they just say to the technical wizard beside them, 'Sharpen that up.' And hey presto, all becomes clear, the murderer is unveiled and the case is closed.

Nope. That doesn't happen, and it didn't here. All we could do was lean in closer to the screen, our noses almost touching the glass (which is daft because you can't focus when you're that close to an object). All we got for our pains was what *might* have been a dark, shadowy figure in the dark, shadowy interior of the Land Rover. But then it might not have been.

'I don't know,' said Nathan, clearly frustrated. 'It does kind of look like it might be a person, but then it could just be the seat back and head rest. It's too dark, and the sun reflecting off the window doesn't help.'

'If there was someone in the car with him, that might explain why he keeps glancing over at it,' I said. 'It might even explain why he changed his phone. Maybe they forced him into taking the drugs and going on the run, and took his phone away to stop him contacting anyone.'

'Except we only have him buying a SIM card, not another phone,' said Nathan.

'True. But...' I stopped. 'No, actually, I've got nothing.'

'No outlandish theory? That makes a change.'

'Don't worry, we've got a two-hour drive from here back to Penstowan. Plenty of time for me to come up with something. And for you to talk me out of it...'

Chapter Twenty

B ut I couldn't come up with anything, despite wracking my brains for much of the drive back to Penstowan. It probably didn't help that the greatest hits station we were listening to was having an ABBA hour, and that despite not being ABBA fans Nathan and I both knew all the words and couldn't stop ourselves singing along (badly).

We arrived back at the station just as 'Dancing Queen' came on. I was about to suggest we sit in the car and wait for it to finish, but I was surprised to see the usually half-empty car park full of people, gathered around a police dog van, none of whom I thought would appreciate our karaoke efforts. Matt, who was talking to the dog handler, looked up and hurried over as we parked and got out.

'What's going on?' I asked. Chrissie joined us.

'Matt told me about the text message Glen Falconer sent,' she said. 'About "the Molly". I know you all assumed that meant ecstasy, but it rang a different bell for me.' She handed Nathan a piece of paper. 'Remember I got a list off the harbour master, of all the boats registered to Stuart Mitchell? Look at the fifth one down.'

I peered over Nathan's shoulder as he studied it. 'The Molly Malone…'

'He was talking about the *boat*, not its cargo,' said Nathan.

'It fits the vague description Walter Finch gave,' said Matt. 'It's bigger than some of the other boats, and it's got room below deck so the crew have somewhere to sleep if they stay out all night.'

'And the dog…?'

'I thought, now we know which boat they've been using, it would be a good idea to get the sniffer dog in. If they really have been bringing in drugs there should still be enough of a residue there for the dog to pick up the scent.' Matt looked pleased with himself. Nathan nodded, impressed.

'Good thinking. Have they been down to the boat yet?'

'No Guv, not yet. We were just about to head down there.'

I'd always loved watching the dogs do their thing. I'd been involved in a long-drawn-out chase once back in London, when a bloke had mugged someone and then took off, not knowing that a colleague and I had been sitting in a patrol car just round the corner. He'd taken one look at us and stopped guiltily, still holding the woman's bag and an evil-looking carving knife, then dived into the labyrinthine passages of a nearby housing estate. We'd jumped out of the car and given chase, my colleague talking into his radio, calling for back-up as I raced ahead. I'd slowed as we approached a dead end, waiting for him to catch up; you don't want to corner a desperate person holding a knife, not when the only way out is through you. But when we entered the dead end, it was empty.

The dog unit had been called – we couldn't have an armed assailant running around the estate – and within minutes the dog (who was called Colin for some reason, and it really didn't suit him) had found him, stuck in a large drainage pipe that led under a nearby playground. He'd obviously thought he could hide there until we left, or maybe he'd intended to crawl through it and hopefully come out the other end, but Colin had barked loudly and when he *still* refused to come out, had slithered down there, grabbed him by the trouser leg and pulled him out. Good old Colin.

This dog was called Lizzie, and she was a pro. Her handler, Anna, proudly told us abouta big drug bust they'd helped uncover a couple of months back – it had made the news, and Lizzie had appeared on *Spotlight* (the regional TV news programme) in their cutesy 'and finally' section at the end of the show. We watched as Anna led Lizzie onto the boat, and then escorted her around, encouraging her to stick her snout into every nook and cranny. They were very thorough, Anna making her do it twice, but at the end of it, Lizzie hadn't barked once.

Anna approached us, patting the dog and making a fuss of her. 'Nothing.'

'No trace of drugs? Not even any residue?'

'No, sorry.'

'The drugs would've been on here last week – is that too long?'

'It doesn't help, nor does the fact it smells of fish round here—' Anna wrinkled her nose. 'But if they were regularly bringing stuff in you'd expect there to be *something* left behind, and she would've picked it up, if it was there.'

'*If* it was there,' I said, looking at Nathan. 'I told you, maybe this isn't about drugs after all.'

'I'm starting to think you might be right,' he said.

We thanked Anna (and Lizzie) and watched her load

the dog into the back of the van, then climbed onto the boat ourselves; grateful that, as one of the bigger boats in the harbour, it was moored in a deeper part of the bay and was accessible from the quayside, and not one of the smaller ones that had been left adrift at low tide, leaning drunkenly to one side in the mud.

'Eww,' I said, holding my nose. 'She wasn't wrong, it really does smell of fish. That poor dog's nose must've been in overdrive.'

Nathan's foot nudged a coil of rope connected to a large net and he grimaced. 'Yeah. Even if they're using it to bring in – whatever it is they're bringing in – they must use it in between for fishing. It would make sense if Tyler and his crew were only going out once every three or four weeks.'

'Yes.' I stopped at the steps that led down to the room below deck. 'Shall we?'

We went down the short flight of narrow steps, ducking to get through the low doorway that protected whatever was down there from the elements. And there in front of us was … nothing. Well, not quite nothing; a tiny galley kitchen to one side, which looked like it hadn't been used for ages – there wasn't even a kettle and a couple of mugs for the crew to make tea. The rest of the space, which was bigger than I'd imagined but low-ceilinged, was empty, save for a couple of unappealing and slightly soiled mattresses, and a pile of blankets.

'Niiice…' I said, unable to keep the disgust from my voice. 'You know those true crime serial killer documentaries on Netflix? I think this might be one of them.' Nathan laughed.

'Yeah, I think you'd have to be *really* tired to sleep down here. But then how long do these boats stay out for? Even if they're out overnight, the crew wouldn't need to sleep, would they? It would just be akin to doing a night shift. They'd sleep back at home during the day.'

'They probably shove the drugs, or not-drugs or whatever, down here while they make their way back from the pick-up point,' I said.

'And then they head to Kevrinva Bay, where they meet up with someone on shore who takes the cargo off them.' Nathan looked thoughtful. 'How would they get to the beach from the boat? Could they wade through the water?'

'Maybe. It depends on the tide, I suppose – not sure how close they could get the boat at low tide, but then at high tide it might be too deep to wade to the shore and back. Especially at night, possibly with their hands full of contraband.'

'True. But their trips don't seem to follow a set time frame or pattern, do they? So maybe that's why. They're guided by the tides. Or those tracks we found on the beach – they could have been made by a dinghy on a trailer, couldn't they? The people on the beach drag the dinghy down the boat ramp and onto the sand, then row out to meet the boat.'

'Yeah, although they looked more like four-by-four tyre tracks to me.' I sighed. 'It might help if we knew exactly what they were bringing over.'

'It could be anything,' said Nathan. 'It *could* still be drugs. I know the dog didn't find anything, but I'm not convinced. It could be explosives, or guns—'

'Woah!' I said, shocked. 'Hang on. I'm struggling to accept Glen and Liam as drug smugglers, let alone gun runners.'

'Yeah, I don't think either of them are likely, but they're possible. It could be as simple as normal goods that are harder or more expensive to get since we left the EU. Import tax and all that has made prices shoot up.'

'Hmmm…'

Nathan snorted. 'I do love the way you don't even pretend to be convinced by my theories.'

'It's not that, I just can't see Mick and Liam struggling to the shore with a large-screen TV or something over their heads. But what about prescription drugs? There have been shortages of some of them recently. There's probably a black market for that, and you could bring in a lot in one go.'

'Maybe…'

'I heard there was a shortage of HRT. There could be some shadowy consortium of really angry middle-aged women who will stop at nothing to get their hands on some oestrogen tablets, and if anyone tries to stop them, SO HELP ME GOD…'

'Well, I for one would just stand back and let them have them,' said Nathan, putting his hands up in defence. 'At least I would've done if they hadn't murdered someone.'

'That's fair.' My phone rang: Daisy. 'Uh oh,' I said. 'What have I not done now?'

'More likely who's your mum offended,' said Nathan with a smirk. I answered.

'Hi, everything okay?'

'You do remember you're giving me a lift into town for the mermaid costume contest later?' she said. I felt a prickle of irritation (or was it guilt); I hadn't been *that* unreliable this past week, had I?

'Of course, I said I would.' I glanced at my watch. 'It's only half three, we've got ages yet.'

'I know, but I thought if you were going to be busy I'd try and get someone else to take us,' she said. 'I felt really bad after making you run around and get my tail last night.'

'Oh sweetheart, that's okay,' I said.

'No, you and Nathan were right, I could be more independent, specially now you're back in the police force—'

But I don't WANT you to be independent, I want you to stay my little girl for a bit longer! I thought, but that was daft. She was growing up. And if I really was back in the force now … my stomach did a funny lurch at the memory of a much younger Daisy, crying as I left for work after finding out about me tackling a terrorist. I'd promised her there would be no more police work, no more danger, and here I was. But how much danger could I possibly be in, in sleepy Penstowan? *Well, you HAVE been involved in at least seven murders since we moved back to Cornwall,* a treacherous but quite reasonable voice in my head pointed out.

'Hey, I'm still your mum. And I'm sorry I forgot yesterday and made a big deal out of it,' I said. 'I promise you I will be back in time to take you to the contest. Apart from anything else, I can't wait to see your costume. I can't wait to see what a "Gothic feminist reimagining of the Siren myth" looks like.' *And I want to give it a good once-over before you leave the house in it,* I added, just not out loud.

She sniggered. 'Oh yeah, I think you'll be surprised,' she said, and I felt a flash of alarm, but before I could say anything else she said, 'See you later, then. Love you,' and disconnected the call.

'Yeah, I love you too,' I said, but it was too late. Never mind. She knew I loved her.

'Jodie! Guv!' Sunil put the phone down and practically leapt up at us as we returned to the station and headed to the office. He reminded me of Germaine, barking and prancing around after I'd been out all day, telling me she'd missed me.

'I take it from your excitement you've got something to tell us?' said Nathan, calmly. Sunil took a deep breath and led us over to the murder board. *This had better be good*, I thought.

'So just after you went down to the harbour with the dog unit, I got a call from the fingerprint team. They found a partial print on the chair Liam Fossett was tied to,' he said. Nathan nodded.

'Yeah, I heard. We assumed it was probably one of the Barracloughs. Was it not?'

'No, Guv. It was him.' Sunil pointed to the board, where a blurred photo – enlarged from the snap Maggie

Mitchell had taken on her phone – had been pinned, under the words *Phone D = Big Boy/Thug*. Sunil rubbed the marker pen off and wrote a name underneath. 'I sent them the photo and they confirmed it. Keith Dawson.'

'*Keith*?' I said in disgust. 'I dunno, thugs just don't have the right names these days. "Keith"! Not very threatening.'

'No, he doesn't look like a Keith… He's got a record, then?'

'Yes, Guv. Aggravated assault, demanding money with menaces, grievous bodily harm.'

'Keith's not a nice bloke, then,' I said. Sunil shook his head.

'No, not very. He used to work for some loan shark in East London, got sent down for picking a fight with someone in a pub, and then he seemed to go quiet when he came out, until now.'

'For "went quiet" read "didn't get caught",' said Nathan. 'And now he's down here.'

'Yes, although maybe not all the time. I did some digging on that unidentified number Mitchell and he called. There's not much information on it as it's another burner phone, but I did manage to locate it. It's in Southend.'

'Southend? Essex?' I asked.

Sunil nodded. 'Yes. I just spoke to a contact in Essex

Police.' He looked justifiably pleased with himself. 'It sounds to me like the loan shark retired from the money-lending business and moved to Essex, where they got into whatever this is. And Dawson is still working for them, probably also based in Essex, but acting as hired muscle and going wherever they need him. My contact knew the name, and said they would see what they could dig up about him and see who he's linked to.'

'Wow,' said Nathan. 'Nice work, Sunil.'

'That's not the best bit though, Guv,' he said. He was almost bouncing up and down on the spot by now. 'I put an alert out on the phones – Mitchell's, Glen's and Keith Dawson's – so I would hear if they pinged. And they all did.'

'What?' I said, sharing a surprised glance with Nathan. 'When? Where?'

'Well, actually, Glen's has been pinging on and off all day,' said Sunil. 'I think you were right before, he never turned it off, just kept going out of range of a phone signal. But he pinged just after midday, while you were on your way back from Salisbury, so we could see he was heading back here, as we thought. Last pinged on the A39 just outside Bude.'

'So he's close… When was this?'

'It pinged in that location about two hours ago. I think he's found somewhere quiet and is lying low again.

But the best bit is that while I was talking to Essex Police, Mitchell's phone came on.' Sunil looked at Nathan. 'You know what that means, Guv? He'll have seen the text message from Glen, about them needing to talk.'

'Brilliant. So hopefully they've arranged a meet... Where was Mitchell at the time?'

'Again, not very far away. Just outside Hatherleigh.'

'Where's that?'

'Country town, about twelve miles away in the opposite direction,' I said. 'Did Mitchell text back?'

'I don't know, I haven't had a chance to chase the phone company yet. But someone must have seen it, because the *real* best bit is that Keith Dawson's burner phone came on about two minutes later, and stayed on just long enough to text or make a phone call. And during that time, Glen's phone pinged again.'

'Bloody hell!' I said. 'He's arranged to meet Glen and get the stolen contraband back.' I looked at Nathan seriously. 'We have to find out where this meet is happening, if it hasn't already. I don't want to have to visit Nina and tell her that her brother's the latest victim in all this.'

'Yeah, I know. And Dawson was where when he made this call?'

'Pinged off the same mobile tower as Mitchell's phone,' said Sunil. 'I think perhaps he was unsure of what to do next. He probably didn't want to admit to his boss that the trail had gone cold. So he decided to turn on Mitchell's phone and see if there was anyone else listed on it who could be the thief. And then of course he saw Glen's text.'

'I didn't even think Glen had Mitchell's number,' I said. 'Mitchell didn't know Glen was going out on the boat, so there was no reason he would have given him his burner number.'

'Mick Tyler could've given it to him when he rang him that Saturday morning,' said Nathan. 'Maybe he told Glen to ring Mitchell and sort it out. Anyway, that doesn't matter. What matters is what happens next.' He turned to Sunil. 'We need to get Uniform appraised of the situation. I think Glen will arrange to meet in Penstowan, on home turf. That's what I would do, anyway. He knows this man's dangerous, so he won't want to meet him anywhere remote. Make sure Uniform all have copies of his photo – the one on his police record might be clearer than that one.' He nodded towards the blurred picture on the board. 'Do you think I can justify calling in extra bodies? We don't know for certain that they *will* be meeting here, it's just a hunch.'

'I think most of them are working this evening anyway,' I said. 'And those that aren't on duty will be around, so we can always ask them to keep an eye out.

It's carnival night, isn't it? Fireworks and the bonfire and everything.'

'Of course! If I was Glen, that's where I'd be arranging to meet; somewhere there are plenty of people around.'

We spent another hour or so looking out for activity from Glen and Keith – come on! *Keith?!!* Hardly a proper gangster name. But there was nothing. Matt had requested access to Glen's financial records, but they weren't much help. He'd used his debit card to take £500 out of the ATM in Fore Street on Saturday, which was probably the maximum he was allowed to withdraw, so we couldn't trace where he'd been staying; possibly a B&B or a motel where he'd paid cash. But he had used the card to fill up with diesel at Sparkford (which we already knew about, of course), and earlier today near Wincanton. It didn't really matter now anyway; as Nathan had said, what mattered was what happened next, and we knew he'd made his way back to Penstowan, or close by, anyway.

'Right,' said Nathan, pushing back his chair. 'I think this meeting's either already happened, in which case we'll know about it when someone finds Glen –' I crossed my fingers, hoping that wasn't the case '– or it's happening later, at the carnival. In which case we should go home and have a break before we head over there.'

'Plus I have to get my little mermaid there in her costume,' I said. Matt snorted.

'Oh yeah, I heard about that. What on earth does a "Gothic feminist reimagining"—'

I cut him short. 'Honestly, Matt, I don't know and I'm not sure I want to find out. But I'm going to.'

Chapter Twenty-One

We got home to find the house eerily calm. Mum and Daisy smiled at us as we walked through the door, which could have just been them being warm and welcoming, but it felt a little bit too much like 'we know something you don't' to me. Maybe I was just being suspicious... Germaine, however, wasn't quite so calm, and she ran up to us barking her head off, aware that exciting things were afoot and no doubt hoping that she would be a part of it.

'Don't worry, sweetie,' I said, bending down to make a fuss of her. 'You're coming too.'

'Is that a good idea?' asked Nathan. 'What with the fireworks?'

'They're silent ones this year,' I said. 'There was a petition after the New Year's Eve display, remember?

They were so loud, it sounded like we were being bombed. They upset everyone's animals. Even the farmers complained, and they're normally far enough out of town that they don't really hear them.' Germaine barked and leapt up at me again. 'Yes, they were *sooo* loud, weren't they, silly old fireworks…' Daisy groaned in disgust.

'Oh my God, Mum, she's your dog, not your baby!'

'I know, but my real baby's too old for me to talk to her like that. Unless you *want* Mummy to start doing it to you, my ickle sugar plum?' Daisy made puking noises. 'Thought not. Then let me have my fur baby.' I stopped and shuddered. 'Oh dear Lord, tell me I didn't just say that out loud? I'll be wearing a "Pugs and Kisses" T-shirt next.'

'You've already got a shopping bag covered in dogs,' pointed out Nathan, grinning.

'Yeah, but I use that *ironically*.'

We had dinner – a bean and sweet potato chilli recipe that I'd picked up from Gino, whose catering van I'd taken over a couple of years ago during an eventful film shoot nearby – and then Daisy headed upstairs to get ready. The costume contest started at seven, and the fireworks would start an hour or so later, just as it was finally starting to get dark. The real problem with having fireworks in the summer that far west was that it just didn't get properly dark until nine or even ten, which was a bit late for the little ones to stay up to.

'Here she comes,' muttered Nathan, as we heard Daisy clumping down the stairs. We looked up and … she was wearing a T-shirt and leggings.

'Oh!' I said, disappointed. 'Where's your costume?'

She held up a large sports bag. 'In here. It's too bulky to wear in the car. I can change into it before the contest.'

Noooo, I need to make sure it's okay first! I thought, but I didn't say anything. She was happy with it, so I needed to trust her.

'Have you seen this costume?' I asked Mum, as Daisy loaded her bag carefully into the boot of the car.

'Oh yes, proper good it is,' she said.

'Hmm.'

'Don't worry, she don't look like you did in your costume,' she cackled. 'State of that!'

'Thanks very much! I'm more concerned about her looking like the other mermaid. Her outfit was a bit … *skimpy.*'

Mum smiled and put her hand on my arm. 'Don't worry. I wouldn't let her go out in public wearing anything inappropriate.'

'Yeah, because you're never inappropriate yourself, are you?'

She cackled again. 'I'm seventy-three this year. I'm

allowed to be inappropriate. Just a shame no one wants to see me in a tiny seashell bra.'

'Don't you believe it, Shirley,' said Nathan, coming over to open the car door for her. 'I've seen Bob the hardware man giving you the glad eye...' Mum giggled like a schoolgirl and I rolled my eyes.

'Please, Nath, don't encourage her or put nasty mental images in my head, I've just eaten.'

The town was heaving when we arrived. We couldn't park anywhere near the grassy area by the beach where the carnival was being held, so we left the car in the police station car park and walked. We spotted Debbie, Callum and their two kids heading the same way and caught up with them.

'Got your costume ready?' asked Debbie, winking at Daisy, who nodded.

'Hang on, what's that wink all about?' I said, looking between my friend and my daughter. 'Don't tell me you've seen it? I haven't.'

'You've been busy,' said Debbie, and although she didn't say it in a nasty or sarcastic manner, it felt like she'd stuck a needle into my heart. 'You've been hunting the *real* mermaid.'

'Yeah, but not *all* the time!' I said.

'Anyway, I haven't seen the finished article,' she said. 'Daisy just needed help sourcing some of the materials.'

'What material is a Gothic feminist mermaid's costume made out of anyway?' I said, slightly grumpily. I knew I was being petty, but – actually there is no 'but', I was just being petty because I felt left out of my daughter's life, even though it wasn't on purpose, and she was getting older and it was bound to happen, and... I just didn't like it.

Debbie looked like she was about to answer, but it was getting more crowded the closer we got to the fair and it was hard to all stay together, let alone talk.

'See you by the stage?' I called, as Debbie and her family got swept away across what was normally the beach car park but was now a fairground. She nodded.

We passed stalls selling candy floss and hot dogs, Germaine growling at the smell, and others selling glow-in-the-dark wands and necklaces, mermaid souvenirs, and all manner of plastic tat. Pop music played over loudspeakers; a couple of local bands had performed earlier on but we'd missed them, although according to Matt, whose brother played in one of them, that was probably a lucky escape. A massive bonfire had been built in a cordoned-off area close to the beach, away from the main fair.

'What time are they lighting the bonfire?' asked Mum.

'They might not be lighting it at all,' said a voice next to us. We turned round and there was Tony, smiling broadly at us. Next to him stood the reason for his good humour: Carmen, looking very happy and relaxed, and 'off duty' without her dog collar. I raised my eyebrows at him and he grinned even more broadly.

'Oh hello Tony love, and hello Vicar,' said Mum. 'What's wrong with the bonfire?'

'This heatwave has dried everything out, hasn't it? Look at the grass, it's like tinder,' said Tony. 'The fire fighters told the festival committee to build it on the beach, but the council wouldn't let them.'

'That's ridiculous! What about the fireworks?'

'The fireworks are on a barge out on the water, so that's safe enough,' said Tony. He smiled at Daisy. 'Where's this costume, then? I hope you haven't changed your mind.'

'Nope, I'm changing into it here,' said Daisy, and as she spoke the pop music stopped and a voice came over the loudspeaker, exhorting all fancy-dress contestants to head to the stage and get ready. There was a squeal nearby as Jade found us, also carrying a large bag, and the two girls rushed off.

'Good luck!' I called, and Germaine barked her own best wishes.

Tony turned to me and Nathan as Mum chatted to Carmen, no doubt 'subtly' pumping her for information about her relationship with Tony – I used those quotation marks wisely, as Shirley Parker was about as subtle as a brick.

'What's going on?' asked Tony in a low voice, or as low a voice as possible given the noise level of the fair.

'What do you mean?'

'A lot of coppers around tonight,' he said. 'More than usual. Even the ones who are off duty look a bit twitchy.'

'Yeah…' I looked at Nathan and he nodded. 'We think whoever's behind Mick Tyler's death could show up here tonight.'

'Bloody hell! Is it safe for everyone to be here?'

'Yes, Tone. It's one bloke, not a homicidal mythical sea creature with supernatural powers that could wipe out the whole town,' I said witheringly.

'I hadn't even thought of that before you said it, but now… Thanks a lot.' Tony looked around at the crowd as if he could spot who was actually a murderous mermaid in disguise. Carmen touched his arm gently.

'Did you tell them?' she asked, smiling.

'Oh, no, I forgot!' said Tony. She gazed at him, with one of those soppy 'what am I going to do with you?' looks on her face, and I thought, *Oh yes, I was DEFINITELY right about her and Tony…*

'A couple of kids found our mermaid and brought it back to the church,' she said. 'They said they found it in a bush, not far from the church actually, while they were out walking their dog.'

'Thank God for that,' I said, and then blushed, because you don't say that in front of a vicar. 'Sorry, I mean—'

Carmen laughed. 'It's all right, that's exactly what I said myself when they brought it back.'

'With any luck it'll stop Jago Thomas and his friends spreading stupid stories about the Siren,' I said. 'I wonder who took it in the first place?'

Nathan shrugged. 'Maybe it was just kids. Bored teenagers, who thought they'd have a bit of fun coming up to Merrymaid Week and scare people with the spooky return of the Siren.'

'I suspect it might well have been the two young lads who brought it back,' said Carmen. 'They were very keen to hand her over and they couldn't look me in the eye. But I told them I didn't care who'd taken her, I'm just glad she's back where she belongs, at St Botolph's.'

'Dammit,' murmured Nathan into my ear. 'If Keith Dawson slips through our fingers I was hoping to be able to pin it all on the mermaid...'

The voice came over the loudspeaker again, this time telling us that the costume contest was about to start. I picked Germaine up and we pushed our way through the crowd to the stage, spotting Debbie down the front. She waved to us and stared at a very tall man who was standing in our way until he let us past.

'There you are!' she started, then stopped as she spotted Tony and Carmen together. She looked at me, mouth open, then shut it quickly.

'I know! They look good together, don't they?' I said as quietly as I could. She nodded, then grabbed my arm and tugged me closer to the stage.

'Come on, you do not want to miss this…' she said, making me feel very nervous. What was Daisy planning, and how come everyone else seemed to know about it?

The MC took the stage. She was an ex-weather presenter from one of the local regional news programmes and was world famous in Cornwall; it was quite a coup to get her. The year before we'd had the bloke who ran the livestock auctions doing the announcements, and he spoke so quickly that by the time you'd worked out what event he was announcing, you'd missed it.

The contestants began to parade out onto the stage, starting with the under-tens. Every single one wore a Disney Little Mermaid costume, complete with orange wig, apart from the two little boys who were dressed up as Aqua Man. Not terribly original, then, but undeniably very cute.

Next up was Daisy's category: the ten-to-eighteen-year-olds. The costumes here had all had a bit more work put into them, but they all still looked like the Disney version underneath. The MC called out the contestants' names as they entered the stage, but I didn't pay a lot of attention; I was just waiting to see Daisy. Until…

'And our next mermaid is… Luke Trevally!' called the MC, and Luke, who I remembered from one of Daisy's school plays, came swaggering out in full drag. He had two large scallop shells stuck onto his bare chest, and a very long blonde wig on. He wiggled across the stage to much laughter.

'Oh dear God,' I heard a woman say behind me. 'I told him not to glue those shells directly onto his skin, they'll be a right bugger to get off.' Next to her, a group of other boys laughed and wolf whistled. Luke turned and blew them a kiss before pouting and posing next to the other mermaids.

'He's the one who found the statue,' said Carmen.

'Is he now?' I said. 'He's also the one who told Daisy it was missing and that the Siren was back, causing mayhem…'

Carmen laughed. 'Cheeky tyke! I'll have to watch out

for him. No harm done though, he obviously just likes a laugh…'

'And our last mermaid of the evening,' said the ex-weather presenter, 'Daisy Parker!'

We all roared as Daisy sauntered onto the stage, and I steeled myself to see exactly what a Gothic feminist mermaid looked like.

She looked beautiful, and otherworldly somehow, despite the fact that the materials her costume was made of were very much of this world. Her tail was covered in transparent scales, shimmering in the lights of the stage, some of them with a slight hint of blue. And some of them seemed to have bits of paper stuck on them. I looked closer; they were cut from plastic water bottles, and must've been an absolute nightmare to put together – no wonder she'd needed help. Her hands were bound loosely together, the plastic rings you get on six-packs of beer encircling her wrists, and she held a large plastic bottle. Her hair was naturally long and a little bit wavy, but she'd threaded strands of coloured rope, string and abandoned fishing line through it. The bodice of her costume was fashioned from plastic bags, a layer of discarded fishing net over it. The net was studded with other bits of junk: metal bottle tops, unidentifiable bits of plastic, broken glass with jagged edges worn smooth by the ebb and flow of the sea. And instead of the big smiles worn by the other contestants, she looked sad, sad enough to make my heart ache, even though I guessed it was an act.

The MC looked a bit taken aback. 'Where did you get the idea for your costume?' she asked.Daisy looked out at the crowd with a determined expression on her face. She bent down and placed the plastic bottle on the floor, then took the microphone from the surprised celebrity's hands.

'I got the idea, and the materials, from all the crap that gets washed up on our beaches,' she said, and I felt a massive wave of pride sweep over me like a tsunami. 'We pride ourselves in Penstowan on having clean beaches, and on looking after the sea and everything in it, but it's not enough. Beaches up and down the country are drowning in the easily discarded detritus of modern living—' *Uh oh*, I thought, *don't get too fancy with the speech, you'll lose the audience.* 'We all just chuck stuff away and buy more, when we don't need it. But we can't buy a new ocean when this one's dead, and we can't buy a new planet either. We need to stop being so selfish and think of other creatures, just like the Siren in the story. The fishermen stopped looking after her, so she stopped looking after them. We need each other. We need—'

The MC managed to wrestle the microphone back from her, and the crowd began to clap. But then Jade appeared on stage from the wings. Daisy bent down and picked up the plastic bottle, lifting it up so we could see what it said: 'CASTROL GTX'. Oil.

'Oh no—' I began, but there was nothing I could do. Daisy upended the bottle over her head and covered herself (and her beautiful costume) in brown goo, while Jade unfurled a banner which the two of them held out : "STOP DEEP SEA OIL EXPLORATION NOW!"

'I hope that's not real oil,' I said, shocked. The crowd was silent. And then suddenly Nathan whooped. I had never heard him whoop before, and I don't think I have since.

'YEAH!! GO DAISY!!!' And he clapped wildly, still whooping. Tony joined in, then Debbie, then Callum, then Carmen and Mum, and finally I snapped out of my paralysis and joined in too.

'That's my daughter!' I said, loud and proud, to everyone nearby. The rest of the crowd began to applaud then, some cheering loudly too, although I did hear a couple of people behind me saying that it was just supposed to be a bit of fun for the kiddies and Daisy had spoilt it. They stopped when Debbie, Mum and I all turned round and glared at them, though.

Chapter Twenty-Two

'You was robbed.' I stood outside the ladies' toilets and consoled Daisy, now dressed back in her T-shirt and leggings. She'd changed out of her mermaid costume and washed what had (thankfully) turned out to be brown paint with flour mixed in to make it more gloopy out of her hair. 'You should've won, but they're all cowards. *COWARDS!*' I repeated loudly, as the ex-weather lady and MC passed by us on the way to the drinks tent. She pointedly ignored us.

'It doesn't matter,' said Daisy, who was proving to be far more mature than me. 'I made my point.'

'I am so proud of you,' I said, putting my arm around her. I expected her to resist and pull away, but she didn't. Not for thirty seconds, at least. 'Why on earth didn't you tell me what you were doing? All this stuff about Gothic feminist reimaginings...'

Daisy laughed. 'That actually was my original plan, but you know how you were asking what a Gothic feminist mermaid looks like? Turns out I have absolutely no idea either.'

'Just as well.'

We rejoined the others, Mum and Nathan both telling Daisy how brilliant they thought her costume was.

'Yeah, it's a shame it ended up with paint all over it,' I said. 'It was beautiful.'

'Beauty is fleeting and ephemeral,' said Daisy.

'I got a photo,' said Mum.

I felt my phone vibrate in my pocket. I couldn't hear it ring with all the noise around us, so I hoped it was a message, rather than a call. Luckily, it was, from Nina.

'Bloody hell, Nathan!' I said, holding up my phone for him to see. *Glen just texted me!!! 'Hey Sis, I'm back, just look out for my halo'. What do you think that means?*

'Good of him not to be all enigmatic, innit?' I said, sarcastically.

'Yeah, very helpful.' Nathan looked around. 'But maybe not as enigmatic as you think. Look...' He looked around. I followed his gaze.

It was finally starting to get dark, and all around us kids and adults alike were wearing or carrying glow-in-the-dark wands and armbands and necklaces – plastic hoops filled with luminous liquid – some worn around their heads like tiaras or diadems. Nathan was looking over at a group of people right on the edge of the fairground, away from the lights. Give it another half an hour, and it would be too dark to see them, save for the glowing halos of light around their necks and heads.

'So he's definitely here, then?' I said, and Nathan nodded.

'I think so, don't you? But he's still not going to be easy to spot…'

Germaine, who Nathan was holding in his arms – the crowd was too dense really to have her running around at our feet – struggled and whined to get down. I took her from him and nodded towards the bonfire.

'Let's head over there and give her a bit of a run,' I said to Daisy and Mum. 'It's emptier there.' I turned back to Nathan. 'And it'll give us space to think…'

'Shame them not lighting it,' said Mum, wandering around the massive pile of timber. Germaine was sniffing around excitedly, glad to be out of my arms. Daisy held the lead tightly to stop her getting tangled up in our legs. 'Even though I don't really see the point of a fire, unless you're baking potatoes under it.'

'Or burning someone on top,' I said. Nathan laughed and grabbed my hand, pulling me towards him.

'Remind me never to upset you,' he murmured, kissing the top of my head.

Germaine darted towards the pile of wood, barking, straining at the lead. Daisy hauled at it, pulling her away.

'Germaine, leave it! What's the matter with you?'

'There's probably rats nesting in it,' I said. 'They'll all scarper as soon as the fire's lit.'

'*If* they light it,' said Daisy.

'Oh yeah. At least we'll still have the fireworks…'

Germaine was still fussing around the bonfire, so we led her away and found a good spot at the bottom of the hill that led up to the cliffs. We were on a bit of a slope, so we were slightly higher than the rest of the crowd, or at least we were until some of the crowd had the same idea as us.

'Never mind,' I said. 'We'll still get a good view of the fireworks from here.'

Finally the display began. Mum put her hands over her ears, until I reminded her that they were using silent fireworks this year.

'It's weird without all the explosions,' said Daisy, and it was, but I wasn't missing the dog whining and getting upset. The almost eerie lack of bangs didn't stop anyone's enjoyment; the crowd all still 'ooh'ed and 'aah'ed at the display.

Suddenly a loud bang, or more accurately a crack,

rang out. Lots of tutting followed and shaking of heads; someone had slipped up and included a traditional noisy firework. I looked at Nathan; something wasn't right.

'Was that a firework?' I asked, and he shook his head slowly.

'I don't think so…' We looked up at the clifftop. I squinted. Above us there was darkness, punctuated by one tiny light. A halo.

'Are there people up there? Is that Glen?' I asked. But Nathan didn't answer, as he was already sprinting up the hill, pulling out his phone and calling for back-up as he did so.

I shouted to Mum and Daisy to stay there and chased after him. Ahead of us, right on top of the cliff, stood three men; two of them, one of whom I now recognised as Keith Dawson, were shouting and waving something around at the man wearing the day-glow necklace, whose hands were held out in a placating gesture. Nathan slowed and put a hand out to stop me before we reached them, gesturing to stay back. The two aggressive men had their backs to us and didn't realise we were there, the cries of delight from the firework crowd masking the sound of our approach.

'That one was a warning,' shouted Dawson. He had a Cockney accent and sounded very, very angry. 'The next one'll be in your head.'

'And then you'll never find her,' said the lone man. Glen. His eyes flicked briefly towards me and I knew he'd seen us, but he was careful not to show it.

'Just give her back,' said the third man. He was calmer than his companion, but his voice still had a low, menacing tone. 'You saw what happened to your mates. We ain't messing about. She's nothing to you.'

'Where's Stuart?' Glen was clearly frightened but he wasn't backing down. Dawson glanced down briefly towards the park, and suddenly I knew exactly where Stuart Mitchell was. He laughed, but it was a humourless sound.

'He's safe. But not for much longer. So you better get your arse in gear and tell us where she is before he starts getting hot under the collar.' Dawson lifted the gun and pointed it at Glen again.

'Police! Drop the gun!' shouted Nathan, running forward, and I thought, *No you bloody idiot, you're not armed, you're not wearing body armour*—

Dawson whirled around and Glen immediately launched himself at him, throwing his whole body weight onto him. Dawson went down, still clutching the gun, but Glen chopped his arm hard, sending the weapon flying out of his hand. I lunged for it, cocking the trigger and pointing it at him. Glen sat on his legs, stopping him getting back up, as Nathan grabbed

Dawson's arms and pulled them up behind his back, handcuffing him. He nodded at Glen.

'Thank you.'

'Nah mate, thank *you*.' Glen's voice was shaky, and so were his legs; he stood up, then abruptly sat down again on the grass.

Meanwhile, the other man had set off down the hillside, but he was greeted by three police cars racing onto the grass to intercept him. Matt leapt out and rugby tackled the fleeing man, his own momentum causing him to topple over into the grass.

'Crying shame only one of you had a gun,' said Nathan mildly, as he yanked the armed man to his feet. 'We've got armed responders here, of course, but they don't get a lot of action. Would've been nice for them to practice on something other than rabbits.'

'Rather them than me,' I said. I still held the gun, and it felt surprisingly heavy. I pointed it down at the ground, hating the feel of it in my hands. I'd never been trained in firearms, and I never wanted to be. Nathan handed the man over to a uniformed officer who had joined us, then reached out a hand to me.

'I'll take that, babe.'

'Please do.'

Excited shouts from down below reached us; it looked like they'd decided it was safe to light the bonfire after all. I called out to the uniformed officer. 'Can you radio the fire marshals down there? I think I know where Stuart Mitchell is…'

'Turn right here,' said Glen. Matt was behind the wheel of the police car, with Nathan in the front passenger seat, while I sat next to the still shaken ex-soldier.

We turned off the A39 and onto a side road that was little more than a dirt track, the car bumping over the rough ground. It was soon pitch dark, the full beam of the headlights lighting up the trees ahead of us but leaving shadows in our wake.

'Are you sure?' asked Nathan. 'There's nothing here…'

'Just a bit further up. I did some work repairing some old farm machinery and this is where they keep it. There!' Glen leant forward, pointing to a small wooden shack in a clearing. A tractor and a few other bits of rusty farming equipment were falling apart outside.

'What a charming hideaway,' I said. 'Because nothing bad ever happened in a remote cabin in the woods.'

The car stopped and we all got out, Nathan raising his eyebrows as I let Glen out. Glen saw.

'I need to do the signal,' he said, and Nathan nodded.

Glen rushed over to the door and knocked three times, paused, then twice, then paused again, then once. 'It's me!' he called, gently. As we watched, the door swung open slowly, creaking on its rusty hinges…

A pair of wide, frightened eyes peered out at us. 'Glen?' The voice was female, scared, with an accent I couldn't place.

'It's all right, it's me,' said Glen, stepping forward to turn on a light inside the cabin. We all blinked at the sudden brightness.

'A real-life Siren…' I said, staring at the woman in front of us. She was young – mid-twenties, I reckoned – with long dark hair and a tanned complexion. She was dressed in a shabby tracksuit, which I guessed was one of Glen's as it swamped her slim frame.

'This is Elira,' said Glen, reaching out to take her hand and lead her forward. 'It's okay, they're friends. They're police—' She drew back, but I smiled at her and moved closer.

'We're not going to hurt you, or arrest you,' I said, although to be honest I had no idea what would happen to her. 'We just want to make sure you're okay.'

'The men—' she asked, hesitantly. I nodded reassuringly.

'Yes, we know about them. They're at the police station now. They can't hurt you.'

Elira turned to look at Glen, who nodded. The frightened woman burst into tears and threw herself into his arms. Glen looked surprised but rather pleased. He held her close while Nathan beckoned Matt and I outside.

'Well I have to say, I wasn't expecting this,' he said. 'We need to call Immigration.'

'Do we, though?' I asked, wheedlingly, but he nodded firmly.

'Yes, we do. You *know* we do. We can't pretend she's not here and none of this happened. There's a body in the morgue, one just out of a coma, and another one very lucky not to have been burnt alive recovering in the hospital, as we speak.'

I sighed. 'I know. It's just … we don't know why she's here. You've got to be pretty desperate to get away from your old life if you pay someone to get you on a boat over here, especially when you see how many boats don't make it and how many get caught.'

'If that's what happened. We won't know for sure until Glen gives us a proper statement. I'll tell you this for nothing, those two blokes we arrested on the clifftop won't tell us a thing.' Nathan shook his head. 'I've met their type before.'

'Okay, but can we at least let the poor woman have a moment to recover? Take her back to the station, let her have a shower and give her a change of clothes? If Immigration deport her, who knows what'll happen to her?' I glanced back inside the cabin, where Glen was talking to her in a low voice, stroking her hair and calming her. I'd always known deep down that he was a nice guy, and I was relieved that my initial drug smuggling theory had proved to be wrong. I turned back to look at Nathan. 'I know her future is pretty much out of our hands, but we can at least treat her kindly while she's with us.'

Nathan smiled at me. 'I can hardly say no to that, can I?'

Back at the station, Elira was led off to the changing rooms by the desk sergeant Sally to have a shower. I'd rung Mum on the way, to let her and Daisy know that everything was okay, and to see if they could find a suitable change of clothes for her. By the time we reached Penstowan my neighbour Nancy had driven down to the station with a pile of clothes and some shoes that might do, in various sizes. God knew where they'd come from; it looked like everyone on our street had donated something. I was touched by their generosity, and so was Elira when she saw them. Her eyes filled with tears.

They filled with tears again when she realised that Glen was being led off to an interview room in the other direction, but we spoke kindly to her and reassured her that it would all work out. Again, we had no way of knowing whether it would, but we could hope.

Glen was nervous – as far as I was aware, he'd never been in any trouble with the police before – but luckily I was able to sit in on the interview, something I hadn't been able to do when I was unofficially poking my nose into my earlier cases with Nathan. I pushed a mug of tea across the table to him and smiled. Nathan was letting me lead this, to start with anyway, as I knew him.

'All right then, Glen. Tell us what you've got yourself into. And properly this time!'

He smiled ruefully. 'I'm sorry I didn't come clean on the phone,' he said. 'I panicked. I didn't know what to do.' He fiddled with the handle of the mug. 'They'll send her back to Albania, won't they?'

'That's where Elira is from, is it?' I asked. He nodded.

'Yeah... I don't really know where to start.'

'From the beginning.'

Chapter Twenty-Three

A djusting to life outside the army is never easy, particularly if, like Glen, you've been forced out before you were ready. Glen hadn't planned to be back on Civvy Street for another ten years at least, maybe longer, but tearing his cruciate ligament had put paid to that. Being injured had meant time away from his usual duties and he was out of his routine, but it still felt like he was being turfed out of his army family, losing that safety net of having most of his everyday life mapped out and taken care of for him.

Losing one 'family' made the decision to move back to his real one in Penstowan obvious, and Helen, his partner at the time, had been all for it. She'd been dreaming of a quaint cottage in a beautiful seaside town, with sunshine and cream teas... Which Penstowan did have, of course, but it also had seagull poop and lots of tourists to contend with in the summer. And the winter brought damp, sea mists that made the smell of fish cling to everything, and no work.

She hadn't lasted long, but in a strange way Glen had found it a relief; the writing had been on the wall for their relationship for a while, so it was one less thing to worry about.

Jobwise, he was luckier than many ex-servicemen in that he had a lot of transferable skills that were in demand in Cornwall. Being an army mechanic meant he was able to service and fix a wide range of vehicles, and he could turn his hand to more or less anything, from boats and jet skis to cars, tractors and other farming machinery. But the work wasn't regular. Most people still took their cars to Rob Trevarrow in town, while the fishermen tended to tinker with their own boats to save money, unless there was a serious problem.

Still, he'd picked up enough work to keep himself going. He had an army pension that paid the small mortgage on his house, and other than that he didn't need much. He enjoyed cooking for himself, and having the family round to dinner regularly. He went to the pub for a couple of pints and to meet up with old friends at the weekend, and the rest of the time he enjoyed going for walks, or swimming in the salt water tidal pool down on the beach to keep himself fit.

'So how did you get involved with Mick Tyler and Stuart Mitchell?' asked Nathan.

'Me and Mick used to play in the school football team,' said Glen. He turned to me. 'You know what it's like here. Everyone knows everyone else from somewhere. You either went to school together, or their sister went with yours, or worked with your mum...' I nodded. 'So I got talking to him one day, while I was having a look at the motor on his boat, and he asked how things were going, money-wise. I said it was all right, but working for myself meant I didn't have a reliable income. I'd heard that he'd been struggling at one point too, but he'd turned it around and seemed to be flush with money these days, so I asked him what his secret was.'

'What did he say?'

'Nothing, at first. He just laughed and said he was lucky. But a couple of days later I ran into Liam on the quay, and we had this weird conversation.'

'You know Liam?'

'Only from seeing him around the harbour. I'd spoken to him a couple of times, in passing, you know? But that day he made a beeline for me.'

'What did you talk about?' I asked.

'He started asking me about my time in the army. He wanted to know where I'd served, and when I told him I'd been in Afghanistan he told me about this group he was part of at university, where they helped teenage refugees settle in and taught them English and that. It felt a bit like he was having a go at me, like it was my fault they were refugees because I'd been in war zones, where a lot of people were displaced.'

'That's rubbish—'

'Is it?' Glen looked at me frankly. 'Because it doesn't feel like that. I might not have destroyed these people's homes, but I didn't save them either, did I? I wasn't there during the fighting, but there were still bombings and shootings and stuff going on when my regiment went there to help keep the peace. I've seen families left with nothing except the clothes on their backs, and there was nothing I could do to help.' He took a deep breath. 'Anyway, I thought he was just this stupid kid who thought he knew everything just because he'd been on a few marches. I got really pissed off with him, to be honest, but I didn't argue with him. I just walked away.'

'But really Liam was sounding you out,' I said. 'And then what happened?'

'And then Mick came round to my house and told me

he had a special job for me a couple of nights later, if I was interested. He said his usual deckhand couldn't come, so he needed someone to cover. And this usual deckhand – who I worked out was Liam – would be leaving Penstowan at the end of the summer to go back to uni, so if I did well I could take over from him.'

'What did you think this "special" job was?' asked Nathan.

'I guessed it was illegal,' said Glen, looking sheepish. 'When he mentioned going out on the boat it was obvious it was smuggling. I said if it was drugs I wasn't interested, because I know people who've had problems with that. Mick just laughed and said I was barking up the wrong tree.'

'Because people trafficking is so much better,' said Nathan. Glen shook his head, angry.

'It wasn't like that! The way Mick talked about it, it was a humanitarian service. He said the first time, yeah, he did it for the money. It was a load of young blokes from Sudan and places like that, who had been living in refugee camps in France for months, and he thought good luck to 'em. But his second run, it was three Syrian families, kids and all, and he said it made him think about his own family, how he'd do anything to keep Viv and the kids safe. He said they were so scared, and so grateful when he showed them a bit of kindness. He really thought he was giving them the chance to find a better life here. Liam felt the same, I reckon.' He sighed. 'I thought it would be a good way to make up for all the shit I'd seen in Afghanistan and Somalia.'

'Did Mick tell you what happened to these refugees after he'd done his bit?' asked Nathan, making notes.

'He said he would drop them off at Kevrinva Bay, and then the people who ran the operation would drive them to London, or Manchester – big cities, where it was easier for them to disappear.' Glen gave a wan smile. 'They'd stick out like a sore thumb in Penstowan, wouldn't they?'

'Just a bit,' I said. 'So you agreed to go out with Mick a few nights before his murder. What happened?'

'We left about nine o'clock. We went out on one of Stuart Mitchell's boats, one of the bigger ones—'

'The Molly Malone,' I said. He nodded.

'Yeah. We followed some of the other fishing boats, but once we got out far enough we headed west, round Land's End, back along the south coast and out quite a long way into the Channel – I'm not sure where exactly, but Mick knew where he was going. A few hours later we met another boat.' Glen paused, and I could tell he was picturing it in his head. 'It was awful, a tiny little boat, no shelter, them all crammed in together. When

Mick said we had to get them all from there into our boat, I thought no way. It was really dark, and the waves are pretty big that far out.'

'But you got them all?'

'Yeah, God knows how. But they weren't families, they were young women, eight or nine of them. They were terrified.'

'Elira was one of them?' asked Nathan.

'Yeah. We managed to get them all below deck. Mick had brought along blankets, and some flasks of tea to warm them up. He was kind to them. We weren't really supposed to talk to them, and they were meant to stay out of sight, but one of them – Elira – said she felt sick, so I took her up on deck to get some air, and that's when she told me they were being trafficked.'

'But you knew that already,' said Nathan. Glen shook his head.

'No, not like that. She said she'd paid some men to help her find work in England. They told her they could get her proper, legal work, cleaning and stuff, so she handed over all of her money and her passport. She said it had all seemed above board. The other girls had done the same. They all came from small villages in Albania, where there was no work, nothing for them there. She didn't have any family. She said young girls were always disappearing, being taken away and sold as sex workers. She thought she was old enough for that not to happen to her.' He smiled sadly. 'Ironic, because that's exactly what they had in store for her, and the other girls.'

'How did she know that?'

'She said once they got them into France, and they had all the girls' passports and ID, they dropped any pretence and made it quite clear they were prisoners now. One girl tried to run away, but they caught her and beat her in front of the others. They were all terrified. She begged me to help them.'

'What did you do?'

'I told Mick. I was bloody furious with him, but he was as horrified as I was. He said he wasn't the one behind it all. He said Stuart Mitchell was the middleman at this end, but other than that all he knew was that the people Stuart was working for weren't very nice. He said we couldn't disappear with all the girls, because he didn't want them coming after his family. But he said maybe we could get Elira away, and I could take her to the police where she could report what had happened. She hated the idea of leaving the other girls, but when we explained it to her, she agreed. We thought if we reported the men Mitchell was working with, you lot or Immigration or whoever might be able to track the other girls down.'

'But you didn't come to the police,' I pointed out gently. 'You ran.'

'We panicked,' said Glen. 'We were supposed to hand the girls over at this cove a couple of miles along the coast from here – Mick said he would row the Molly's dinghy over to the shore with them – but we jumped off and swam ashore near the beach first.'

'You swam?' I said, incredulously. 'That would've been incredibly dangerous, surely? It must still have been dark.'

'Yeah, it was. But the surf hut is always lit up at night, so it gave us a point to aim for. Mick got as close as he could to the shore. I'm a very strong swimmer, and with Elira in a life vest it meant I could tow her to the beach if she got tired. But I think the adrenaline had kicked in and she didn't really need me.' He shook his head, musing. 'She was amazing.'

'And then?'

'And then we went back to my place. It was still dark, so I thought it was safe enough to walk. Mick said he was going to tell the traffickers he went out on his own – they knew it was usually two of them – and that there'd been an accident with Elira, she'd fallen overboard during the hand over, or trying to get away or something. He said they would probably check with the other blokes doing the handover, so they'd find out

337

eventually, but it would stall them. So we went back to my house and lay low, not really knowing what to do. And then Mick rang me on Saturday and told me to run, because the traffickers didn't believe him and they were coming back to look for her. He gave me Stuart's number and told me to either ring him and arrange to hand her over, or to get as far away as possible and tell the police.'

'But you *still* didn't go to the police,' said Nathan.

'No, I know, and we should have. I'm sorry. But Elira was traumatised. I was as well a bit, to be honest. I just wanted to get her away. So we threw some stuff in a bag and left.'

'And went to Salisbury.'

Glen looked surprised. 'Yes. So much for me changing phones and covering my tracks. I wasn't sure how well connected these people were, if they'd be able to trace me or something. I wanted to see an old friend of mine—'

'David Sinclair.'

'You've spoken to him? He's an old army mate. I wasn't thinking straight and I knew he would know what to do. But he wasn't there. So we found this B&B near Wincanton and just hid for a bit.' He smiled. 'We spent a few days just going for walks, having picnics by the river. Elira had been cooped up in a house, and then a truck, and then the boat, for almost two weeks by the time I met her. You know those flowers that close up overnight, and then open again during the day? It was like that. Elira had been all tense and closed in, and spending that time with her was just like watching her relax and unfurl...'

I looked at Nathan and exchanged an unspoken *Oh this boy's got it BAAD* with him.

'Anyway...' I said, clearing my throat. 'Why did you come back? You must've known you were in danger.'

'After I spoke to you that day, when you told me that Mick was dead, and about poor Liam in hospital, and that Stuart was missing... I couldn't believe all that had happened because of me. I knew I had to make it better, but I wasn't sure how. I texted Stuart's number and told him we needed to talk, hoping that whoever had him would see it. And then that thug rang me, wanting to meet. I'd already started to head home, because I knew we couldn't carry on as we were. Even Elira knew it. She felt bad for leaving the other girls.'

'So why not just finally come and talk to us? Why put yourself in danger by meeting up with them?' asked Nathan.

'Well ... I wasn't sure if I actually wanted you to catch us, because I'm going to get into trouble now and Elira will probably get deported. But I did it mainly because I didn't want them to get away. There wasn't much I could tell you about the traffickers, nothing that would help you track them down, so I thought the best way was to get them here, but once I got here myself I realised how out of my depth I was. I texted Nina, knowing that she'd call you straightaway.' He smiled at me. 'I'm glad you worked out Stuart was in that bonfire before they lit it.'

'You can thank my dog for that,' I said.

Chapter Twenty-Four

I sat on the stone wall at the back of my house, enjoying the evening breeze and thinking about an interesting phone call I'd had earlier that day. It had been a long twenty-four hours, interviewing Glen and Elira (who were both very helpful), and Keith Dawson and his mate (who were not – the phrase 'blood out of a stone' would have been an understatement, and it had taken ages just to get Dawson to admit that was his name). The heatwave hadn't let up, and it had been so hot that it was worth braving the midges that hovered around the gorse bushes on the other side, waiting for someone (me) to nibble on, just to feel the slightly cooler evening air on my bare arms.

'Here you go,' said Nathan, joining me. He passed me

a mug of tea (the British will drink hot tea whatever the temperature, even in the middle of a heatwave), then sat next to me, sipping at his own. 'Am I imagining it, or is Daisy not talking to me?'

'She's annoyed with both of us,' I said. 'Me for running towards the sound of a gunshot, after I promised her I wouldn't put myself in danger again, and you for not stopping me.'

'Like I'd have been able to…'

'What do you think will happen to Glen?' I asked. Nathan shrugged.

'That's out of my hands now the National Crime Agency have got involved. But without him they wouldn't have a lead on the traffickers. With any luck the worst he'll get is a suspended sentence.'

'And Elira?'

'I just spoke to Matt about her. He said she's going to claim asylum, and the Fossetts have offered to sponsor her, give her a job and somewhere to live. Liam's awake, and he told them all about the trafficking. I don't know if it'll cut any ice with the Immigration department, but it's a start.'

'Good. I just hope they find the other girls.'

'They will. Dawson is apparently still keeping shtum, but his mate has started singing. They'll track them down.'

'What'll happen to Stuart Mitchell's fishing fleet?' I asked. 'He employed a lot of people. Life's tough enough for the fishermen round here as it is.'

'I don't know,' said Nathan. 'The NCA are all over the business's books, but I reckon most of his business was actually above board. Supplying the pubs and fish and chip shops, for instance. He paid his taxes regularly, and to all other intents was a model citizen. That was how he managed to hide what he was doing for so long. But Mitchell's looking at a jail sentence, and that might mean they can confiscate his boats as illegal proceeds from the smuggling. If that happens I reckon someone else'll come in and buy the whole business.'

'Maybe some of the lads down at the harbour could get together a consortium to buy it,' I said. 'They could form a co-op.'

We sipped at our tea in companionable silence for a moment. I nodded towards the small construction site in front of us. The granny annex (which I wasn't allowed to call it in front of my mum) was coming along, but it was still hard to imagine the finished building.

'I miss my garden,' I said, although to be honest I wasn't much of a gardener and all that I'd really lost was a patch of lawn that, in this dry weather, would've been brown and desiccated anyway.

'It'll be worth it,' said Nathan. 'This'll cheer you up.

Hang on…' He stood up and took something long and thin from his pocket, then turned away so I couldn't see what he was doing. When he turned back he had two sparklers in his hand. I laughed as he passed one to me. 'Sorry, they're a bit bent where I sat on them.'

'I've always loved sparklers!' I said. 'What's this for?'

'We missed the fireworks, didn't we? We were a bit busy.'

'True.' I waved my sparkler around, leaving a trail of brief but bright light in its wake. 'You can write stuff with these,' I said, waving it around a bit more.

'Can you read this?'

I turned to watch Nathan, attempting to write in the air. I smiled. 'I think that's "u evol I",' I said.

He frowned. 'Bugger, I forgot you're reading it back to front…'

'It's okay, u evol I too,' I said, leaning in to kiss him, careful to avoid stray sparks. 'This is so sweet. What are you after?'

He laughed. 'You are so suspicious, Parker. I was just trying to be romantic. And to commiserate.'

'What for?' I asked, surprised.

'I got a phone call today, from Superintendent Hansen. He told me about the auxiliary trial…'

'They decided it wasn't working, having me floating

between different stations. I know. He rang me earlier too.'

'I'm sorry, I did try and get him to change his mind…'

'It's not your fault, it's mine,' I said. 'I didn't think it through. I was so flattered to be recruited I didn't consider what it would be like, not for Daisy or Mum, but particularly not for you.'

'For me? It was fine for me—'

'Of course it wasn't! You had to try and treat me the same way you treat Matt and everyone else. But how could you ever really do that? We live together, we "evol" each other. This is why they don't let married officers work together,' I said. 'I'm surprised they turned a blind eye to our relationship in the first place.'

'I suppose they thought it would be okay, what with you just being an auxiliary,' said Nathan.

'He's offered me a full-time posting in Exeter CID,' I said. Nathan looked shocked.

'What? Really? That's – that's incredible…'

'It's tempting,' I admitted. 'But how would that affect us? We'd end up on different shifts, never seeing each other. And Daisy – I promised her my policing days were over, and I've already broken that promise quite enough. And then there's my catering business.'

'I'm sure we could find a way to make it work—'

'Let's not,' I said. It was suddenly obvious to me what we should do; because I'd realised that what I really wanted out of life was not, as it turned out, to be a police officer again. Nathan looked at me in surprise. 'Let's get married instead.'

Nathan's jaw dropped, and with it my stomach. What if he didn't want to marry me? But I needn't have worried, because he reached out and took my sparkler-free hand.

'Is that really what you want? Because that would make me the happiest man alive. But marrying me doesn't mean you have to sacrifice your career.'

'I know that.' I remembered what Sergeant Adams had said, back at the birthday party. 'But I've realised there's more to life than being a copper. Maybe I just needed to get it out of my system, once and for all. It's been fun being a DS, but I reckon it could be just as much fun being a Mrs. Although,' I added hastily, 'I won't be changing my name. No offence, but "Withers"? It's not great.'

'I'm aware of that, thank you,' said Nathan wryly.

'You could always change *your* name,' I said. '"Nathan Parker" has got a nice ring to it.'

He laughed and took the now spent (but still hot) sparkler from my hand, placing it carefully on the stone wall next to him. He pulled me towards him.

'If it's really what you want, I'd marry you tomorrow,' he said.

'It might take a bit longer than that to organise the wedding,' I said, snuggling into him. 'Good job I know someone who can do the catering.'

Acknowledgments

Bringing a book to publication is a collaborative process, so as ever there's a *long* list of people I need to thank.

First of all, thank you to the **Great British Bake Off** for existing and inspiring me. I'm watching it as I type this (oh my God, Jürgen just dropped his vegan sausage rolls on the floor! What a nightmare!). I'm not a good enough baker to compete, so this book is probably the closest I'll ever get to a technical challenge. And I've just realised I missed a trick by not including Death by Chocolate as one of the recipes (or the murder weapon). Goddammit.

To my agent, **Lina Langlee**, and everyone at **The North Literary Agency**; I feel very lucky to have you behind me! I try not to give in to the old 'creative temperament' too often, but when I do you know exactly how to calm me down/gee me up/give me some tough love. I do occasionally need to be told to pull myself together...

To my editor, **Bethan Morgan**, and the team at **One More Chapter**; thank you for your confidence in me, and your continued support of Jodie and the Penstowan gang. We appreciate it! And we *adore* the new covers…

To my writing besties, **Carmen Radtke, Jade Bokhari, Sandy Barker, Andie Newton** and **Nina Kaye**; you are my sisters from other misters and I literally could not do this without you. I love talking to you ladies every day, our brainstorming sessions, our putting the world to rights, and our downright silliness.

To my husband **Dominic** and son **Lucas**; thank you for humouring me, making endless cups of tea, and always having my back. I love you!

Jodies's tried and tested recipes #6

Mocha Choc Chip Cookies

I was trying to think of a recipe that everyone would like, so I thought to myself, okay, who doesn't like cookies? No one, that's who. NOBODY hates cookies. Nobody worth worrying about, anyway. There are two types of people in the world: those who like cookies, and monsters. MONSTERS, I tell you!

And who doesn't like coffee? Well, actually, I'm not that keen. Give me a cup of tea, milk, no sugar, any day (and none of that poncey Earl Grey or green tea malarkey, either; good old builders' tea, or what our overseas cousins call "English Breakfast", despite the fact it's not grown in England and we don't just drink it at breakfast). But while I might not be a big fan of coffee the drink, I do like the scent and the flavour; coffee and walnut cake is seriously yum, and of course coffee goes well with chocolate, which I am a BIG FAN of. But you already knew that.

And if you're even less of a fan of coffee than I am, you could actually leave it out of this recipe altogether and your cookies will still taste amazing. In fact you could even substitute the coffee for another flavour, like a couple of teaspoons of orange zest or maybe a few drops of peppermint, because they both go amazingly well with chocolate. Be warned that that's just a suggestion; I haven't tried swapping those in myself, because I'm a sucker for the mochalicious combination of coffee and chocolate (and a few nuts).

ON WITH THE RECIPE! And this time, for all my US readers (and anyone who prefers using cups to measure ingredients with, which I actually do), I've used both units of measurement where I can. If you want to double check (or go back and try recipes 1-5!), just Google 'grams to cups converter' - there's loads of them online.

1. Cream together **120g (1/2 cup) butter, 50g (1/4 cup) caster sugar** and **100g (1/2 cup) soft brown sugar**. The brown sugar adds a slightly caramelly taste to the cookies, but if you don't have brown sugar, don't worry, just use all

caster sugar. Make sure you use real butter, rather than margarine. I know you can use them interchangeably in a lot of recipes, but this one just doesn't work as well with soft margarine.

2. Add **1-2tsp ground coffee** according to taste. You can use powdered coffee, or if like me you have granulated, grind it up into a powder in a pestle and mortar. You can leave the granules whole if you want, but you'll end up with spotty cookies!

3. Add **1 egg** and in the words of Michael Jackson, beat it.

4. Fold in **240g (strictly speaking this equates to 1.92 cups! So just under 2 cups) plain flour, 1/2 tsp baking powder** and the ubiquitous **pinch of salt** (don't ask me what *that* is in cups, lol).

5. Add **170g (1 cup) milk chocolate chips**. This is a serious amount of chocolate chips – we're not messing about here – so don't skimp!

6. Shape the dough, which will be quite stiff, into a large sausage shape (you're going to slice this into cookies later, so make sure it's the same size all the way down the sausage, if you know what I mean. No one wants a lumpy

misshapen sausage or cookies of all different shapes and sizes), then roll it up in baking paper and chill in the fridge for at least 30 minutes. At this point, you could put the dough in the freezer and save the cookies for another day (you can cook the dough from frozen, it'll just need a little bit longer in the oven), but let's face it, I never do that, I want cookies and I want them now!

7. Can I just point out that I managed to get all the way through the previous bullet point without making a smutty joke or double entendre about stiff sausages? I must be growing up. Finally.

8. Preheat the oven to 180°c/350°f.

9. While the dough is chilling, I normally get a **handful** (maybe **1/4 cup?** I've got small hands...) of **almonds** or **hazelnuts** and chop them into small chunks, but this is optional.

10. Take out the dough and slice it into rounds. Place them onto a lined baking tray, leaving a bit of space between them as they will spread a little while they cook. I like to stud the cookies with the chopped nuts before they go into the oven.

11. Bake for around 12 minutes, but keep an eye on them as this can depend on your oven and you don't want them to burn. Take them out when they're golden and let them cool. They'll still be a bit soft, but they'll harden up as they cool.

12. Tell yourself you're only going to have one – possibly two – and then **EAT THEM ALL!** They are seriously lush and one is never enough.

Have you read the other books in the
Nosey Parker series?

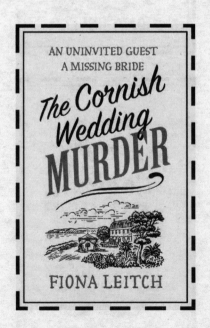

Have you read the other books in the Nosey Parker series?

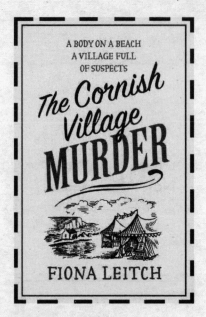

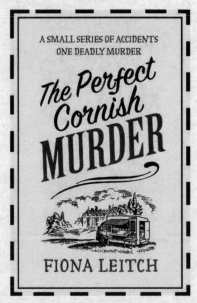

Have you read the other books in the Nosey Parker series?

TWELVE GUESTS
ONE SNOWSTORM

A Cornish Christmas MURDER

FIONA LEITCH

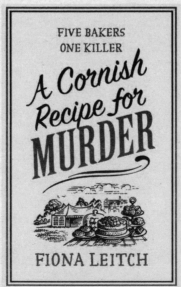

FIVE BAKERS
ONE KILLER

A Cornish Recipe for MURDER

FIONA LEITCH

YOUR NUMBER ONE STOP

ONE MORE CHAPTER

FOR PAGETURNING BOOKS

One More Chapter is an
award-winning global
division of HarperCollins.

Sign up to our newsletter to get our
latest eBook deals and stay up to date
with our weekly Book Club!
<u>Subscribe here.</u>

Meet the team at
<u>www.onemorechapter.com</u>

Follow us!

🐦 <u>@OneMoreChapter_</u>
ⓕ <u>@OneMoreChapter</u>
📷 <u>@onemorechapterhc</u>

Do you write unputdownable fiction?
We love to hear from new voices.
Find out how to submit your novel at
<u>www.onemorechapter.com/submissions</u>